SHIFTER IN THE SWAMP

SHIFTER IN THE SWAMP

ACADEMY OF NECESSARY MAGIC™ BOOK ONE

MARTHA CARR

MICHAEL ANDERLE

This book is a work of fiction. All of the characters, organizations, and events portrayed in this novel are either products of the author's imagination or are used fictitiously. Sometimes both.

Cover Art by Jake @ J Caleb Design
http://jcalebdesign.com / jcalebdesign@gmail.com

A Michael Anderle Production

LMBPN Publishing
PMB 196, 2540 South Maryland Pkwy
Las Vegas, NV 89109

First Version, January 2021
eBook ISBN: 978-1-64971-433-6
Print ISBN: 978-1-64971-434-3

From Martha

To everyone who still believes in magic and all the possibilities that holds.

To all the readers who make this entire ride so much fun.

To Louie, Jackie, and so many wonderful friends who remind me all the time of what really matters and how wonderful life can be in any given moment.

From Michael

To Family, Friends and
Those Who Love
To Read.
May We All Enjoy Grace
To Live The Life We Are
Called.

THE SHIFTER IN THE SWAMP TEAM

Thanks to our Beta Readers

Allen Collins, Mary Morris, Larry Omans

JIT Readers

Dave Hicks
Dorothy Lloyd
Jackey Hankard-Brodie
Wendy L Bonell
Diane L. Smith
Deb Mader
Jeff Goode

If I missed anyone, please let me know!

Editor

Skyhunter Editing Team

CHAPTER ONE

I'm never gonna be able to sleep like this.

Amanda Coulier lay in her twin-sized bed in room 228C and stared at the plain white ceiling panels above her. In the low light of her dorm room, they looked more gray than white, studded with rows of tiny black holes. Now, her racing mind was forming shapes in them.

A crossbow.

A hunting knife.

A flat-bottom airboat that disappeared as soon as she made it out.

A coonhound.

That last one made her snort.

Makes it seem like I wanna be back at that cabin with them. Guess that's all I know about actual combat—hunting with a bounty hunter.

The twelve-year-old shifter drew a deep breath and let it out in a heavy sigh before a slow, eager smile spread across her face. *Tomorrow, I get to learn* more. *In an actual class.*

The only thing she knew about the upcoming combat training class was that it started bright and early the next morning. The teachers wouldn't say anything more than that, and Amanda didn't think they'd answer her even if she'd bombarded them with all her burning questions.

It has *to be about actual fighting, right? And weapons. What the heck else could it be? This is a dang bounty hunter school.*

That was what Amanda liked to call it in her mind although the *teachers* preferred to refer to this place as The Academy of Necessary Magic. Sometimes the Academy. They called stuff around here all kinds of weird names as if they were trying to pretend this place wasn't exactly what it was. Amanda knew, though. She also knew the guy who'd started the school in the first place, with two other bounty hunters who were apparently top-level like Johnny Walker.

She was Johnny's ward, after all. Practically his kid.

Rolling over on her side, she glanced at the digital alarm clock resting on the built-in desk across the room.

After midnight? She puffed out a sigh and flipped onto her back again before rubbing her hands down both cheeks. *Jeeze, I would've gone out for a run if I'd known I'd be lying in bed like this for two whole—*

A door quietly opened and shut.

Amanda sat up and blinked in the darkness. On the second and third floors of the girl's dorm building—and yeah, Johnny had called these the barracks once or twice—all the other girls were asleep in their beds. Lights Out was at 10:00 p.m., and most of the students at the Academy had figured out how strictly the teachers enforced that rule. For the most part.

Still, none of the other girls were shifters like Amanda. None of the boys were, either. So Amanda was the only student in the building who could hear that door open and shut in the middle of the night. Against the rules. When everyone was supposed to be asleep or at least still in their rooms.

She bolted out of bed and walked swiftly and silently on her bare feet to the door. Footsteps echoed up the enclosed staircase at the front of the building—a little louder than the sound of the dorm's front door but still muffled through at least three walls and two stories.

Not only one pair, either. With wide eyes, Amanda turned her head and rested her ear against the door of her room. *Two people coming up the stairs. Who the heck would try to sneak into the dorms?*

Then the muffled timbre of a female voice reached her ears. She rolled her eyes. *Great. Principal Glasket. Must be super important if it got her out of her sleep mask.*

Smirking, the girl set both hands on the door to steady herself and pressed her ear a little closer.

The *squeak* of the door to the staircase at the front of the building came through loud and clear. Oddly enough, there were plenty of creaking doors and squeaky hinges and handles or windows that stuck. It always made Amanda chuckle because the Academy's campus was only six weeks old, built brand-new from the bottom up.

I bet Johnny told the builders to do that on purpose, just to be funny.

The staircase door *thumped* against the third-floor hallway's wall, followed quickly by the *click* of Principal Glasket's two-inch pumps on the tile floor. "Here we are. Third floor."

Amanda frowned. *Nobody gives a tour at midnight. We don't even have tours.*

A heavy sigh joined Principal Glasket's steady breathing. "Don't you guys have elevators here or something?"

Glasket let out an attempt at an empathetic hum. "No, those were left out of the building plans, I'm afraid."

"You could, like, make a magical elevator or something instead."

"And give every student at this school open access to an elevation charm from the very start? I don't think so."

"These stairs are brutal."

Glasket's unamused chuckle filled the hallway. "If *I* can walk up and down a few flights of stairs without getting winded, Miss

Flannerty, I'm sure you and your much younger body will quickly grow used to it. Come on. Your room's down the hall."

Despite the odd topic of conversation, Amanda's smile grew even wider.

Her room? Didn't know this place was taking new students the second official week of classes. Cool.

The two sets of footsteps grew louder as Principal Glasket and this new girl, whoever she was, moved down the hall toward Amanda's room. Glasket's sharp clip with her pumps, and the girl's slow, hesitant shuffle. Probably due to a suitcase or whatever kind of luggage she'd brought with her to her temporary home for the next four and a half months.

Or she's slow...

"All right. Here we are." Glasket stopped across the hall two rooms down from Amanda's and drummed her fingers on the door. "233C. This is you."

"Great." There was no enthusiasm whatsoever in the one-word statement.

The hallway fell silent, then Glasket smacked her lips. "Well, I gave you the key at the station, so now would be the time to use it. I imagine you could use a good rest after your...ordeal today."

"You don't have a key?" the girl asked.

"Of course not. This is a magic school, Miss Flannerty. Not prison. Every key on this campus is charmed to work only when the *owner* is in possession of it. So no swapping or trading or stealing of keys."

"You can't break into my room?"

"I don't have a key to it. However, any of the faculty here could most certainly force entry if there was a good enough reason. I hope you don't plan on *giving* us a reason to break down the door of your bedroom."

"Depends on your definition," the girl muttered.

Principal Glasket cleared her throat. "What was that?"

"Nothing."

Amanda had heard it. She leaned slightly away from the door and frowned. *Whoever she is, it doesn't sound like she wants to be here. Who* wouldn't *want to be here?*

The rustling of a hand through a nylon jacket pocket filled the hall, then a key scraped against the lock of the dorm room, and the handle turned.

"There." Glasket didn't sound any more amused now that they both knew the new student's key worked. "Now, let me see. Bathrooms are at the end of this hall. The first floor is a common area, open for use until Lights Out at ten o'clock. Personal items tend to grow legs and walk off if they're left in common areas, so if that's a concern of yours, I recommend keeping all your belongings in your room. Other students are welcome to gather in the common area of either dorm, but the second and third floors of each are *not* co-ed, so no sneaking boys up into your room and vice versa."

The new girl snorted. "Yeah, 'cause *that's* something I'd want."

"Meals in the outdoor refectory three times a day, as long as the weather permits. The kitchens are off-limits at all hours. So is the faculty building and the west wing of the main building. Classes start at seven-thirty in the morning. You'll get your textbooks and whatever required materials in your classes tomorrow. There's no uniform or official dress code, but we expect all our students to dress appropriately for the weather *and* their various classes. I gave you your schedule, didn't I?"

"Yep."

"Good." Glasket let out a heavy sigh. "Any questions for me now before we turn in?"

"Yeah, just one." There was a long pause, then the *thump* of the new girl slinging a duffel bag or a backpack off her shoulder and through the doorway into her new room. "You guys have a three-strike policy too?"

"I'm sorry?"

Amanda stepped away from her bedroom door and wrinkled her nose. *Going right for the worst-case scenario, huh?*

"You know, like detention or being expelled or whatever."

The principal cleared her throat. "I'd like to think you're coming into this with a little more optimism and would actively *try* to stay away from racking up any strikes at all, no matter what our policy is."

"I'm only trying to figure it out." The new girl must have leaned up against the wall beside her room; the *swish* of nylon and the soft *thump* of weight rose all too clearly through Amanda's door.

"Figure what out, Miss Flannerty?" Now Glasket sounded like she'd rather be anywhere else but right here introducing a new student to the Academy.

Like, snuggled up in her bed. I thought she went to sleep at nine or something.

"Well..." The hint of amusement in the new girl's voice was all too clear, and Amanda forced herself not to open the door to see whether the girl smirked as she imagined. "I mean, I hit my limit at the last place, so I got shipped off and sent here. So if anyone strikes out here, do they get shipped off to, like, a workcamp or something? Or is this the last stop?"

"By *last stop*, you're referring to..."

"Like, Juvie without the *classes* or something. I don't know. I guess that's pretty much what this place is anyway, right?"

"Miss Flannerty—"

"Or did you guys build a brand-new prison for underage magicals somewhere in this dump too?"

Amanda's eyes widened, and she stifled a surprised laugh.

Holy crap. She's really pushing it.

When the hallway fell tensely silent one more time, she leaned toward the door again and listened intently.

Principal Glasket sighed, and the *click* of one footstep followed. "I realize this is a big change for you. I do. Plus, the circumstances of you coming to this school were less than ideal."

"That's not an answer."

"I'm not going to answer that question, Miss Flannerty, because it doesn't warrant one. If you do the work, focus on your classes and on learning what you're here to learn instead of looking for shortcuts—"

"Oh, that's what they're calling it, huh?"

"—then you'll do fine," Glasket continued, ignoring the sarcastic interruption. "We wouldn't have accepted you into this school if we didn't believe you have the potential to be more than what you've shown so far. There's no point in trying to prove us wrong."

The girl scoffed but didn't have any new comeback for that.

"I'm going to go to bed now," the principal added. "You should do the same. Get as much sleep as you can before wake-up at five forty-five—"

"Are you freaking *kidding* me?"

"Other students are sleeping on this floor, Miss Flannerty. Please keep your voice down."

"What kind of insane person wakes up before six in the morning? Ever?"

Two quick clicking footsteps, then Principal Glasket lowered her voice into a warning sternness. "Let me make this clear to you right now. This is a school for magicals like you who are here to learn and hone their talents in a variety of magical disciplines, whatever they happen to be. Just like the other schools around this world—"

"Not *just* like the other schools."

"Whatever you might have heard, Miss Flannerty, I suggest you put your preconceived judgments of this place aside and focus on *learning*."

"Or what?"

Another long pause followed.

When Principal Glasket spoke again, Amanda could practically see the witch's tight grimace of a smile as clearly as she heard it in the woman's voice. "You spent a year at the School of Necessary Magic. You're used to their rules and regulations, their teaching methods, *and* the way they discipline their students. Maybe you're even a little *too* familiar with that last one. Believe me when I say we run things differently here at the Academy. If you're already intent on pushing the envelope here too, go right ahead. In my opinion, that's taking what seems like the easy way out to learn the same lessons the *hard* way. Still, if you have to answer your questions through personal experience, then that's your prerogative. Good night."

Glasket headed back down the hallway toward the closed staircase without waiting for a reply, her pumps clicking harshly across the tile floor. The squeaky door opened, then closed again, and the principal's echoing footsteps faded down to the dorm's first floor.

Whoa.

Blinking quickly, Amanda stepped away from her door and huffed a quiet, disbelieving chuckle.

Here I thought Glasket finished showing her angry side after the first month at this place.

Out in the hall, the new girl sighed in disgust, walked into her room, and shut the door. Not quite a slam, but not exactly quiet, either.

Amanda waited and listened, but everything was quiet again.

Someone from the School of Necessary Magic got sent here? *Before the second week of school? Jeeze. She must've screwed up pretty badly.*

Turning slowly to face her bed, she chewed on the inside of her bottom lip. It was after midnight. She was used to waking up early. Even *before* everything that had happened that spring, before meeting Johnny and going to stay with him and the hounds, she'd regularly woken up before six because that was what her parents did.

A hard lump formed in her throat, and she swallowed.

Waking up early for a hunt in the swamp is a heck of a lot better than waking up early just to read the paper.

The girl glanced at her alarm clock again—12:24 a.m.

Definitely time to sleep.

With a determined nod, she approached the side of her bed and sat.

The second her backside touched the mattress and she looked up at the door, the energy that had kept her up this late thinking about combat training in the morning flared through her again. Only now, she'd be wide awake even longer thinking about this new student across the hall who'd gotten *kicked out of magic school.*

Amanda closed her eyes, drew a deep breath, and counted to ten, her fingers absently drumming on her thighs.

Time to chill out and go to sleep. Relax. Chill...

Her eyes flew open, and she popped up off the bed to her feet.

Screw it. If I'm gonna be awake, might as well see who the heck this new girl is.

CHAPTER TWO

The door opened slowly and silently, and Amanda peered through the three-inch opening to check the hall. Sure enough, Principal Glasket was gone, and the new girl had retreated into her room and closed the door behind her.

After waiting and listening for another five seconds, Amanda widened the opening enough to slip quickly through and didn't bother closing it again. She wouldn't be out here long.

Best way to find out about someone is to go through their stuff. Second-best way is to listen in when they think nobody can hear.

She'd done plenty of that before. It had been harder with her parents and Claire; they'd all had an uncanny and infuriating knack for being able to find Amanda whenever she tried to spy on them, no matter when or where or how. Perks of being a shifter in a shifter family. She'd done the same thing with Johnny too, and while he'd never picked up on her *listening* to him, the bounty hunter hadn't enjoyed her going through his things.

The thought of his scowl and bristling beard almost made her laugh, but she shoved it back down.

Forget about Johnny right now. This is Mission New Girl.

Fortunately, the floors hadn't been built to creaky specifications, so she didn't make a sound as she slowly padded barefoot across the hall toward room 233C.

The second she reached the halfway mark, the new girl's door opened as slowly and silently as Amanda's had. A head of jet-black hair poked through, followed by the rest of the young witch with a smartphone clutched in both hands and her gaze fixed intently on the screen.

Amanda froze in a half-crouch, her eyes wide and arms comically lifted at her sides in sneaky-shifter-girl fashion.

The new girl stepped into the hall, frowned at her phone, then looked up. She gave Amanda a quick once-over and tilted her head. "What are you doing?"

Clearing her throat, Amanda straightened and dropped her arms at her sides while shooting a glance down the empty hall. "What are *you* doing?"

"Oh, I get it." The girl shoved her phone into the back pocket of her cargo pants and smirked. "They put on some kinda hall monitor duty, right?"

"What?"

"Sent you up here to *keep an eye on me?*" The girl widened her eyes and waggled her head with thick sarcasm. "Well, go ahead. Run back to Glasket and make your report."

Amanda wrinkled her nose and couldn't help a small chuckle. *Good thing I have experience with grumpy jerks.*

"No one knows I'm awake. Except for you."

"Good for you." The new girl swiped her black bangs away from her eyes—Amanda couldn't tell if they were blue or gray—and shrugged. "So what are you doing?"

"That's my room." Amanda stuck her thumb out toward her slightly open door.

"And?" The girl folded her arms.

"I heard you and Glasket come up here. I got curious."

"Whatever. Feel free to get un-curious." Grumpyface gave her another once-over, then headed down the hall toward the back of the building.

Amanda tried to hold it back, but the bubbling questions flooded up out of her as they usually did. "You came from the School of Necessary Magic, right?"

She took two quick steps forward and stopped when the new girl turned halfway around to frown at her. "That's none of your business."

"Well, it's not like you were exactly quiet about it." Amanda shrugged and couldn't help a small smile. "What'd you do?"

"Look...whoever you are." The girl pointed at the end of the hall. "I'm kind of about to go do some stuff, so maybe save the questions for someone who feels like talking."

"Yeah, okay." Folding her arms, Amanda watched the girl walk off and waited until just before she reached the corner of the narrow hallway that formed a T-intersection in the back. "I guess you know how to turn off the alarm wards, right?"

The new girl froze, her back stiffening beneath the black zip-up hoodie. "Wards?"

"Yep. They go up around the dorms after Lights Out. Come back down in the morning. Not as bad as being shocked by a cattle prod, but most people don't know what that's like."

"I'll think I'll take my chances."

"Sure. The last girl I saw trying to sneak out at night hit the ground and didn't get up until *noon* the next day. I mean, unless you're trying to *do some stuff* in the supply closet back there. I'm pretty sure that's clean."

With a heavy sigh, the new girl turned and rolled her eyes until her gaze landed on the short, wiry, brown-haired girl standing in the middle of the hallway. "Fine. What do you want?"

A grin broke out on Amanda's face. "I wanna know what got you kicked out of that other school in...Virginia, right?"

Slowly, the girl's frustrated scowl melted away into a small smirk. "You came out of your room in the middle of the night to ask me what kind of delinquent I am?"

"Actually, I figured I'd listen through your door for a while." Amanda shrugged. "You'd be surprised how many people talk to themselves when they think they're alone. It's a *lot*."

The new girl snorted. "You're weirdly honest."

"Yeah, I get that a lot. So hey, while we're *standing* here..."

The smirk widened into a smile. "I blew up the power generator. Plus the backup generator. And probably killed whatever those creepy plants were that needed all that UV light twenty-four-seven."

Amanda barked out a laugh, then clapped a hand over her mouth. "Why would you wanna blow up the power generator?"

"I mean, I wasn't *trying* to. It happened to be right next to this secret room one of the teachers thought he could keep me out of by putting a reinforced door over it. Honestly, he had it coming."

"Did you...get in?"

The new girl wrinkled her nose and glanced at the ceiling. "Almost."

"Then they sent you *here*."

"Yeah. Third strike and everything." The girl tossed her bangs out of her eyes. "I didn't think they'd go through with it. Didn't think those potions would make such a huge explosion, either. What are *you* in for?"

Amanda narrowed her eyes. *Jeeze, she makes it sound like we're locked up in a jail cell together.*

"I came here 'cause I *want* to be here."

The girl rolled her eyes again and scoffed. "Oh, come on. Nobody *wants* to be here. You get shipped with everyone else, or what?"

"No. I mean, I started the first day when the other kids showed up for the Opening Ceremony."

"Cute. So what'd you do?"

"I...said, 'Yes, I want to go to the Academy.' Then I packed up and moved into my room." Amanda chuckled. "Shouldn't be that hard to believe."

"You're playing the game. I get it." The other girl leaned back against the wall and huffed out a wry laugh. "You don't have to keep sugar-coating it. I bet your story's not that different from anyone else's here. You screwed up one too many times, and your parents said they were fed up, they were shipping you off to the Academy in the freakin' swamp, and you'd go to school *here* to learn your lesson."

Amanda swallowed. *Awesome. First conversation ever, and we're talking about parents.*

"That's not what happened. I came here by choice."

"Yeah, I bet." The girl leaned forward and glanced up and down the hallway before lowering her voice. "You realize this place is pretty much Juvie for magicals, right? Trust me. If I had somewhere else to go, I'd run away from this dump as fast as I could."

I do have somewhere to go. And I still wanna be here. Amanda studied the other girl's haughty smirk. *This is all just an act.*

"How long were you at the School of Necessary Magic?"

The girl shrugged. "A year. Plus a week, technically."

"Well, that's something, at least. Most of the other kids here stopped going to school after, like, first or second grade."

"Ya think?"

"So...are you *from* Virginia, or went there for a year and a week?" When she got no reply, Amanda shrugged. "I grew up in New York. Up north. It was weird to come down here to the Everglades at first. Swamps and everything. Bet it's pretty different than Virginia, too. Or wherever you live—"

"Look." The girl nodded at her with a grimace, then turned toward the open door of 233C. "Nice chat and everything, but you're trying too hard. I didn't come here to make friends, so... Maybe take it down a notch."

"Uh-huh." Amanda tried to copy the girl's scowl, but a tiny smile broke through.

"Yeah, you can quit staring at me too. I'm gonna go pass out."

"My name's Amanda."

The girl had grabbed the doorknob and held the door halfway open as she frowned into the hall. A flicker of amusement—or maybe gratitude—flashed across her face, and she sighed. "Summer."

She doesn't look very summery.

"Cool." Amanda let herself smile a little more. "Hey, if you need any help figuring out where you're going tomorrow, like for classes and stuff, I can show you around. This place kinda seems like a maze at first."

"I'm good." Then the door shut not-so-quietly and left Amanda standing in the middle of the hallway, smiling like a goof at the closed door of 233C.

She waited another minute, listening to Summer root through her things and climb onto the slightly squeaky mattress in her twin-sized bed.

Sure, now that she knows I was trying to listen, she's not gonna talk to herself.

With a small chuckle, Amanda spun and headed back to her room. She slipped inside, pulled the door shut again with a soft *click*, then crossed the room to her bed and flopped down on her back.

Summer, huh? I bet she and Johnny would hate each other.

That made her laugh, and she whipped the sheets and comforter up over her legs before snuggling down and dropping her head onto the pillow.

She's trying to be tough. It would suck to get kicked out and sent here without a choice. Wonder if she knows how to hunt.

Amanda tossed in her bed for another hour, way too excited for the morning and unable to fall asleep. Because of Combat Training, obviously. Also because she wasn't the only kid here anymore who hadn't been coaxed out of the tunnels under LA and shipped out here by a team of bounty hunters.

CHAPTER THREE

The blaring magical alarm echoing across the Academy's entire campus and seeping in through the walls made Amanda groan. The amplified wake-up call included a different song every morning—probably so they wouldn't get used to it and sleep right through. Today, the obnoxiously upbeat tune of *Roar* by Katy Perry weaseled its way into her head and finally made her sit up with a frustrated grunt.

Who picks *these stupid songs?*

She jerked the covers off herself and swung her legs over the side of the bed. Her shoulders slumped, and she hunched over to rub her cheeks.

Four hours of sleep is definitely not enough. That's what I get for being excited.

The song played all the way through to the end, and when it finished, Amanda's shifter hearing picked up the scattered groans and dragging footsteps of the other girls in the dorm getting out of bed to start their day.

She shuffled across the room toward her dresser and wearily pulled open the drawers to pick her clothes. Her eyelids drooped as she reached blindly inside to feel around for a pair of shorts and a tank top, and she let out a massive yawn.

I should've stayed in bed instead of trying to meet the new girl and thinking about Combat Training—

A gasp escaped her, and her eyes flew open to stare at the dresser. "That's right! Yes!"

Grinning now, the shifter girl jerked off her pajamas and hopped around the room as she shoved her limbs into her clothes.

Yes, yes, yes! Combat Training! I hope they let us use knives in the first week. Probably not. Oh man, Petrov's gonna crap himself when he sees my throwing aim.

She jammed her feet into her favorite pair of sneakers—the ones Lisa had loaned her in the Manhattan hotel and had never bothered to ask for their return. Then she snatched up her mostly empty forest-green backpack, slung it over her shoulders, and quickly tied her long brown hair back into a messy ponytail.

This is gonna be awesome.

She made her bed in under two minutes, then flew through her door and practically skipped into the hall. The other girls in the dorm looked up at her with groggy expressions. Some of them laughed and shook their heads at her wide-eyed excitement. Three, she noticed—Candace Jones and her two yes-brats, Emma and Megan—looked the shifter girl up and down with sneers of mock-disgust before rolling their eyes and heading down the hall toward the stairwell.

Amanda stared after them for a moment, then smirked. *They have no idea what I can really do.*

After a glance at Summer's door—which was closed and didn't open—and another to scan the faces of the other girls heading down the hall, she shrugged and made her way through the zombie-like teenagers to the stairs. Breakfast was waiting for them out beside the kitchens, and although they had until 7:00 a.m. to make their way down there before the kitchen pixies cleaned up and closed down for the morning, Amanda had learned the hard way that the best stuff went first and quickly—and she was always hungry.

By the time she burst through the front doors of the long, narrow building of the girl's dorm, the first orange and yellow glow of sunrise filtered through the oaks and mangroves studding the campus. Crickets and cicadas still buzzed heavily in the swamp, birds sang at each other in every direction, and the constant wet *plop* of frogs darting into the water punctuated it all. The air was still cool enough this early in the morning to make Amanda feel energized all over again.

She raced down the outside of the dorm toward the large stone building of the kitchens and the pavilion behind it on the northwest side filled with picnic tables and a covered salad bar. There was only salad in it at lunch, but in the morning, the serving pans were filled to the brim with ice and held pitchers of orange juice, cranberry juice, ice water, and milk.

Amanda eyed the pitcher of milk and wrinkled her nose as she got in line at the breakfast buffet table. Not her thing, but some of the other kids seemed to like it.

"Every morning."

"What?" She turned to find Jackson Pris standing behind her with his arms folded, scowling at the salad bar turned refreshment stand, and shaking his head.

"With the milk. I don't get it. I can't think of anything that grosses me out half as much as that stuff."

"To each their own, right?"

"Yeah, but they're not taking that far enough." He tossed his shaggy, sun-streaked brown hair out of his eyes. "Should be 'to each their own young, and let's stop taking this crap away from baby cows.'"

Amanda barked out a laugh and stepped toward the table as next in line. Fortunately, there were only two other kids in front of her. "You don't *have* to drink it, you know."

"No. I have to watch Corey slobber it down like he can't survive without it." Jackson nodded toward the first picnic table under the pavilion, where they both had a clear view of the ridiculously large, half-Kilomea Corey guzzling down the rest of one clear plastic glass of milk. The kid's belch echoed across the yard. He wiped the milk mustache off his entire mouth with a forearm, then grabbed his second glass and drained it five seconds.

"Huh."

"Don't try to tell me that stuff 'builds strong bones.'"

She smirked at Jackson and finally reached the table to pick up a plate and get down to business piling it high. "Seems to be working for *him*, though."

The thirteen-year-old wizard standing behind her snorted. "Have you ever wondered *why* no one wants to sit next to him? It's 'cause he drinks so much milk."

"I thought it's 'cause he always tells everyone to get lost."

Jackson grabbed a plate and shook his head. "It's disgusting."

Amanda tried to hide a smile as she moved down the buffet table and scooped up large spoonfuls of the best scrambled eggs in the world, sausage links *and* bacon, fruit salad, yogurt, toast already dripping with melted butter, and a cinnamon roll bigger than her fist—just to start.

"Dude." Jackson shot her plate a sidelong glance. "Are you really gonna eat all that?"

"Are you kidding?" She jammed a piece of bacon into her mouth, then stuck two more on her plate to take its place. "This is round one."

"You got some kinda medical condition or something?"

Snatching up two napkins and a fork, she turned to look at

him and cocked her head. "No, but if I did, it'd be none of your business."

"Only trying to look out for you, Coulier. That's all."

"Yeah, well, I'm pretty good at looking out for myself, thanks. Especially when it comes to food."

The boy laughed as she hurried away from the table to pour herself a glass of orange juice at the salad bar. Amanda was smiling too, but it faded as she focused on filling the cup.

I've been here for almost two months, and no one's picked up on what I am. There's no way they wouldn't bring it up all the time if they knew.

The Academy's carefully selected faculty and staff all knew who Amanda Coulier was—and what she was. It would've been impossible to keep the fact that she was Johnny Walker's ward a secret for very long. The other students knew that much, at least. Ms. Ralthorn had approached Amanda on her first week on campus, way before the actual school year had officially started, and asked if she "needed special allowances to use her abilities in private."

Amanda had told the woman no right away but didn't have the heart to ask the Light Elf teacher if she knew anything about shifters at all. It wasn't like she couldn't control herself and had to go running through the swamps to kill something on a full moon or anything. After six weeks of being here, she still hadn't shifted in front of anyone else. Not after what had happened the last time she'd changed in front of strangers.

Not like any of the kids here are trying to kidnap me from my house or come after me in the middle of Nowhere, Everglades. If I don't have to shift to get through school, I won't.

With a firm nod of determination at the ice-buried pitchers of juice and milk, Amanda snatched up her plate again and headed toward one of the picnic tables beneath the pavilion. She dug into her eggs and sausage the second her butt hit the bench, then the usual crowd of what she'd almost come to think of as her friends joined her.

"Every single meal, Amanda." Grace Porter laughed and set down her plate across from the shifter girl. "How do you go through so much food all the time?"

"I'm hungry," Amanda replied through a mouthful of eggs, then tried to catch the bits falling out of her mouth. "The food here's really good."

"I don't know about *that...*" Grace tucked her short blonde bob behind her ears and shrugged. "But sure. It's better than whatever we managed to...borrow back in LA."

"Borrow, huh?" The orange juice was so cold, Amanda braced herself for a brain-freeze as she gulped down her second mouthful.

"Yeah. *Borrow.*" Grace smirked and stabbed a bunch of cut melon onto her fork. "With an extended timeline for returning it when we're done."

"Not our fault if the stores didn't want it back in its new form." Jackson stepped over the bench and sat beside Grace. "Not that we ever really *tried...*"

"Breakfast, Jackson." Amanda pointed at her plate. "We're eating breakfast."

"Hey, it's not like I painted a super detailed picture or anything." The wizard turned over his shoulder toward the buffet table, which now had a much larger line growing steadily longer by the minute. "Alex! Grab me an extra cinnamon roll!"

The half-Wood Elf with his dark brown hair tied back in a long ponytail reaching the middle of his back raised an eyebrow at their table. "Should've thought of that before you sat down, man."

"I ran out of room! Come on. Just one."

Alex rolled his eyes and slowly shook his head as he made his way down the breakfast table.

"Ran out of room?" Grace snorted and gestured at Jackson's plate. "That's, like, a half-full plate."

"No…that's a perfectly segregated plate, okay?" Jackson touched his fork against each of the neatly separated piles of different food. "They touch even a little, and I can't eat it. The whole thing's ruined."

"You have some serious issues to work out." Grace looked up at Amanda and grinned. "Hey, you know any other magicals with OCD?"

"Um…" Amanda wrinkled her nose and instantly thought of the oddly organized way Johnny operated in his home despite the fact that she'd seen the bounty hunter blow up more than anyone's fair share of buildings and creatures. "I don't know."

"Maybe he's the first."

"Hey." Jackson shot the witch a playful frown. "Because I like to keep things clean and organized doesn't mean I have a *problem*."

"Yeah. *Okay*."

Amanda was already halfway through her breakfast but started yawning again before she got to the cinnamon roll.

"Whoa." Grace leaned away and looked Amanda up and down. "You're usually running around like you drank three Red Bulls first thing in the morning. What's up with *you*?"

"Didn't get much sleep." Amanda rubbed her eyes, then dug into the rest of her bacon and yogurt.

"Aw…" Jackson leaned forward over the table with a frown of mocking concern. "Little kid still scared of the dark?"

He laughed when Grace elbowed him in the ribs.

"No." Amanda cocked her head at him. "I don't have a problem with milk or my food touching, either."

Grace burst out laughing, and Jackson shook his head while narrowing his eyes at the shifter. "Are you *sure* you're only twelve?"

"Last time I checked." She shoved the last two pieces of bacon into her mouth and shrugged. It didn't bother her one bit that she was *almost* the youngest student at the Academy. Jimmy took the blue ribbon on that one; he was only eleven. None of the other kids knew what kind of magical he was or even his last name. She'd picked up from random conversations that the other kids who'd all lived together beneath the city of LA had tried to figure out anything else about Jimmy, but he barely talked, and even the teachers couldn't get him to say more than two or three words at a time.

She glanced across the outdoor cafeteria and found the tiny kid standing in line between a tall, thin wizard she thought was named Ben and an equally tall seventeen-year-old girl she recognized but didn't know. Jimmy stood with his hands in his pockets, occasionally leaning sideways to peer around the much taller kids in front of him to get a good look at the buffet table.

I bet even Jimmy's not afraid of the dark. Not after living in tunnels for whoever knows how long.

"What kept you up, then?" Grace asked.

"I bet she was trying to get herself in trouble." Jackson snorted and carefully lifted a forkful of eggs to his mouth. "You know, trying to fit in with the rest of us."

Amanda shot him a crooked smile and finally dug into her cinnamon roll. *Just because I didn't drop out of school to live underground doesn't mean I haven't seen some shit.*

"It's not a competition," she muttered.

Grace barked out a laugh and slapped Jackson's arm with the back of her hand. "You're really digging yourself a hole, here."

"Yeah, I know." Jackson pointed at the shifter girl. "I'll get you to crack eventually."

"You can try." She bit off a huge chunk of cinnamon roll and waggled her eyebrows at him.

"Try what?" Alex rounded the table with his full plate and sat next to Amanda.

"To crack her open like an egg," Grace said. "He thinks she's *fragile*."

"Trying to figure her out is all." Jackson shrugged. "I know you have secrets, Coulier. Only a matter of time 'til they're out in the open."

"Yeah, okay." Amanda tried to smile but focused on her cinnamon roll. *Secrets are secrets for a reason. Not gonna happen.*

"Hey, sweet!" Jackson stood and reached across the table toward Alex's plate. "Thanks, man."

"Dude. That's mine." Alex glared at the cinnamon roll the wizard had snatched right off his plate.

Jackson froze with his mouth open and the cinnamon roll poised for a bite. "Come on. I asked you to get me one, and you brought two."

"Yeah, for myself."

"Here, I'll split it with you—"

A green light flashed on the grass behind the wizard, then two snaking tendrils of thick brown roots burst from the lawn and wrapped themselves around Jackson's belly.

"What the—" He looked down at his middle before the roots squeezed and made him cough up a wheezing grunt. "Dude..."

"Mine." Alex flicked his fingers toward the stolen cinnamon roll, and it zipped out of Jackson's loose grip before plopping down on the half-Wood Elf's plate.

With a sharp *snap*, the vines unwound themselves from around Jackson's middle and slithered back into the gaping holes in the grass. The wizard gasped and slammed a fist down on the table. "Not cool, man!"

"Then don't take my stuff." Alex's deep brown eyes flashed with a pale green light as he stared at the other boy and took a huge bite of the returned cinnamon roll.

"Jeeze." Jackson rubbed his stomach and cleared his throat. "You're trying to kill me."

"OCD *and* paranoid." Grace shot Amanda a crooked smile.

"Whatever." The wizard focused on his plate and crammed food into his mouth, chewing angrily.

Amanda glanced around her small group of friends. "Hey, you guys excited for Combat Training?"

"What?" Jackson looked sharply up at her. "What the hell is that?"

"Our first *class*." Grace snorted. "You don't pay attention to anything, do you?"

"Aw, come on. We haven't even had a stupid class yet. How am I supposed to know what everything is?"

"The schedule," Alex muttered.

"What schedule?"

"They handed them out two days ago." Grace frowned at the wizard. "After dinner. In the center field. You don't remember?"

As the other kids at her table argued over the when, where, and how of knowing the classes they'd be taking for the Academy's first-ever official semester, Amanda tuned them out and stared across the outdoor cafeteria.

Summer had finally arrived from wherever she'd been since wake-up, and now Candace, Emma, and Megan surrounded her. The trio of older girls had their heads bent toward Summer as they viewed the now crowded buffet table and pavilion.

Great. She's getting the grand tour from the saltiest girls in the whole school.

Then Summer's sweeping gaze landed on Amanda at the picnic table and stayed there while Candace kept chattering away in her ear.

Amanda gave the new girl a small smile and raised her hand in a mostly subtle wave. Summer's upper lip twitched, and she rolled her eyes before turning away and facing forward at the end of the breakfast line.

Grace turned around to look behind her and frowned. "Who are you waving to?"

"New girl."

"There's a new girl?" Jackson whipped around on the bench and scanned the line. "Where?"

"End of the line."

"Oh…" With a sigh, the wizard faced forward again and scowled. "Candace already snagged her up to be her new slave. Figures."

"You know her?" Alex stared at Amanda as he chewed his food.

"Not really. She's right across the hall from me, though."

"Huh. Wonder what got her *here.*"

"She looks pissed off about something," Grace added. "No wonder Candace and the yes-brats swooped in."

Amanda kept her mouth shut and quickly finished the rest of her breakfast. *Not my place to tell someone else's story. Guess we'll find out what she can do in class.*

CHAPTER FOUR

The entire student body of the Academy of Necessary Magic gathered in the center field of the campus just after 7:00 a.m. for Principal Glasket's little opening speech for their first day of school. A deafeningly loud alarm like a fog horn blared across the field, making everyone duck or cover their ears or grimace. Glasket jolted and stumbled forward against the podium on the small stage, making the microphone buzz with static before erupting into a loud shriek. She fumbled with the mic, finally got the sound to stop, then shot a burning glare toward the congregated teachers standing off to the side. "Mr. LeFor—"

"Yeah, I'll get that fixed." The tall, wiry wizard who would be teaching Augmented Technology rubbed his short, fiery-red hair vigorously until it stood on end in every direction. "Still working out the kinks."

"The kinks? You—never mind." Glasket waved him off, then faced the gathered students again and broke into a wide grin. "Good morning, everyone. You've all been here for quite some time and have gotten to know the campus and the various rules that keep this place running. Now it's time for your first day of classes. I wanted to tell you that I'm so glad each one of you is here, and I'm very much looking forward to seeing how your skills, abilities, and knowledge develop over this first semester at the Academy of Necessary Magic.

"Just a reminder. You all received your first-semester class schedules on Friday. Every schedule was assigned a color. Green for freshmen. Yellow for sophomores. Purple for juniors. Red for seniors. You'll be in these same classes for the entire year, with the same students on the weekly rotation through your studies. So." Glasket glanced at her bright-pink wristwatch. "You have about fifteen minutes until classes begin. Your teachers for Block One will show you where to go with your year's assigned colors. Enjoy the rest of your day, and let's have a great first year."

When the principal clapped, the mic shrieked again. She quickly righted it, cast another scathing glance at Mr. LeFor, and the students covered their ears, grimaced, or laughed.

"Freshmen!" Mr. Petrov barked. "Eyes on me!"

He marched across the back of the central field toward the long concrete building on the southeast side of the campus. When he stuck his finger high above his head, a shower of green sparks burst from the tip and shot five feet into the air.

Grace gently elbowed Amanda and muttered, "Guess we better fall in line, huh?"

"Yeah, before he throws the sparks at *us*." Chuckling, Amanda headed off toward Mr. Petrov, her heart fluttering at the thought of starting her first class on the first day of bounty hunter school with Combat Training.

"You guys have any idea what we're about to get into?" Jackson glanced across the field at Mr. LeFor throwing up red sparks, Ms. Calsgrave tossing a spiral of purple, and Mrs. Zimmer shooting a thin stream of yellow.

"If it's with the lieutenant, it's gotta be good," Alex offered, shrugging as the group of friends made their way toward Mr. Petrov.

"How do you know he's a lieutenant?" Amanda shot the half-Wood Elf a playful frown.

"The guy barks orders like one."

"Which I honestly expected a lot more of at a bounty hunter magic school," Alex added. "Thought this place was gonna be more like boot camp or something."

Or a Quantico for magical kids. The thought made Amanda smirk. Johnny had called it that once too. More than once, actually, but it hadn't turned her away from wanting to come here and learn whatever she could to be the best at everything she did.

When they reached their combat teacher at the far end of the center field, they turned to watch the rest of the designated freshman class come toward them while the rest of the students shuffled toward their other teachers for the day's first class.

"Oh, my God." Grace's pale blue eyes grew wide.

"What?" Jackson stared at her, then fervently searched the field.

"Look at Jimmy."

Amanda scanned the field for the small form of the youngest kid on campus. When she found him, he was shuffling along in a crowd of other kids toward Mrs. Zimmer.

"No way." Jackson's mouth fell open, then he turned toward Grace and gestured at the sophomore class gathering by the alchemy teacher. "The baby's starting as a *sophomore*?"

A small frown flickered across Alex's eyebrows. "Interesting."

"It's not *interesting*, man. It has to be a joke. What is he, *eight*?"

"Eleven," Amanda muttered.

"Not much better, Coulier."

"We all got tested." Grace shrugged. "Guess he's been holding back on us."

"If that little shrimp can skip grades, *I* should be in that class too." Jackson folded his arms and scowled at the sophomores following Mrs. Zimmer toward the main building for indoor classes.

"You didn't even try to fight me at breakfast." Alex watched with a blank expression as the other students finished separating into their various classes. "Probably 'cause you couldn't think of any spells to try."

"No, probably because I couldn't *breathe*." Jackson scoffed. "You think Jimmy could've fought you off?"

"He can obviously do *something* better than the rest of us." Grace nodded at the hulking half-Kilomea kid stalking toward the freshman group with a scowl. "Doesn't look like everyone tested up, though."

"You gotta be kidding me." Jackson turned away and shook his head. "We shouldn't be lumped in with *that* guy."

"Baker!" Mr. Petrov shouted. "What the hell are you doing over here? Get to your color."

"I did." Corey stopped at the edge of the group of freshmen and folded his arms. He stood a full head and then some above everyone else and glared at the combat teacher.

Mr. Petrov looked the huge kid up and down and grunted. "Let me see your schedule."

Corey removed a crumpled sheet of paper from his pocket and handed it to the teacher when the man approached and held out a large, calloused hand.

Petrov grimaced as he unfolded the schedule sheet, scanned it, then handed it back. "Huh. Looks like you got some work ahead of you. All right. Everyone shut up and pay attention. When I say fall in line, that's what you do. So fall in line and be quick about it."

The freshmen shuffled around into some semblance of a line that petered out at the end. The man looked them over, sighed, and rolled his eyes. "Good enough. Let's go."

Then he took off toward the squat, square building on the southeast edge of campus, practically marching the whole way.

Amanda looked up at the back of Corey's head three kids in

front of her, then turned over her shoulder to whisper to Grace, "Isn't he eighteen?"

"I think so. Or almost, anyway." The blonde witch shook her head. "As I said, we all got tested."

"Yeah, and Coulier got to skip a few grades too," Jackson added, peering over Grace's shoulder. "When was the last time *you* were in school?"

"Beginning of this year." Amanda faced forward again and followed the line of freshmen following Mr. Petrov. She'd finished seventh grade in New York in May, only three and a half months ago. Back when her life had been as normal as it could have been for a shifter girl and her shifter family. Back when she'd thought it would stay that way forever.

Don't get all sappy, Amanda. They're gone, and nothing's ever gonna change that. Time to be someone else now.

She grabbed the straps of her mostly empty backpack and squeezed tightly, steeling herself to focus on classes and not the past she couldn't change. Besides, things hadn't turned out as badly as they could've—because of Johnny and Lisa, and now because she had the Academy.

When the freshmen rounded the corner of the low building Mr. Petrov led them behind, they gazed up at a huge obstacle course constructed of wooden beams, ropes, steel panels, and a few gadgets bolted at various heights.

"Sweet." Jackson bobbed his head and gazed at the ropes and ladders and precarious-looking platforms. "We get a playground."

"Don't get stupid with me, Mr. Pris," Petrov barked. "All you hoodlums had your fun running around LA like it was your playground, but this isn't baby school anymore. *This* is the Academy. Every one of you is gonna master this course by the time you finish your first year here."

A small, mousy girl standing at the front of the group timidly raised her hand.

Petrov glanced at her. "What?"

"What happens if we don't?"

"Christ, and we're already asking the dumb questions." Petrov rolled his eyes, and the girl dropped her hand immediately. "If you whiny little punks *fail* my class, you're starting over. Anything else anybody wants to waste our time with, or can we get started?"

"See?" Alex leaned toward Amanda with his eyebrow barely raised. "Lieutenant."

"Apparently." Part of her had expected Mr. Petrov's rough orders and semi-military mannerisms to fade a little once classes started, but that obviously wasn't happening. *Johnny did call them drill sergeants instead of teachers. Does the military even have magicals?*

"Great." Mr. Petrov folded his arms and nodded toward the obstacle course. "Now that you're all finally quiet, listen up. You're gonna run this course over and over again until you—"

He stopped when his gaze landed on the building behind the freshman class. When he just kept staring, some of the kids turned to look over their shoulders, Amanda included.

Summer rounded the corner to join them, scowling like this was the last place she wanted to be. She glanced at Amanda, then stared straight ahead and folded her arms.

"Who the hell are you?" Petrov barked.

"Summer."

"Last name, kid. Don't make me tell you to speak up."

"Flannerty." Summer looked up at the teacher and shrugged.

"Why the hell are you showing up late to class, Flannerty? You trying to ruin the first day for everyone?"

"I'm not supposed to be here."

"Then why *are* you?" When the new girl didn't answer, Mr. Petrov looked her over and rubbed his chin. "That's right. You're the new kid." He snapped his fingers and waved her forward. "They gave you a schedule, right?"

"Yeah."

"Hand it over."

Summer glared at him. "I didn't bring it."

"Look at you. Already off to a winning start." The man folded his arms. "What's your color?"

"Green."

"Then you're exactly where you're supposed to be. Fall in with the rest of the class."

The girl's fists clenched at her sides. "I'm not a freshman. I spent a whole year at—"

"I don't give a slime-toad's fart where you've been or what you were doing before you came here, Flannerty. If your color's green, you're a freshman at *this* school. Fall in line."

Everyone was staring at the new girl with black hair and a bitter grimace drawing her lips tightly together. Amanda almost wanted to go to her and say it was okay, that Corey was eighteen and he'd still only tested in at this grade, that things were different at the Academy than anywhere else.

That's why she was running around with Candace this morning. They all assumed she'd be in the sophomore class. Did they put her with us because she blew up her old school?

When Summer shuffled toward the rest of the freshman, her jaw visibly clenching and unclenching, Amanda decided to stay where she was. She had a feeling the new girl wouldn't want an eager twelve-year-old freshman trying to make her feel better.

She'd tell me to take my pity somewhere else. I need to focus on myself.

Jackson gently nudged her in the back and muttered, "Did you know they'd lumped her with *us*?"

Amanda shook her head.

"If you newbies don't quit making noise," Petrov barked, "you'll never pass this class. So listen up, 'cause I'm only gonna say this once. Whatever you did before coming to this school, forget about it. That has nothing to do with why you're here. You're here because every single one of you is magically talented in one way or another. That means some of you will find my class easy, and some of you will have to push yourselves to the edge of your physical limits and your sanity to get through."

He paced back and forth in front of the freshmen with his hands clasped behind his back, scrutinizing each face as he passed. "Since the *traditional route* every other kid on this damn planet takes obviously isn't for you, you're at the Academy of Necessary Magic. Where *we* get to teach *you* how to channel your talents in a way that will be more useful to you. Not to mention the rest of society."

"When do we get to start fighting?" Tommy jerked his chin up at the teacher with a smirk.

"You don't, Brunsen," Petrov barked. "Not yet."

"It's *combat* training—"

"None of you are ready to get to the actual *combat* until you know the basics!" Spit flew from the teacher's lips as he shouted, then he wiped his mouth with the back of a hand and straightened. "This isn't about learning how to lose your shit and beat people up because you feel like it. It isn't about how much damage you can inflict in a fight, whether or not you're the one who starts it. It's about physical control! Of your body. Then your mind. Then your magic. If any of you get that far, *then* we'll work on the fighting part. That starts with defensive martial arts, but none of you little twerps are even remotely ready to start there. First, you need to warm up."

Petrov pointed at the obstacle course. "You're gonna run this course 'til you can't stand on your two feet. We'll see who has the chops to make it through. If you can't, you won't be in Combat Training for the rest of the semester. You'll be in Obstacle Course Running until you *do* make it. Understood?"

No one said a word.

Amanda stared up at the ropes and wooden platforms of the course and narrowed her eyes.

Doesn't look that hard.

"Now, I'm only gonna do this once, so if you're not paying attention, don't expect me to repeat the demonstration. You'll have to figure it out on your own." Petrov glanced over the two dozen faces staring back at him, then flicked a hand in the air. A yellow light burst from his fingers then grew beside him, morphing into a square window of light in the air. Red numbers appeared in the window: 00:00:00.

He turned and headed toward the rope ladder at the start of the obstacle course. Then he snapped his fingers and took off at incredible speed toward the ladder.

The magical timer floating in front of the freshman class started, counting up the seconds as Mr. Petrov hauled himself up the ladder and climbed.

Jackson snorted. "Like we can't figure out how to climb up onto a—"

A loud *pop* sounded from one of the gadgets bolted to the top of the wooden pole on the other side of the rope ladder. The gadget's head swiveled, then an orange orb launched from it and headed straight for Petrov. The wizard summoned a shield of white light in front of his face to deflect the attack, then scrambled up onto the platform and leapt up to grab the metal bars in front of him and swung across by his hands, bar after bar.

Two more gadgets activated and launched different-colored attacks at him, and he avoided each with either a quick evasive maneuver or a defensive spell.

"Yeah. A playground." Grace shot Jackson a sidelong glance and raised her eyebrows. "When was the last time *you* got attacked by the monkey bars?"

The wizard ruffled his hair and grimaced. "Crap."

CHAPTER FIVE

Mr. Petrov completed the course with a leap and a forward flip in the air. When he landed steadily with both feet planted firmly in the grass, the last blast from the magically-rigged weapons on the obstacle course crashed into the ground two inches behind his black boots. Then he stood, snapped his fingers, and rolled his shoulders back. The magical timer stopped at 02:31:28.

The training field was utterly silent.

"That," he barked, pointing at the timer, "is the record you have to beat before you can move on to anything else. If you fall off, you start at the beginning. If you get hit by any of those fun little training cannons, you start at the beginning. If you freeze and think you can't finish the course, you'll either fall off or get hit, and you start at the beginning. Anyone refuses to jump in with both feet, and you'll run laps around this course for the rest of the class. That's two and a half hours, just so we're clear. When you finish this course, you won't want to start again, but trust me. Every single one of you *will*. It's up to you how long you're willing to keep screwing around before you get it right."

He stopped in front of the wide-eyed freshmen and raised his eyebrows. "What are you waiting for? Form a line!"

The kids scrambled to do as told, most of them trying to find a spot toward the end of the line or at least the middle.

"What—hey!" Tommy spun and grabbed Evan Hutchinson's shoulders as they struggled with each other to push the other one to the front of the line. "Dude, you can't—"

"*I'm* not going first," Evan hissed. "And you *owe* me after last week."

"Last week had nothing to do with—"

"You're up, Brunsen!" Mr. Petrov barked and snapped his fingers. The magical timer blinked, and the numbers reset to zero.

Tommy froze at the front of the line, his back rigid, and stared at the obstacle course with a grimace.

"You wanna get down to the fighting? Go ahead and prove you're ready." Petrov snapped his fingers again. "Clock's ticking, Brunsen. Go!"

With a groan, Tommy raced off toward the rope ladder and started to climb.

In the line of anxiously waiting students, Grace turned to look at Amanda with wide eyes. "This is not what I expected."

"Yeah, me neither." Amanda shrugged. "You think you can do it?"

"I have no clue." The witch glanced at Mr. Petrov, then shook her head. "It's better than running laps for two and a half hours."

Tommy shouted in surprise when a blue orb crashed into him on the top of the first platform. The spell whisked him up off the obstacle course, flung him to the side, then turned him upside down and dropped him onto the grass. He landed with a *thump* and a groan.

"Back of the line, Brunsen," Petrov shouted. "Hutchinson, you're up!"

Behind Amanda, Jackson cleared his throat. "Better than running laps? Speak for yourself."

None of the freshman class made it through the obstacle course before the blaring alarm cut across campus to signal the fifteen-minute break before Block Two. Even Corey, who was bigger and stronger and older, got tossed off two-thirds of the way through. Most of the kids barely got past the monkey bars. Jackson had opted for running laps although Petrov had failed to tell them beforehand that if they chose that, they'd be chased around by another levitating gadget that spewed painful low-level shocks if they slowed or stopped to catch their breath.

Amanda had finished almost three-quarters of the obstacle course before finally hitting the grass. That was because she'd lost her footing on the teetering seesaw of a platform to avoid one of the magical blasts.

She could have shifted right then and there to regain her balance, but she didn't. So she'd landed awkwardly on her backside and now tried hard not to rub it in front of everyone as the alarm blared and the freshmen class let out a collective sigh of relief.

"All right!" Mr. Petrov shouted. "That was an impressively pitiful display for the first day. If any of you start seeing double or can't feel your extremities, wait 'til the end of Block Two before you run to the med ward. Most of the effects wear off in an hour. I expect a hell of a better attempt from all of you on Wednesday. Now get out."

Rubbing their sore bodies, groaning, and covered in sweat, the freshmen headed around the training building toward the central field, where all the grades would essentially trade places and follow the other teachers to their next class.

Jackson panted as he swiped at the sweat pouring down his forehead and flicked it aside when Grace and Amanda caught up to him. "Totally not fair..."

"Why? 'Cause you tried to take the easy way out?" Grace

flexed her hand over and over. An orange orb had hit her and cramped the muscle until she'd had to let go of the monkey bars.

"Let me tell you something." He pointed at her. "That was *not* the easy way out."

"Obviously." Alex swept his long brown hair back into a new ponytail and quickly retied it. "You gonna try the course next time?"

Jackson glared at him. "I…have no idea. Surprised *you* didn't get some kinda prize, though, Coulier."

"What?" Amanda laughed weakly and peeled her sticky, sweaty tank top away from her skin. "I didn't finish, either."

"Yeah, but you made it farther than anyone else." Grace shot her an encouraging smile despite her deeply flushed cheeks. "That was pretty cool."

"No idea how you managed to do that." Jackson puffed out an exhausted sigh and shook his head. "You some kinda crazy acrobat or something?"

"No." Amanda stared straight ahead and saw Summer marching furiously away from them toward the central field. "I… run a lot, and I've done a lot of hunting—"

"*Hunting*!" Jackson barked out a laugh. "How does *that* help?"

"You know, chasing down an animal, kind of…predicting where it's gonna go next. Stuff like that, I guess." She wrinkled her nose and shrugged. *Sure. Chalk it up to hunting with Johnny and two coonhounds. Not to the fact that I'm a shifter.*

"Where did you go hunting?" Alex muttered.

"Here. In the swamp."

All three of her friends burst out laughing. Jackson stopped abruptly and bent over to prop his hands on his thighs and catch his breath.

"You're full of surprises, aren't you?" Grace playfully shoulder-checked the younger girl.

Amanda let out an uneasy chuckle. "Yeah. I guess."

"Hey," Jackson called after them, still winded. "Wait up."

"How about you *hurry* up?" Alex said without turning around.

"You know what—" The wizard jogged to catch up with them and wiped more sweat off his forehead. "You know what I don't get?"

"Everything?"

Jackson punched Alex in the shoulder, but it was a weak attempt. "Why the heck do they have us in Combat Training first thing in the morning? 'Cause now all I want is to jam a whole pizza in my face and take a nap."

Grace snorted. "So your bacon can't touch your eggs, but a pizza's okay?"

"Hey, everything's *supposed* to touch on a pizza—" A yawn interrupted him, and he shook his head. "The rest of the day's gonna suck."

"I think that's the point." Amanda finally let herself rub her still-sore backside for a moment before readjusting the straps of her backpack. "I think you're right, though. What's our next class?"

"Um...Alchemy, I think." Grace pulled her neatly folded schedule out of her pocket and glanced at it. "Yep."

"Mrs. Zimmer is shooting up green sparks now." Jackson pointed with a limp finger toward the tall brunette woman with her hair braided down her back. "I seriously hope she doesn't make us run another obstacle course."

"With alchemy?" Grace shoved the schedule back into her pocket and shot him a curious frown. "I'd love to know what that's supposed to look like."

"How should *I* know? I'm saying what I *don't* want."

Alex cleared his throat. "She's still married, right?"

Amanda and the other two turned to look at the half-Wood Elf, who stared straight ahead at the teacher for their next class.

"Dude, are you *still* on that?"

Alex shrugged. "Just checking."

"She brought her husband out here with her." Grace lowered

her voice as they passed the students from other grades milling across the central field to get to their next teachers. "I'm pretty sure that means they're still married and in this together."

"Yeah, but he doesn't *do* anything." The half-Wood Elf peeled strands of long hair away from his sweaty neck. "You never know. Teaching a bunch of kids some crazy magical stuff could put a strain on anybody."

"You're unbelievable."

Amanda shot him a small, knowing smile. "You have a crush on Mrs. Zimmer?"

"Great insight into the obvious, Coulier." Jackson clapped a weak, sweaty hand on her shoulder, and it immediately slid off again.

"No, I don't." Alex swallowed. "I'm just…curious."

"Gross." Grace grabbed Amanda's wrist and pulled her quickly forward. "Come on. If we're first into her classroom, maybe we can find a seat where we don't have to watch him drooling through the whole class."

"I don't drool." He shoved his hands into his pockets but didn't take his eyes off their next teacher.

Amanda let the young witch drag her to the front of the freshman group gathering around Mrs. Zimmer. "Any idea what alchemy is?"

"Not even a little. It has to be better than climbing a jungle gym while being shot at, right?"

Alchemy was held inside an actual classroom in the main building's north wing. The second they stepped inside, the freshmen sighed in relief under the air-conditioning pumping through the building, still wiping sweat off their aching bodies. Amanda laughed when the cold hit her, and Grace shot her a confused glance. "What's so funny?"

"I thought it got hot in LA."

"You ever been to California?"

"No."

"First of all, it's dry." Grace tucked her bob behind her ear. "This place is like living in someone's armpit."

Amanda snorted. "It's not that bad."

"It's awful. I don't care how long you've been here. Second, it's a lot cooler underground."

Right. Because they all used to live in tunnels.

"How did you guys even—"

"All right, everybody." Mrs. Zimmer clapped as they filed into the Alchemy room, where sleek stainless-steel tables broke up the room's center in four long rows. "Grab a seat wherever you like and settle down. We have a lot to cover today."

The woman's long braid swung back and forth across her back as she hurried toward her desk at the front of the room. The kids shuffled toward the tables, and Amanda willingly followed Grace toward the second table from the front. Chairs scraped across the linoleum floor, backpacks and bags slid off shoulders to lie on it, and the students all slumped in their seats in exhaustion.

As Amanda settled into her chair, she caught sight of Summer walking past her table to take a seat in the first row directly in front of the teacher's desk. The girl noisily scooted her chair out and quickly plopped into it.

Huh. Figured she would've taken a seat in the back.

Mrs. Zimmer glanced briefly at the new girl, then blinked and eyed the other students settling in. When the last freshman entered the room, Zimmer flicked her hand toward the door, and it swung shut on its own with a soft *click*. "I'll wait 'til everyone's sitting, but I'd appreciate you being quick about it. Yes, Mr. Everly. I'm talking to you."

A few sniggers rose at that. Some of the kids turned to watch Brandon the half-Crystal shuffling across the back of the room.

He ignored the stares and ruffled his hand through his blond hair that was so light it was almost white. Chips of ice scattered to the floor around him, tinkling like glass.

"Mr. Baker." Zimmer pointed at Corey as he neared the front of the room. "How's your eyesight?"

"What?" The giant kid looked up at her with a blank stare.

"Can you see across the room?"

"Uh...yeah."

"Good. Then please take a seat either at the end of the rows or in the back. I want everyone else to be able to see too."

The half-Kilomea frowned in confusion, paused and searched for an empty seat, then lumbered back to the far row of tables and sat. The metal chair with a plastic seat and back groaned beneath his weight as he lowered himself into it.

Amanda studied the room. Stainless-steel shelves lined both side walls. Those on the right held glass beakers and titration tubes, vials, copper bowls, and Bunsen burners. The shelves on the left were stuffed with jars and larger vials, all of them of clear glass and filled with powders and liquids of various colors. Two low sinks took up the far right corner, each with two spouts aimed toward each other. A tall glass case stood six feet high on the left of Mrs. Zimmer's desk, and behind its glass door were even more beakers and jars and vials of different-colored liquids although these glowed with more intensity than any of the others. A round bowl with a tightly sealed lid contained a silver, mercurial liquid that pulsed every thirty seconds with silver light.

She leaned toward Grace and muttered, "So this counts as our science class, then."

Grace tried to hide her smile and shrugged.

CHAPTER SIX

"Okay." Mrs. Zimmer rested her fingertips on the surface of her desk and leaned forward, scanning her students' faces. "Now that everyone's settled let me start by saying it's obvious that all of you are exhausted from your first class of the day. I get it. However, if you're going to learn anything in *this* class—not to mention make it through the full two and a half hours without blowing yourselves up—I expect you to stay on your toes. Alchemy is one of the most volatile, unpredictable, and dangerous disciplines taught at this school. Or anywhere else, for that matter. It's also one of the most rewarding if you do it right."

"So we're basically in a Potions class." The blonde girl named Jasmine—Amanda thought she was a witch or at least a half-witch—drummed her fingers on the tabletop.

Zimmer raised her eyebrows, and a tight, unamused smile made one side of her upper lip twitch. "No, Miss McVar. Alchemy and potions are definitely not the same things. Please raise your hand the next time you have a burning desire to interrupt me during this class, and if I'm finished and ready to start answering questions, *then* I'll call on you."

Jasmine slumped back in her chair and folded her arms.

Someone in the front row snorted, and when Mrs. Zimmer glanced down at the culprit, Amanda realized that someone was Summer.

"As I was already planning to explain," Zimmer continued, raising her eyebrow one more time at Jasmine, "there is a very clear difference between alchemy and potions. First and foremost, I'd say potions is simply a way for those with far fewer skills in casting spells to achieve their intended effect with magic. Can't cast a ward on your own? Sure. There's a potion for that. Need a healing spell but can't mend a cut or a broken bone on your own, even if your life depended on it? Yes. Potions for that too. They're time-consuming, messy, and don't pack nearly as much of a punch as the time, energy, and resources required to concoct them might otherwise make you assume. I don't enjoy potion-making so we won't do any of that here."

The classroom fell silent. Summer's chair creaked when the girl leaned forward over the front table and stared eagerly up at their teacher.

"Alchemy, on the other hand, is quite the opposite." Zimmer swiped a few stray hairs away from her face and drew a deep breath. "Alchemy is the *science* of transmuting pre-existing magical properties from their dormant forms into new forms, reagents, and vessels to actively repurpose those properties into something anyone can use."

Corey grunted in the back. "What?"

"It means you'll learn how to transmute and harness magic that already exists outside yourselves to use it on your own. Without spells. Without potions. Often without any of your magic at all. Don't worry about trying to wrap your heads around all this at the very beginning." Zimmer chuckled. "It's an advanced science. Highly useful. Much faster and more potent than spells or potions. Also much easier to screw up."

The teacher walked away from her desk and pulled a large keyring from the pocket of her dark green shorts. She stopped in front of the glass case to unlock it, pulled out a jar of something that looked like perfectly round black stones, and locked up again before bringing the jar with her to her desk. Then she pulled a large plastic tub from beneath her desk and set it on top. "Maybe a little demonstration will connect the dots for you a little more succinctly. Mr. Everly."

"Uh..." Brandon jolted upright in his chair and gaped at her.

"I need one of your hairs."

"You...my...what?"

"You can have one of mine," Alex piped up, pointing at his head. "I have lots."

"Thank you, Mr. Montoya. If you were a half-Crystal, I'd gladly accept. I asked Mr. Everly."

Alex's shoulders slumped, and Jackson thumped him in the arm. "Tough break, man."

"Shut up."

"We're all waiting, Mr. Everly." Zimmer stuck one hand on her hip and held the other out toward the half-Crystal sitting in the second-to-last row.

"Okay..." Brandon had to try twice before he managed to pluck a few strands of hair. His chair scooted back loudly when he stood, and he hesitantly made his way up to the front of the classroom before depositing them in the teacher's open palm.

"Thank you. Return to your seat."

A few kids sniggered at Brandon as he headed back, pausing every couple of steps to look at Zimmer over his shoulder.

The witch was already busy preparing the items for her demonstration—a bottle of clear, slightly blue-tinted liquid from the plastic tub, a measuring spoon, an empty glass vial, and a box of matches. "It's commonly understood that the science of alchemy was first introduced and used on this planet for creating the kemanas across the globe. Or at least that's as much as we've come to understand since no one truly knows the time, place, or method in which they were created. Anyone who was here for the kemanas' inception is, of course, dead. The crystals powering each of these haven cities are, in and of themselves, transmuted reagents for much more powerful and long-lasting magic straight from Oriceran. Magic harnessed and funneled directly into a different object so anyone and everyone with the capacity to use it can do so."

Zimmer pulled the stopper from the empty vial and dropped Brandon's hair into it. "There *are* ways to reverse the effects of alchemical work on any physical vessel, but that is better left to the professionals. I've seen more than my fair share of incredibly stupid and arrogant magicals lose a few limbs trying to accomplish such a feat. Some of them are dead, too."

"Jesus," Jackson whispered. Someone in his row shushed him.

Amanda couldn't take her eyes off Zimmer's quick, precise movements with her tools.

"When done correctly, alchemy allows us to turn anything into a useable power source for whatever magic we choose to work with. Like that of a Crystal, for instance." Mrs. Zimmer unscrewed a small vice bolted to her desk, and the thin metal clamps opened enough for her to set the vial between them before she quickly screwed it shut again. "Dormant magic in Mr. Everly's hair, of course. His very DNA. Add to that the stripping agent—"

"*Stripping?*" Brandon's voice broke, and most of the class burst out laughing.

"Not of *you*, Mr. Everly." The teacher didn't look up from her work. "I'm sure I speak for all of us when I say no one wants to see that."

More laughter filled the air as Zimmer carefully poured the blue-tinged liquid into the measuring spoon.

"You will learn the exact measurements necessary for transmuting any amount of magic into your new reagents, and I expect each one of you to memorize these measurements before we move on to more complicated procedures. Yes, there will be tests."

A collective groan rose from the students. Amanda frowned and shot the kids sitting in her row a sidelong glance. *What, they've never had tests before?*

The Alchemy teacher funneled the small amount of blue liquid carefully into the vial and removed it from the clamp. Then she shook the vial vigorously. "This is the simplest way to strip down the inactive magical properties. The most effective in a pinch. It doesn't work for every type of reagent though, and I also expect each of you to know the difference between which items you can successfully handle this way and which ones will only waste your time if you try to work with them in simple terms like this. Or which ones will kill you if you get it wrong."

Someone in the back gulped.

By the time Zimmer finished shaking the vial, the stripping agent had turned a bright electric blue, and Brandon's hair floating in the substance was now a visible silver strand within the glow.

"I need a volunteer."

Summer smacked the table and raised her hand instantly. The sound startled some of the other students, and Zimmer looked down at the new girl for a fraction of a second before scanning the other hesitant faces. No one else raised their hand.

"Miss Cameron."

"What?" The small, wide-eyed witch named Blake sitting at the end of Amanda's table blinked furiously and blushed a deep shade of red.

"Come up to my desk, please."

"I...but *she* raised her hand." The girl turned to stare at Summer.

"I did. It's still up," Summer said eagerly. "I'll come help."

Zimmer ignored her. "I'm asking *you*, Miss Cameron. Don't make me ask again."

Blake's chair scooted back noisily as she stood, then she walked rigidly to the Alchemy teacher's desk, her blush gone and replaced by a ghostly white.

Summer scoffed and slumped back in her seat, her hair falling into her lap.

Amanda frowned at the back of the new girl's head, then quickly wiped the expression away. *Since when does she care so much about being picked?*

"Take out one of those pumice stones, please." Zimmer nodded at the jar of perfectly round, semi-porous stones.

Blake struggled to remove the jar's lid, then hesitated with her hand poised over the opening.

"They're rocks, Miss Cameron. They don't bite."

Some of the students giggled, and now a deep flush battled with the terrified blanch in the witch's cheeks.

"At least not yet. We'll cover those later in the semester." Mrs. Zimmer smirked as she gently rocked the glowing vial back and forth. "Go ahead."

Blake reached into the jar and snatched up a rock, then held it away from her at arm's length with a grimace.

"Describe what's in your hand, please."

"What?"

Zimmer sighed. "I'd intended this to be a quick and painless demonstration, Miss Cameron. Don't hold us up on the very first day."

"It's…it's a…rock." The witch slowly brought the stone closer and turned it over in her hands. "N-not that heavy. Lots of little holes all over it."

"Good." Zimmer drew a thickly padded glove from the plastic box on her desk and set it down. "Now throw it."

"What?"

"Maybe you should pay a visit to the med ward after class, Miss Cameron. I'm sure Nurse Aiken would be happy to help you discover what's wrong with your hearing. I said throw it!"

Blake jumped with a little squeak, turned, and chucked the rock blindly at the side of the classroom. The stone rose in a small arc, fell, and bounced twice on the linoleum floor. A round of laughter filled the room, and the witch tucked her brown hair behind her ears with jerky motions as she scowled at her classmates.

"That's fine. Please take your seat." Zimmer pointed at the rock on the floor, and it zipped through the air right in front of Blake's face, making her jump and squeak again before the teacher caught it deftly.

Then the girl scrambled back to her chair at the end of the table and tried to hide by slinking down so far in her chair she almost slid right off it.

"Now you've seen it," Zimmer continued. "A simple pumice rock. Not that heavy. Lots of little holes in it. We call that *porous*, Miss Cameron. For future reference. Yet, it's still strong enough not to break beneath that astounding display of strength in your throwing arm." The woman's voice was flat as she set the rock on the desk and uncorked the glowing vial. "Alchemy allows us to change the physical and magical properties of anything around us, sometimes even at the molecular level."

She upended the vial over the rock until every last drop had trickled from the glass. When she finished, a puff of white smoke—or steam—rose from the stone, followed by the *crackle, hiss,* and *creak* of what sounded a lot like splintering ice. The rock wobbled slightly on the desk and a sheen of icy crystals formed around the surface.

"*That's* a neat trick," Tommy muttered.

"That's science, Mr. Brunsen." Zimmer pulled on the thick glove and grinned. "*Magical* science."

She picked up the stone with her gloved hand and turned it around in the light. "I've alchemized Mr. Baker's Crystal magic into a perfectly natural stone as a new reagent."

"What's the point?" Jasmine asked.

Without hesitation, Zimmer stepped beside her desk and chucked the ice-encrusted stone at the floor. It shattered with a loud *pop* and sent shards of ice scattering across the surface. The students sitting closest shied away, hauling their feet off the linoleum to avoid the shrapnel. A puff of frigid air and steam rose from the cracked-open center of the pumice rock, and the students gasped and muttered in various degrees of surprise.

"The point, Miss McVar, is to gain an understanding of the way alchemy works. With that understanding comes a *much* better grasp of how to use what's around you to harness and use the magic you couldn't possibly wield on your own."

"Hey, Brandon," Evan shouted. "She turned your hair into a Crystal bomb!"

The kids laughed.

Amanda turned to look at Brandon, who sat with his arms folded and glared at the shattered ice-rock on the floor. He didn't look too happy about being the teacher's demonstration guinea pig. When she faced forward again, Summer turned over her shoulder to look at her and waggled her eyebrows.

What's that *supposed to mean?*

"So you're gonna teach us how to make magical bombs," the new girl stated.

Some of the other freshmen cheered in excitement. A small handful shrank farther into their chairs.

Zimmer glanced at Summer with a raised eyebrow. "That's only one of the applications, Miss Flannerty. As I'm sure you already know. *Magical bombs* are reserved for advanced-level alchemy. Unfortunately, you'll have to wait a few years to wrap your head around that kind of knowledge." She returned her attention to the rest of the class. "Now, I want each of you to grab a textbook from that shelf over there—in an *orderly fashion,* which at the very least I hope you've learned how to accomplish since you first got here—and return to your seats. We're starting on page four."

With a collective groan, the freshmen pushed away from the tables and rose to do as instructed.

"When do we get to the actual *alchemy* part?" Summer asked, still firmly planted in her seat.

"Not today, Miss Flannerty." Zimmer nodded toward the textbooks on the shelf. "If you don't get up to grab your textbook, I'll have to transfer you to a different class for Block Two. As far as I know, the only opening at this time of day is Combat Training."

Summer hissed and shoved herself out of her chair to get in line.

As Amanda filed down the row of tables to join the other students, Grace leaned forward to whisper, "What's up with the new girl?"

Amanda shrugged. "She likes bombs."

So does Johnny. He had somebody make a Crystal-magic bomb for him too, only in a crossbow bolt instead of a rock.

CHAPTER SEVEN

Two and a half hours of Alchemy class went by a lot faster than two and a half hours of running an obstacle course and getting barked at by Mr. Petrov. When the alarm blared at 12:45 p.m. to signal the lunch break, every kid in the class shoved their textbooks into their backpacks and stood abruptly.

"No homework for this first week," Zimmer shouted over the chaos of scooting chairs and zippers and heavy footsteps heading toward the classroom door. "Don't get too comfortable. That'll change real quick!"

"Man." Jackson shook his head as he joined Amanda and Grace in the hall. "They need to make these classes shorter. What kind of idiot picked two and a half hours?"

Grace shrugged. "Probably the Light Elf, right?"

"What Light Elf?"

"The woman. You know, one of the bounty hunters who started this school."

"Leira. Jasper Elf," Amanda muttered, hiking her backpack higher on her shoulders now that the Alchemy textbook weighed it down.

"Yeah, her." Grace shot the shifter girl a sidelong glance and a quick smirk. "You say her name as if you know her."

"I mean, she was standing up there with Johnny and…that big guy on our first day here. We all saw her."

"*Johnny*." Jackson let out a low whistle. "Listen to you, Coulier. First-name basis with all the top bounty hunters, huh?"

"Well, when I *live* with one of them…"

"Yeah, yeah. We get it. You're a twelve-year-old freshman who's super special and knows all these important magicals. You live *here* now, don't you? Like the rest of us."

Amanda snorted and shook her head. "Because I want to be here."

"Same old story, Coulier. You know what? I still have no idea what you are."

"A super special twelve-year-old freshman."

Grace cracked up laughing.

Jackson scoffed and turned to look over his shoulder down the hall. "Where the hell is Alex?"

"Probably mooning over *Mrs.* Zimmer," Grace quipped.

"He's not that stupid—oh. Yeah, he is."

Alex filtered out of the Alchemy classroom with a dreamy smile on his face, lugging his backpack in one hand by the strap so it dragged across the floor. Zimmer stepped out of the room behind him with a raised eyebrow and leaned back against the doorway, folding her arms.

"You think he tried to put the moves on her?" Jackson asked.

"That would be seriously stupid on the first day of class." Grace stared at their teacher, then finally turned around. "She doesn't look too happy, though."

"Hey, Goo-Goo Eyes!" Jackson tossed a hand in the air. "If you don't hurry up, all the food will be gone before I get to tell you to grab me seconds!"

Alex started, blinked, then finally saw his friends in the hall and hurried after them. "I'm not getting you anything."

"Yeah, like you didn't get anything from Mrs. Zimmer, huh?" Jackson slung his arm roughly around the half-Wood Elf's shoulders.

"Get off me." Alex shrugged away from him and tossed the rest of his long brown ponytail over his shoulder. "I don't know what you're talking about."

"Sure you don't."

Amanda's stomach growled so loud, all four of them could hear it over the other conversations and loud footsteps of so many students moving through the halls of the main building. Her friends stopped and stared at her, and she looked straight ahead.

"Damn, Coulier. Sounds like you haven't eaten in a week."

"You watched me stuff my face this morning."

"I thought *I* was hungry. You got some kinda feral animal in there or something?"

She shot Jackson a glance and tried to laugh it off, but her smile felt tight. "No."

"I'm screwing with you." He clapped a hand on her shoulder and grinned. "Better hurry up and get to lunch before you end up eating one of us. Race ya!"

The wizard took off down the hall with a wild laugh and disappeared through the crowd of students all heading that way.

Alex rolled his eyes and picked up the pace, finally slinging his backpack over his shoulder.

"He *was* joking." Grace playfully nudged Amanda with her elbow. "You know that, right?"

"Yeah, I know." Amanda walked beside the witch and couldn't bring herself to look at the other girl. "It wasn't funny."

"He never is. Should we tell him?"

"And have to deal with a grumpy Jackson all day?" Amanda shook her head. "That'd be even worse."

"Ha! Very true."

A small smile returned to Amanda's lips, but she couldn't stop thinking about what the wizard had said. *A feral animal inside me. He has no idea how close he was.*

For a brief moment, she started to beat herself up about being so afraid to tell the other kids she was a shifter. Then she remembered what happened to her and why. Kidnapped from her home and sold at auction to the highest bidder at that stupid Monsters Ball. Or *almost* sold. Good thing the highest bidder had been Johnny Walker the bounty hunter, and there was no way he'd "paid" for her after the way he and Lisa had crashed that scumbag party. What really got her was the memory of the thugs who'd hunted her down a few miles from Johnny's cabin in the swamp and attacked her right out in the open, even when she'd shifted to tell them she was a girl and not a wolf.

They didn't care. None of them made it out alive after that.

She caught sight of Jackson slipping through the double front doors of the main building and wrinkled her nose.

Does he really think shifters eat *people or was that another joke?*

The outdoor cafeteria swarmed with students finally let out of their classes, all of them vying for a place in line in front of the buffet table and seats around the picnic tables.

Fortunately, the Academy of Necessary Magic had less than a hundred and twenty students enrolled for its first year. If they took on any more than that, they'd seriously have to rethink the way they did mealtimes.

Amanda piled her plate high with two massive sections of the giant sub sandwiches laid out across the length of the table—one with turkey and cheddar, the other with ham and provolone. Then she scooped up a heaping pile of potato salad, another of regular salad, and snuck an apple and a banana into her backpack just in case.

"Coulier!" Jackson shouted from a table under the pavilion. "You getting some of that pudding?"

She glanced at the giant glass bowl of chocolate pudding and shrugged before whacking down a large spoonful of it onto her plate.

"Hey, get me some too!"

"Dude. You already have some." Alex pointed at the wizard's plate.

"Can't ever have enough pudding. Coulier!"

"Sorry." She grabbed a spoon and lifted her plate. "It's already touching the potato salad."

Jackson slumped over onto the table. "Damnit."

Grace shook her head and grabbed two napkins from the end of the table. "I bet we can find a few seats at a different table."

"No, that's okay. I'm gonna—"

"Oh, *that's* right." The witch shot Amanda a playful wink. "Lunchtime's private."

"It's not *private,* exactly..."

"No, I get it. Trust me. It was hard enough to find alone time back in LA. Not like we had walls and bedroom doors underground or anything. If you need your space, you need your space." Grace laughed as she headed toward the guys' table. "See you after."

"Okay." Amanda watched her friend walk off, then glanced around the outdoor cafeteria and scanned the faces of the other students cracking down on lunch.

It wasn't that she didn't like having friends at the Academy. She did, although she would've been happy running around the swamps with Johnny, Rex, and Luther if coming here for school hadn't been an option. Still, she could only take so much of being constantly surrounded by other kids who had no idea who she was or what she'd been through to get here. They only had an hour for lunch, and over the last six weeks while the other students got used to living in real buildings and sleeping in real beds again, Amanda had gotten used to spending lunch on her own.

She turned away from the buffet table and the kitchen building and headed almost directly north toward the edge of the campus.

The Academy of Necessary Magic had been built right in the middle of nowhere in Florida's Everglades, which formed an easily recognizable boundary around the school's campus—the natural border of the swamps themselves. Amanda had already picked her favorite spot by a group of mangroves, which offered enough privacy from anyone else who might bother to walk to the edge of the campus. She didn't mind being seen—if anyone ever saw her. Mostly, it was to get away from the noise.

Funny. I spent my whole life in New York and only two months with Johnny, and I'm already trying to cut out the noise.

Not that she couldn't hear most of the other students' conversations from here anyway. Her shifter hearing made sure of that. At least here, at the edge of the swamp, she could also hear the birds and the wildlife moving through the reeds and the waterlogged flora. She could think about how nice it would be the next chance she got to shift and run around the swamp as she'd spent two months doing with Johnny's coonhounds.

Johnny had tried to backtrack a little on the first day of the Academy's opening—in his gruff and still weirdly shy way. He'd tried to tell her she didn't *have* to be here if she didn't want to, but Amanda had shot that thought right out of the air.

"I'm at an academy learning to be a *bounty hunter*," she'd told him. "This is the coolest thing I've ever done!"

"It might not always be cool, kid," he'd said. "You know that, right?"

Yeah. She knew that. The dwarf had probably meant it in a completely different capacity than she was feeling now—that being a bounty hunter wasn't all explosions and fistfights and getting the bad guys on the first try. That was fine. Amanda didn't expect the job she'd eventually get when she graduated to be *easy,* of course.

She hadn't expected being around this many kids, all while keeping her shifter blood a secret—not to mention what she'd been through in the last three months—to be so *hard.*

That part wasn't cool, either.

She set her plate down on the grass beside her and snatched up one of the sandwiches. It disappeared in three bites, and she quickly wolfed down the second before feeling even remotely full.

Ha. "Wolfed down." The puns don't get any better, either.

Halfway through the potato salad, something skittered across a soggy berm thirty feet in front of her. A brown-red streak darted across the mound of earth poking out of the swamp water, followed by a grunt and a squeal of terror before something snapped.

Amanda watched the berm until the red fox trotted through the reeds, a large rabbit dangling limply from its jaws. The animal turned toward her and met her gaze, its flanks heaving after the quick scuffle for its lunch.

Everybody does what they have to do. She nodded at the fox, and whether or not it understood the gesture, it darted through another stand of reeds and thick ferns and disappeared. *Including me. Whatever it takes to get through school here so I can finally get the assholes who killed my family and stop anyone else from doing the same thing. After this, I won't need a bounty hunter's help anymore. I'll* be *one.*

She inhaled the rest of her potato salad, the regular salad tossed with a sweet vinaigrette, and all the pudding before she set the scraped-clean plate aside and let herself daydream. A run tonight would be perfect.

CHAPTER EIGHT

Their only class after lunch was the last class of the day—Illusions. Amanda slumped into her seat in Ms. Calsgrave's classroom in the main building, already dreading whatever the course would entail.

The rest of the freshmen slowly filtered in, looking wiped out after a giant meal and the ridiculously long class periods. Grace claimed the desk next to Amanda and shrugged her backpack to the floor before sliding into the seat. "Finally. Something that makes sense."

"How's that?" Amanda rested her elbow on the desk and propped her chin up in one hand.

"Illusions. Spells. Actual *magic* this time." The witch unzipped her backpack to pull out a notebook and pen. "I don't care what they're trying to call this place or what we're supposed to be *training* to be at the end of it. It's a magic school. Gotta be *some* kind of magic taught here. You know, beyond jungle-gym-climbing and bomb-making."

Amanda snorted, but she still didn't feel any better about this class. Practicing actual *magic* wasn't something she had experience with, even *before,* when she'd thought she was merely another relatively normal kid with a relatively normal family.

Besides, it's common knowledge that shifters can't *do spells.*

Ms. Calsgrave sat quietly at her desk, her face hidden behind a black hardcover book with an engraved pentagram on the front that had been filled in with gold paint. The other students quieted on their own as the minutes ticked by and their Illusions teacher kept flipping through the pages.

Grace leaned toward Amanda and whispered, "What is she doing?"

"Reading?"

"Yeah, but… I mean, that's not a *school* book. That's for, like, humans who want to pretend they're witches."

Amanda shrugged.

Someone in the back of the room coughed loudly.

"Because my face is hidden behind a book doesn't mean I can't see you, Miss Porter." Ms. Calsgrave's voice didn't come from the front of the room at her desk, but from the back by the open classroom door that none of the students had bothered to shut behind them. "Because you see me up there doesn't mean that's where I am, either."

All the students turned in their chairs when the door swung swiftly closed with a loud *thunk.* The air in front of the door shimmered, and Ms. Calsgrave appeared from thin air with her hand still on the doorknob.

"What the—" Jackson jumped in his desk chair at the back of the room, glanced at the same teacher sitting behind the desk, then pointed at Calsgrave standing four feet away from him. "You…"

"This *is* Illusions class, Mr. Pris." Calsgrave eyed him with bright blue eyes and a soft smile. "So the first lesson, of course, would be not to believe everything you see."

She pointed at the second version of her sitting behind the desk, and the illusion shimmered away into nothing.

"Wait, we get to learn how to be *invisible*?" Jasmine's mouth hung open.

"That's awesome!" Evan shouted.

Ms. Calsgrave shook her head as she headed down the side of the room toward her desk. "Awesome? Definitely. Not this year, though. Eventually, you'll get to this point, but everyone has to start at the beginning. A cloaking illusion is *not* beginner-level magic."

"Man, that's creepy." Jackson shuddered. "How long were you standing there?"

The teacher either didn't hear his question or didn't think it was worth answering. She merely sat behind her desk and looked up to gaze across the faces of her students. "Illusions are often overlooked in discussions of *useful* magic, especially within the disciplines all of you are here at this school to master. What is most important for you to learn here is the power of your *resourcefulness*. When all else fails, illusions are a resource you can always call upon to use. Combat and weapons technology and alchemical arms are all very well and good. However, what happens if you're stripped of your ability to use any of those skills? It's hardly plausible to carry around a stripping agent in your back pocket for the rest of your life. *Illusions* can't be taken from you, stolen, broken, or manipulated, as long as you learn how to master their various forms for whatever purposes you want."

"Yeesh." Tommy sniggered and jerked his chin at Evan sitting beside him. "Sounds like somebody's trying to one-up Zimmer."

"What it sounds like, Mr. Brunsen, is you're not paying attention."

Tommy sat up straight in his chair and immediately faced her.

"The Academy's curriculum wasn't chosen by some arbitrary want to pit various disciplines against each other. Every one of the classes you'll take during your four years at this school is *essential* for a well-rounded education in...*alternative* life choices.

Which we all know is already ingrained in you. That's why you're here. So yes. You'll learn how to defend yourself physically and with magic. You'll also move up through your classes to discover how to use what you've learned for offensive tactics as well. *This* class is about how to make sure you don't get caught with your pants down.

"Obviously, now that magic has been out in the open for the last few decades—and I *am* talking about humans' awareness of our existence—most magicals think the art of casting illusions has lost both its luster and its necessity. They're wrong. There's a delicate balance between using illusions for fun and casting them so precisely and accurately that no one can tell the difference between what's real and what you've created. My demonstration, for example. Both cloaking and reproduction illusions will be second-nature to you by the time you graduate."

"So you *will* teach us how to make ourselves invisible," Jasmine reiterated.

Calsgrave blinked and cocked her head, her chestnut-colored hair hanging loosely over her shoulders. "First, we start with the basics. Manipulating light to change colors. Come up here and take a piece of paper. *One* each. Then we'll start."

She gestured at the stack of construction paper piled neatly on the corner of her desk, each loose leaf a different color.

"Oh, great. It's a magical art class."

Amanda had no idea which boy said it, but most of the students laughed and looked at Calsgrave to see how she'd respond.

She didn't. Ms. Calsgrave simply gazed over the faces of her students and sat back in her chair. "We're here for two and a half hours. If you feel like wasting all our time, be my guest. I *was* told before taking this job that I'd be teaching a bunch of rough-and-tumble kids who probably wouldn't make it through the first week of class, let alone an entire four years. So either you can live up to the very low expectations set for you, or you can exceed them. Your choice."

Amanda frowned at the woman, who opened a drawer in her desk, pulled out the same black book with the golden pentagram on the cover, and started to read. *I bet any other school would fire a teacher for talking to students like that.*

This wasn't any other school, was it?

Slowly, the freshmen stood from their desks and shuffled toward the front of the room to grab a piece of construction paper. Ms. Calsgrave didn't look up once from her book, not even when Mark DeVolos paused with a sheet of blue paper in hand and muttered, "We get scissors and glue sticks too?"

"Feel free to take it up with Principal Glasket, Mr. DeVolos."

"What?"

"While you're there, make sure she knows I sent you there with crystal-clear instructions to explain exactly how well-equipped your attitude is. Maybe a little chat with her can help you funnel some of your staggering wit into actual usefulness."

Mark stood there with a smirk, staring at the back of her book. "Aren't you supposed to be—"

"I said get out!" Ms. Calsgrave pointed at the piece of paper in his hand, and two dime-sized fireballs launched from her finger. The sheet burst into flames.

"Ah! Are you crazy?" Mark leapt away. "You could have—"

"I did exactly what I wanted, Mr. DeVolos. I teach illusions, but that doesn't mean I'm useless in more destructive spells."

"You're sending me to the principal's office? I was *joking*—"

"Principal Glasket is expecting you, and we'll both know if you choose to screw around and do anything other than instructed. Out." The whole time, Ms. Calsgrave's eyes never left the pages of her book.

"Jeeze." Shaking out his hand that hadn't been remotely burned, Mark turned and stormed back to his desk to grab his backpack. "This place is nuts."

"It's better than where you were," Calsgrave called after him. Then she finally looked up at the next student in line and glanced pointedly at the stack of construction paper. "Keep going. There's enough for everyone."

Amanda watched Mark stomp out of the room, then met Grace's gaze. The witch grimaced, her eyes wide, and shrugged before they moved up in line.

If the juvenile delinquents act up, light their materials on fire. Perfect solution.

At least their Illusions teacher didn't make them run laps.

"No, this isn't art class." When everyone sat with their construction paper, Ms. Calsgrave stood from her desk and pointed at a poster hanging on the wall behind her. "If you're going to have a working understanding of how to manipulate light with your illusion charms and spells—and yes, sometimes even wards, like those around this school—you have to understand how colors work. Everything we see with the naked eye falls within the light spectrum. Colors. Find the color of your paper on the color wheel behind me. Whatever lies directly opposite that should match the new color of your paper by the time this class ends. Any questions?"

"Yeah, aren't you gonna tell us how to do that?" Corey muttered from his desk on the far side of the room.

"You're jumping ahead of me, Mr. Baker. If that's the only question, we'll move on." Calsgrave raised her hand and closed her eyes. "It's all about finding the energy inside yourself and blending it with your intention. At least, that's how the simplest illusions start. See in your mind's eye what's in front of you, then bring into your awareness what you want that thing to *look* like. In this case, the different color. Don't force it. *Feel* it."

"Feel it," Grace whispered, glancing down at her paper. "How are we supposed to feel a color?"

"You're feeling for your inherent magic, Miss Porter," Calsgrave replied, her eyes still closed. "No incantation or ingredients or reagents for this. Only your ability. I can't imagine you haven't used your magic for *something* in your life. Tap into that, and focus."

Amanda stared at the dark red paper centered on her desk and wrinkled her nose. *What, she wants us to meditate our way into changing colors?*

"Feel free to close your eyes," Ms. Calsgrave added. "If it helps you focus. Keep practicing on your own, and I'll make my rounds to check on your progress."

"Is it supposed to be something *everyone* can see?" Brandon squinted at his paper. "Or only us?"

"If you were the only one who could see it, Mr. Everly, it wouldn't be an illusion. A *delusion*, maybe."

A few chuckles rose at that.

"Now get busy. Anyone who feels like screwing around until that final alarm bell sounds can join Mr. DeVolos and Principal Glasket." The Illusions teacher returned her full attention to her book and left the students to fend for themselves with their first attempt at manipulating light and color.

No one said a word as they focused on figuring out how the heck to do the assignment.

Amanda closed her eyes and tried to focus on *visualizing* her dark red paper into a bright blue. The heavy sighs, throat-clearing, and fidgeting from the other students around her made focus almost impossible.

Feel my magic, huh? That would result in me shifting. Not something I wanna do in class. How the heck am I supposed to do this?

"Purple, purple, purple," Grace whispered.

Amanda opened one eye and glanced at her friend. The

witch's eyes were closed, her chin lifted, and both hands hovered over her yellow sheet of paper.

"Come on, magic." That was Brandon muttering under his breath although she heard him as well as if he stood behind her and whispered in her ear. "Help me out. I'm more than an ingredient factory for alchemy bombs."

Someone let out a long, slow *hiss* behind her.

A girl sitting in the front row of desks brushed her hair away from her face and sniffed.

Can't even concentrate when everyone's so loud*!*

Amanda opened her eyes, lowered her hands into her lap, clenched her fists, and glared at her paper.

Just do it already.

CHAPTER NINE

An hour later, Ms. Calsgrave finally returned her book to the open drawer of her desk and stood to make her way around the classroom. With her arms folded, she paused beside each student's desk and didn't even look at their construction paper. She was looking at their faces.

"Don't grit your teeth, Mr. Zendry. Relax."

"No, Miss Cameron. If you're *afraid* of the paper, how are you supposed to make it do what you want? Sit up straight. Dive into it. Make it do what *you* say."

"Mr. Montoya, I did say pick the *opposite* shade on the color wheel. Not different shades of green—Whoever's humming needs to stop right now."

A few students chuckled but immediately returned to focusing on their papers and the apparently impossible illusion-casting.

As the teacher neared Grace's and Amanda's desks, Grace let out a long, heavy sigh, her head lowering until her chin practically touched her chest. Then she sucked in a sharp breath and looked up. "Oh my God. I did it."

"What?" Amanda looked sharply up at her friend's desk,

which was now covered by a deep violet sheet instead of the previous canary yellow. "Whoa."

"I did it!" Grace sat up straight in her seat and started to raise her hand before she realized Ms. Calsgrave was literally right there. "I changed it! I did the illusion!"

"Which everyone else is still attempting to do, Miss Porter, so please keep your voice down." Calsgrave unfolded her arms as she stopped beside Grace's desk. "Very good." She tapped the paper with her index finger, and the purple switched immediately back to yellow.

"Hey—"

"Now do it again."

"Oh..." Grace's smile faded when she realized the teacher was serious. "Great."

Amanda quickly shut her eyes and tried to at least pretend intense focus as Ms. Calsgrave slowly stepped toward her desk next.

"Which part's giving you the most trouble, Miss Coulier?"

Crap. Now I get called out too?

"Um...all of it?" she muttered, forcing herself not to look up and search the other freshmen's faces. Not like she was the only one who couldn't do this, but that didn't make her feel any better.

"That's as good a place to start as any," Calsgrave replied gently. "So focus on feeling your magic. Remember, it's about manipulating *light* first and foremost."

"Yeah, I heard that part." Amanda's fists clenched even tighter in her lap, and she cleared her throat. "I guess it's harder than I thought."

"No, it's not. Close your eyes. I didn't say clench them shut, Miss Coulier. Gently closed. Doing what seems impossible at first *will* be impossible if you stay all clamped up like that. Take a deep breath. Think of a time when you used your magic for something you're truly proud of."

"I don't—"

"You don't want to tell me you hadn't done *anything* useful before you came to this school. That's not true. You have a memory in mind. Use it."

The only thing flashing through Amanda's mind was the memory of shifting in the back of a white van—leaping out of her clothes *and* the handcuffs binding her, clamping her jaws down around the throat of the guy who was supposed to be holding her at gunpoint in the back seat and ripping out his jugular before darting into the front to tear off the hand of the asshole in the passenger seat.

Sure, that helped me then. *Not helping now.*

"Feel your way through it, Miss Coulier," Calsgrave continued. "Use that sensation to visualize—"

The overhead lights flickered once.

The teacher looked up and frowned. "Hmm. What are you thinking about?"

Like I'm gonna tell her in front of everyone. Yeah, right.

"It's private," Amanda muttered.

"Well, there's another hurdle to get over. If you've stuffed the feeling of your magic so far down inside that you can't access it now, no wonder this is so hard for you."

"I didn't stuff anything down."

"Then go ahead. Tell me what you're thinking about."

Nobody wants to hear about that. I'm not only the girl who got kidnapped... Focus on the stupid color!

"Miss Coulier?"

Amanda's cheeks flushed hot, and the overhead lights brightened with a growing buzz before two of them popped and shattered, raining glass down all over her desk and those immediately around her.

"What the—"

"Hey!"

"Ow! Why is there glass everywhere?"

The class stared at the broken lightbulbs, then looked at Amanda.

"Sorry," she muttered.

Ms. Calsgrave brushed a pile of glass off the shoulder of her gray cardigan. "Well, that was…something."

"Hey, talk about manipulating *light*, right?" Tommy barked out a laugh. "Amanda took it to a whole new level—"

She slammed her fists down on the desk and lurched from her chair toward where the half-wizard sat. "I'm *trying*!"

Her voice came out as a growling snarl that didn't quite sound like her, and the tingle of her magic at the start of a shift raced through her body and into her limbs. She cut it off before it could go any farther.

Tommy shrank away from her, tightly gripping the sides of his desk to keep him from falling sideways out of his chair. "Dude. Your *eyes*."

I gotta get out of here.

He looked up at the teacher, then at all the students staring at her. "Did you see her *eyes*? That was the freakiest thing I've ever—"

Amanda stood the rest of the way, her thighs knocking against the desk and almost shoving her back into the connected seat as the legs screeched noisily across the floor. "I can't do this."

"Miss Coulier, that's not—"

"I need some air." She snatched up her backpack and rushed behind her desk to get out of the row.

Grace reached out for her but was too slow. "Hey, what happened?"

Amanda ignored her friend and caught sight of Summer at the end of the last row of desks. The new girl widened her eyes and grinned as Amanda stormed past her. "That was cool."

Nothing to say to that, either.

"Miss Coulier, you haven't been dismissed from this class."

"Then I'll go see Glasket. I get it."

"That's not what I said. You were on the verge of something. Miss Coulier. *Amanda.*"

With her face burning hot, Amanda tore open the classroom door and slipped into the hall. *Feel my magic? Yeah right. I'll end up breaking more crap. Probably sliced somebody open with shattered lightbulbs. What's* wrong *with me?*

Her feet propelled her quickly down the empty hallways until she reached the double doors and shoved them both open. The muggy heat of late August washed over her like a thick, cloying blanket after the air-conditioned building, but she welcomed it. It felt way more normal than the frigid air inside, and in under a minute, she couldn't even feel the flush in her cheeks anymore compared to the rest of her body.

She'll probably still send me to Principal Glasket anyway. I ran out of there like a little kid.

Her anger and frustration died as she hurried across the empty central field and the outdoor cafeteria, heading for her favorite spot beneath the mangrove branches at the edge of the swamp. Her backpack hit the grass with a *thump,* then she sank into the grass and pulled her knees up to her chin.

That class is stupid anyway. I don't need an illusion. I'll keep walking around looking like a human until I lose it and everyone sees what I am.

Tommy had mentioned her eyes. Probably because they flashed silver in any shifter right before they transformed, and Amanda wasn't an exception to that rule. She'd thought she could be the exception here at the Academy, that she could fit in like everyone else. But there wasn't another shifter here, and now the entire freshman class knew she couldn't cast spells and that something freaky happened with her eyes when she got frustrated.

Breathe, Amanda. Come on.

She closed her eyes and rested her chin on her knees.

If the teachers thought you couldn't handle this, you wouldn't be here. They didn't let you in because Johnny told them to. You want *to be here.*

A large bird took flight from somewhere ahead of her in the swamp, rustling the branches with its fluttering wingspan and leaving a wide ring of thick ripples moving across the water toward her. Amanda stared at the water lapping at the bank, swirling with bits of mud and broken reeds floating on the surface.

Ms. Calsgrave knows what I am. She shouldn't have pushed me.

Then Johnny's words came back to her again with a whole new meaning: "It might not always be cool, kid. You know that, right?"

"Yeah, I know," she muttered and looked out over the swamp.

I still have to try. It won't be a heart-to-heart chat, but I should at least tell her what happened. Later. When I'm not so pissed off.

CHAPTER TEN

Amanda stayed beneath the mangroves for at least the next forty-five minutes until the alarm bell shrieked across campus to signal the end of the last class for the day. It was a little weird that half their days during the week at the Academy ran until 4:30 p.m., but the whole school was a bit odd. At least tomorrow, they only had two classes in the morning and the rest of the day to do whatever they wanted.

I could stay here until everyone goes to bed. Then I won't have to deal with all the questions.

The sound of over a hundred students filtering out of their last class for the day raced toward her across the campus. It was quickly followed by the growing scent of some kind of pasta and meat sauce wafting toward her from the kitchens, and her stomach rumbled fiercely in response.

No. She had to eat dinner at the very least. She couldn't run away and hide and ignore everyone for the rest of her four years here. It was only the first day.

Puffing out a sigh through loose lips, she pushed herself to her feet and grabbed her backpack.

I have to make sure I don't lose it again trying to cast illusions. If I even can...

Amanda made her way back across to the outdoor cafeteria, her mouth watering as the smells reached her already overactive sense of smell. She glanced at the open window on the side of the building and saw Fred standing at the sink. The large, burly, severely hairy pixie in a black apron and hairnet looked up from washing his hands and caught sight of her. With a knowing smile, he shot her a thumbs-up—what she'd come to know as his sign for, "You're going to love what we're whipping up next."

With a wry chuckle, she nodded and returned the gesture before passing the building toward the central field. There was still an hour left before they'd all head out here for dinner. At least she had good food to look forward to. Plus Fred and the other kitchen pixies to remind her of it.

The other kids ran around in the field, shouting to each other or standing around in small groups to talk about their first day of real classes. Maybe even about Amanda's slip-up, despite how much she hoped that wasn't true.

"Where did you slink off to?"

Amanda froze, then slowly turned to see Summer standing there, scratching an itch on her calf with the toe of her opposite sneaker. The new girl was smiling at her.

Probably 'cause she thinks she can use it against me.

"Nowhere," Amanda muttered and kept walking.

"Hey, that's cool. I get it. Just trying to get away from all this crazy and take a breath, right?" Summer chuckled and strolled after her. "Honestly, it's a good thing you left when you did. That kid Tommy would not *shut up* about your *eyes*—"

"So you thought it was a good idea to tell me about it?"

"What? No, I'm only saying." Summer jogged to catch up with her. "Calsgrave finally told him that if he didn't stop, she'd make him go blind for a week and still mark it against his grade when he couldn't see for any of his classes."

"She did?"

"Oh, yeah. You know, for a witch who tries so hard to sell the whole 'feel your magic' bullshit, she's kinda scary."

Amanda snorted, and the corner of her mouth lifted in a tiny smile. "I think she's trying to figure out how to teach a bunch of kids who have no idea what she's talking about."

"Ha. Yeah, I bet she meditates and does a bunch of yoga and stupid crap like that in her apartment. Or whatever they give the teachers here to live in. You think their building's like the dorms?"

"No clue."

"I bet they have suites. Figures. Like they don't think we need any more than a tiny room and a tiny bed—"

Amanda turned quickly around to face the other girl and raised her eyebrows. "Was there something you wanted to say to me?"

Summer blinked, her blue-gray eyes wide. "What?"

"I mean, you spent all day acting like you have no idea who I am. Or actually, more like you think I have the plague or something. Why are you trying so hard to be nice all of a sudden?"

Quickly pressing her lips together, Summer swallowed. Her hands slid into the front pockets of her long jean shorts, then she smirked at the shifter girl and shrugged. "I don't know. What you did with the lightbulbs was pretty cool."

"Not when I was trying to turn a red paper green. I don't wanna keep talking about it." Amanda took off again toward the central field teeming with students who had an hour to kill before dinner.

"Hey, hold on. I wasn't done." Summer darted after her and fell in line with Amanda's relatively fast pace. "You're a shifter, aren't you?"

Amanda stopped again and glanced around. Nobody seemed remotely interested in their conversation. *I can't believe she's trying to talk about this right now. Or ever.* She turned slowly toward Summer and frowned. "What makes you think that?"

"Oh, come on. You growled at that Tommy kid, and your eyes flashed silver. You couldn't even chill out enough to *feel your magic*, and you did the best on the obstacle course this morning. Hell, you probably would've finished it if you hadn't slipped off. Still pretty impressive. Not to mention the fact that *nobody* here knows what you are."

"Wait, you've been *asking* about me?"

Summer tossed her black bangs out of her eyes and scanned the crowded field. "Not exactly. I hear things. I think it's awesome, though. Never met a shifter before—"

"Hey, maybe keep it down." Amanda glanced around them again. "Did you ever think maybe there's a *reason* nobody knows?"

"Of course there's a reason." The other girl laughed. "So...come on."

"What?"

"Tell me. Why are you making it such a secret?"

Amanda shook her head. "I'm not—"

"Honestly, you might be the only good thing about this school. It wasn't a *rule*, but there weren't any shifters at the School of Necessary Magic when I was there. Like, at all. So how'd you get them to take you here, huh?"

"I already told you I'm here because I *want* to be—"

"Yeah, yeah. You wanna be a bounty hunter when you graduate. Blah, blah, blah." Summer pointed at her. "Oh, *I* know. You're the poster child for this place, aren't you?"

It took a second for that last bit to sink in, and Amanda's frown only deepened. "I have no idea what you're talking about."

"Come on, Amber. It's Amber, right?"

"Amanda."

"Whoops. Amanda. Listen. Everyone knows shifters aren't *magical*. Not the way the rest of us are, at least. So this school is gonna groom you and stick you under the spotlight as the shifter who went through the first four years of this place. Start bringing in all the attention and probably more money, right? 'Cause a lot of your kind tends to fall off the side of the road into the gutter, know what I mean?"

"Still no."

"You know, like crime and gangs and all that. Unless they have a pack and—whoa. Do you have a *pack*?"

Amanda drew a deep breath and held the other girl's gaze. "No. I really don't wanna talk about this."

"Yeah, sure. We can pick it back up later when no one's around."

"No, I mean, like, ever. Okay?" Her cheeks grew hot again, but she forced herself not to look away from Summer's eyes. "Please don't tell anyone else."

The new girl snorted and looked out over the crowd of students again. "Please. I'm not a snitch."

That's probably as close to a promise as I'll ever get out of her.

Amanda readjusted her backpack's straps and looked for Grace or Jackson or even Alex. Maybe if one of them saw her, they'd come over here and help her out a little. Summer was suddenly becoming way too much. However, she couldn't find any of them.

"Hey, question for ya." Summer slapped Amanda's arm with the back of a hand.

"Okay…"

"You know where they keep the potions and ingredients or whatever for alchemy?"

Amanda looked up at the girl and narrowed her eyes. "Yeah."

"Wanna help me get in there later?"

"What?"

"You know, to get my hands on a few things." Summer grinned. "That Light Elf teacher isn't gonna let us *touch* the good stuff probably 'til we're seniors, which *should* be only two years away for me if these dumbasses hadn't held me back a year. Stupid, right?"

"I mean, we all took the same test—"

The girl scoffed. "Tests don't tell anybody anything. I'm not waiting around for years to use the stuff they have locked away, not being used. So how about it?"

Amanda's frown deepened. "No. Sorry."

"Aw, come *on,* shifter girl. Don't tell me you haven't broken a few rules since you got here." Summer leaned toward her and lowered her voice. "I heard it's bad for shifters to go a long time without, you know, *shifting*. You have to get out sometime, right?"

Crap. Why does she have to put all the pieces together now?

Stepping away from the new girl, Amanda shook her head. "I'm not breaking rules like *that.*"

Summer laughed. "Like what?"

"Like...breaking into a storage room for stuff we aren't supposed to touch."

"Look, they have so much stuff in there, they won't even notice a few things missing. What's the big deal?"

"Isn't that why you got kicked out of your last school? And sent here?"

As she rolled her eyes, Summer's smile faded a little. "They're all way too uptight out there. It wasn't a big deal."

"Maybe not for you. I *really* don't wanna get kicked out of *this* school. So whatever you do, I guess you'll have to do it on your own."

"Huh." The new girl blinked and ran her tongue over her top teeth with a squeaking, sucking sound. "Wow. You know, I'm a little disappointed, shifter girl."

"Don't call me—"

"I thought you were badass." Summer wrinkled her nose and shrugged. "Guess I was wrong. You're just another goody-two-shoes at another stupid school full of sheep. Except you got a wolf in you."

She smacked the back of her hand against Amanda's shoulder much harder this time and stormed off into the center field.

Wherever she went next, Amanda didn't see. She was too busy being stunned into confusion.

What the heck is her deal*? I lose it and almost shift, and she wants to be partners in crime? What I get for trying to be nice to the new girl.*

"Hey, Amanda!" Grace's shout and wave from the crowd caught her attention. "Get over here."

Choosing to ignore Summer's hot-and-cold vibes, she smiled at the witch and headed through the crowd toward her, Jackson, and Alex. They wouldn't bombard her with personal questions now after six weeks of knowing she didn't want to talk about her past that was still way too fresh. At least *these* friends still looked happy to see her. Even if they were pretending.

CHAPTER ELEVEN

That night after Lights Out—the only thing for which there wasn't an obligatory alarm blaring across the entire campus, in case a few teenagers decided to go to bed before 10:00 p.m.—Amanda lay in her bed and stared at the ceiling again.

This time, she listened intently to the sound of the other girls in the dorm slowly settling in for the night. Their first few weeks here had been a little more lax with the rules. They could still talk and hang out with each other in the dorm after Lights Out but weren't allowed to leave the building. As they'd gotten closer to the first week of classes, the Academy's staff had started to crack down on "offenders" who left their rooms after 10:00 p.m.—although it didn't come without a warning beforehand. Those who'd been caught had been sent to the kitchens the next day to help wash dishes after meals or to Mr. LeFor's office at the back of the main building.

She'd heard *that* punishment was worse; Mr. LeFor liked to use his unwilling "assistants" as test subjects for whatever new gadget he was working on. Mandy Kaylek said he'd tested some kind of anti-gravity sphere on her, and she'd stumbled around the campus with her balance all out of whack for a week afterward.

Amanda figured the teachers had set up some kind of noise sensors as their so-called security system although she hadn't been able to find any proof. It didn't matter. She could be deathly quiet if she wanted to be, and she *was* every time she snuck out of her dorm room to go for a run after everyone else had fallen asleep.

Or maybe they know it's me and haven't bothered to dish out punishment.

Still, that wouldn't explain the small hole she'd found in the electrically charged wards around the dorm building. It was way in the back on the first floor, on the opposite end of the building from the front doors. Not exactly conveniently located *in front* of the back door beside the closet of cleaning supplies, but Amanda had quickly discovered how to get through it. It only took a little premeditating and finesse. Which, when she was a wolf, she fortunately still had enough to get the job done.

It seemed to take forever for the other girls to settle down into a chorus of steady breathing, heavy snores, and the occasional flopping over on a mattress. She gave it an extra half hour to be sure, then glanced at her alarm clock—11:14 p.m.

Plenty of time to slip out for a quick snack. That apple and banana didn't do anything.

In the silence, she double-checked that her room key was safely stuffed into the front pocket of her shorts, then headed across her room and opened her door. No one in the hallway, either. Not even Summer.

Good. She'd wake up the whole floor trying to ask me about being a shifter.

Amanda pulled her door shut behind her with the barest whisper and almost inaudible *click*, then headed barefoot down the hall toward the closest staircase. She'd figured out that if she pulled up on the handle when opening *that* door, the hinges didn't squeak. Then she headed down the enclosed stairwell for two flights until she reached the first floor.

All the lights were off except for the large overhead bulb in the middle of the common room, which dimmed on a timer but didn't have an actual switch. After a quick scan of the empty area, she turned toward the back of the building and headed for the narrow metal door with "Exit" painted on it in thick white letters.

Finding the hole in the building's security ward had been an honest mistake during her third night at the Academy and her first attempt at shifting while no one else was awake to see it. The faint smell of a lit match grew stronger the closer she came to the wards, which were invisible until someone stepped into them and got zapped hard enough to discourage a second attempt. It stung, the buzzing aftereffects lasting for almost an hour, but no, it wasn't hard enough to knock someone out until noon the next day, like she'd told Summer.

She doesn't need to know. Especially if she's trying to sneak out and break into the alchemy supplies.

Amanda sniffed at the air beside the back door, and her shifter senses zeroed in on the place where the sulfuric stink of the wards gave way to the salty, slightly sweet nighttime air of the swamp. That was how she'd found the hole, and that was how she tested them every time she stepped out for one of her mini escapes.

I guess someone forgot to make sure they sealed it all the way. Or they got lazy.

She quietly opened the supply closet beside the back door and took out the small tin pail that was always right there inside the doorway.

Or they wanted to leave an open escape route for me because they knew I'd need to get out. Yeah, right. No special treatment for the shifter. Not after the way Calsgrave pushed me today.

Shaking that thought out of her mind, Amanda concentrated

on opening the back door. The opening in the wards wasn't large —not quite a foot wide—but it was enough to open the back door without triggering a massive magical jolt to her system. The tin pail fit neatly between the door and the frame to keep it propped open for her.

When she had everything in place, she stepped back and drew a deep breath.

Definitely need to get out.

She shifted. Her whole body tingled—all the way to the tips of her dark-brown hair that she felt only for an instant before short gray hair covered her head instead.

Stepping quickly out of her clothes, the small gray wolf sniffed one more time at the wards, then gathered the articles into her mouth and positioned herself directly in front of the foot-wide opening in the door. Her skin tingled again when she leapt gracefully over the pail and landed outside in the grass, raising her hackles and making her shake herself.

A hole in the wards doesn't mean I can't still feel something.

She took another quick sniff in the air but only caught the tangy, half-briny scent of the swamp water, the last traces of two rabbits that had darted across the field, and the faint odor of cigar smoke mixed with strawberry rhubarb pie. That would be the pixies.

Amanda dumped her clothes onto the ground and shifted back into her human form, then quickly tugged them on beneath the overhanging rooftop of the dorm building. She'd gotten this part down to a science too—getting dressed again after shifting back. It grew easier every time, but she wished she didn't have to risk being spotted butt-naked in the grass behind the building.

If I could cast any actual spells, that wouldn't be a problem with an illusion. Except for maybe the draft.

After one more glance around the open grass studded with oak trees behind the dorm, she headed northwest to take the long way around the building toward the kitchens. She stopped only once to glance around again when her stomach let out a furious growl that seemed way too loud in the silence, even with all the nighttime sounds of the swamp to mask it.

Nobody can hear your stomach through concrete walls, dummy. Keep moving.

Still, she stuck close to the buildings and the slightly darker shadows of the trees dotting the campus, despite the moon being only a waxing sliver in the late-August sky. The smell of cigar smoke and pie grew stronger as she darted across the outdoor cafeteria and headed for the back door of the kitchens—or really the only entrance.

Her knuckles rapped against the metal to the beat of "Shave and a Haircut," which had been her first joke with Fred. He'd responded to her very first tentative knock in the middle of the night with that little rhythm from the inside of the door, and now it was how the kitchen pixies knew Amanda Coulier was standing outside, waiting for them to let her in.

The door opened slowly, and a puff of cigar smoke wafted right into her face. Choking back a cough, she waved the smoke away and blinked. "Wow."

"Well, look who it is." Fred chuckled and held the door open with one hand as he lifted a plastic cup to his mouth with the other. Ice clinked together as he took a long sip and looked Amanda over.

So the first day of class makes them wanna drink too, huh?

Amanda wrinkled her nose and swatted one more time at the receding smoke. "How's the whiskey?"

Fred choked down his drink, then barked out a laugh. "How do you know what I'm drinking?" He pulled his cup away to frown at it. "You see through walls too?"

"Shifter nose, remember?"

"Nothing gets past you, does it? Still showing up to a professional kitchen barefoot, I see."

She shrugged. "I'm quieter without shoes. Plus, they're a little harder to carry when I don't, you know...have hands."

"Ha!"

"You gonna stand there all night, man, or can we at least finish this hand first?" A skinny pixie with a shock of neon-orange hair sat at the high, stainless-steel prepping table in the center of the kitchen, one shoe hooked under the rung of the stool beneath him and his other foot propped up on a second stool. A shimmer of sparkling orange light rose around him like a full-body halo.

Fred turned slowly toward the table while gesturing for Amanda to step inside. "I'm allowed to welcome our late-night guest, aren't I?"

"Sure you are. Hey, kid."

"Hi, Carlos."

"I know what you're trying to do," the orange-haired pixie added. "No matter how you spin it, buddy, I'm still getting that sweet activation ring of yours in the pot. With everything else you sorry sonsofbi—"

"Watch your mouth!" Sitting across from Carlos, Gloria swatted the table and glared at the other cook.

"What?" He spread his arms and finally rolled his eyes when the pixie woman's warning stare didn't let up. "Fine. Point is, I'm taking the pot. So hurry the hell up, Fred, huh?"

"Listen to him." Gloria shook her head and shot Amanda a playful frown, her bubblegum-pink curls bouncing across her shoulders. "No control."

"I didn't say anything..."

"It's okay." Amanda chuckled and stepped farther into the kitchen as Fred shut the door. "I've heard worse."

"From that bounty hunter guardian of yours?" Carlos snorted. "Yeah, I bet."

"That doesn't mean *you* can talk like a dirty-mouthed pixie in front of her," Gloria admonished.

"I *am* a dirty-mouthed pixie." He raised an orange-glittering hand and gestured around the room. "Hiding in a kitchen. Where no one else is supposed to hear or see me, right? No offense, kid."

Amanda raised both hands and shrugged. "None taken."

"Come on, then." Fred nodded toward the counter on the other side of the kitchen. "Got somethin' laid out for you and ready to go."

"You already made me something?" Despite the cigar-smoke smell, the scent of pie plus the *thought* of it made her mouth water even more.

"Sure we did. You're our favorite visitor."

"You're our *only* visitor, honey," Gloria added.

"Still."

"How'd you know I was coming?"

Fred chuckled. "It's been four days since the last time, girl. Figured if you weren't out here tonight, it'd be tomorrow."

"Yeah, and *we'd* have the pie to go with our drinks," Carlos added. "Man, will you hurry up already?"

"Don't put it all on me. We're still waiting for Greg."

"Greg!" Carlos pounded a fist on the table, making the stack of playing cards jump. "You fall in or something?"

Pounding footsteps came from *below* the kitchen floor, and Amanda hurried toward Fred and the pie counter as a trapdoor opened two feet behind her with a *bang*. Greg's unruly blue hair poked up from the hidden staircase underground, followed by the lit and smoking end of a massive cigar dangling from the side of his mouth. "What're you yellin' 'bout, you glowin' orange fu—oh. Hey, 'Manda."

"Hi." She grinned at him and slowly backed away to join Fred by the counter, where the giant pixie pulled out a devastatingly sharp kitchen knife to slice the pie. "Nice night, huh?"

"Is it? I couldn't tell." Greg climbed through the trapdoor and left it open, taking three long puffs on the cigar. Then he exhaled, working his lips like a gaping fish out of water, and blew out a string of white star-shaped clouds. "Spent the whole night tryin' not to wring Carlos' scrawny little neck."

"Only because I'm about to take you for everything you're worth."

"Here you go." Fred handed her a plate and a fork, thin tendrils of steam still rising from the pie's center. "Got ourselves our very own taste-tester, huh?"

"Smells great." Amanda leaned against the counter with the plate in hand and took a long, deep sniff. "It's—"

She couldn't hold back her coughing any longer and shook her head.

"That bad, huh?"

"Damnit, Greg," Gloria snapped, completely forgetting her rule about not cursing in front of a student. "Open a window, will ya?"

"Huh?" Greg looked back and forth between Amanda and the pixies at the table, frowning. "I *did*."

"Well, then put that thing out, will ya? The poor girl can't breathe in here."

"Looks to me like she's breathing just fine."

"Don't make me come over there." Gloria wagged a finger at him. "You won't like where I put it out for you."

Greg stomped toward the wall with a groan, grabbed a machete dangling from a hook beneath the pots and pans, and swiped it down on the end of the cigar. The thing cut cleanly just beneath the burnt end, which sailed straight into a bucket beneath the window used as an ashtray. Then he turned toward Amanda and pointed the tip of the machete at her. "Don't think I'll forget this, kid. And remind me to thank you later for forcing me out of my bad habits."

She chuckled and couldn't look away from the point of the machete.

"Don't worry about being polite, either," Fred added. "If you don't like strawberry rhubarb, I can pull out something else for you. Just say it."

"What? Oh, no. It smells amazing."

"Then eat the damn pie!" He roared with laughter, and the other pixies joined in, shaking their heads.

Amanda dug in, consuming her first three bites without actually tasting it and ignoring the fact that the gooey center was still hot enough to burn her tongue. "It's perfect," she said around a huge mouthful.

"That's what I like to hear." Fred slapped the counter. "Clarissa's recipe finally got some love. Hey, tell her it worked."

Greg leaned over the open hole beneath the trapdoor and shouted, "Clarissa!"

"*What?*"

"Kid likes your pie."

"And?"

Greg looked up at Amanda and shrugged. "You want some?"

"No! Shut up!"

The blue-haired pixie burst out laughing, throwing his head back and waving the machete around like a lunatic. When he finally settled down again, he kicked the trapdoor shut with a loud *bang*.

"I said shut up!" Clarissa shouted, her voice muffled through the floorboards.

"Eh, she'll be back to her usual self again. It's that time of the month."

Amanda choked on her next bite of pie and stared at him.

"Don't listen to him, honey." Gloria waved him off. "He doesn't know what he's talking about."

"I don't know what *you're* talking about," Greg replied. "'Cause it's true."

Carlos snorted and shook his head.

"It's the new moon," Gloria clarified. "Makes her shut herself up in her room for about a week. Then she's up here as bright and chipper as ever."

"Huh." Amanda swallowed and had to try a second time to get all the pie down. "So *that's* where you guys sleep."

"Well, it sure as hell isn't on the prep table!" Carlos slammed his hand down on the table to emphasize his point, and the pixies broke into another round of laughter.

"You want some water with that, kid?" Greg cocked his head and pointed at her plate.

"Oh, my bad." Fred reached toward the stack of freshly washed plastic cups. "I'll get it for ya. Fix your eye, man. You're gonna scare this girl away from ever paying us another visit if you keep letting yourself go like that."

"Shit." Greg looked at Amanda, and she noticed his left eye was turned so far to the outside, she could barely see the dark-blue iris. Then he slammed the heel of his palm against his temple twice—really hard—and the eye flashed with blue light before correcting itself. "Damn enchanted eyeball."

"I *told* you to get the warranty," Carlos added.

"I *know* what you told me. The guy seemed legit!" Blinking furiously, Greg straightened and focused on Amanda again. "There. Better?"

She couldn't help but burst out laughing, struggling to keep the remains of her pie from sliding off the plate.

"Aw, see? Give the kid more credit, Fred. Nothing scares *her*."

Huffing out a laugh, Fred waited until Amanda's fit died down before he handed her the water. "Sure. If a few washed-up kitchen pixies don't scare you away, I don't know what will."

"Who you callin' washed-up, you hairy beast?" Carlos slapped the table again. "Now get your ass over here so we can finish this hand and I can whoop *all* of you."

"You better not be looking at my cards."

"Man…"

Amanda finished draining the water and let out a loud, contented sigh. "Thanks."

"Sure thing, kid. I'm glad to see somebody enjoying that pie the way you did."

"You can take it with you if you want," Gloria offered.

"Yeah…I don't think I can get back into the dorms with a whole pie." Amanda shrugged. "Thanks. You want me to put the dishes in the—"

She stopped when the quick patter of feet outside reached her ears—fast, not very covert, moving in rhythm to the owner's heavy breathing.

Fred and Greg climbed back onto their stools at the makeshift card table, and all the pixies stared at her. "You gonna finish that thought?"

"What?"

"If you were gonna say 'put the dishes in the sink,' you'd be right on point. We'll take care of it after that."

Carlos waved his hand in the air. "It *is* our job, isn't it?"

"Yeah… Yeah, okay." She quickly dropped the dishes in the huge sink below the window facing the outdoor cafeteria and frowned. *That did* not *sound like a teacher. Who else would be running around in the middle of the night?*

"You okay, honey?" Gloria asked as she picked up her poker hand again. "You look a little distracted."

"I'm good. Should probably get back to my room, though. Thanks for the pie. It was great."

"Any time." Fred took a long drink of his whiskey.

"You know us, kiddo. We live to *serve*." Greg shot her a mocking bow from his stool until Gloria smacked him on the shoulder.

"Have a good night," Amanda mumbled as she headed quickly for the door.

"You come back any time, Amanda. We got you."

"Thanks." As she slipped out of the kitchen door, the pixies returned to their poker game.

"She's a good kid," Gloria said.

"Good at sneaking out of the dorms at night," Greg added. "How'd she manage that, you think?"

"Who cares?" Carlos shouted. "Play the damn hand!"

The door shut behind her, muffling the pixies' voices, and Amanda stepped across the dark grass, listening intently for the same pattering footsteps across campus. The faint *creak* of a door opening made her turn, but then the sound disappeared beneath the humming buzz of cicadas and the chirping of crickets.

Anyone stupid enough to try breaking into this school should be stopped, right? If I'm the only one who knows...

She took off slowly toward where she'd heard the creaking door, which could have come from any of the buildings.

I should at least see who it is first. Maybe no one else has *to know.*

CHAPTER TWELVE

It took her less than two minutes to pick up the scent of the "intruder," and when she did, Amanda stopped and cocked her head.

Summer? How the heck did she get out?

She followed the scent across the campus, lost it once in the central field when a mouse scurrying through the grass stole her attention, then found it again. It led right to the front doors of the main building.

I thought they kept all the doors locked at night.

As she approached the front doors, a loud buzz rose behind her, particularly loud for how far behind it was.

Amanda looked over her shoulder and saw a purple streak of light blazing into existence beside the dirt road that was the only way in and out of the Academy campus—at least by land. The buzz grew louder, the flickering purple light flashed brighter, and a spray of purple sparks burst into the air before filtering down to the dew-studded grass. She sniffed and found the same sulfuric tinge in the air, this one with a sweet undercurrent.

Weird. For a brand-new school, this place has a lot of loopholes with its wards. Guess it's all trial and error.

When the invisible wards around the school's perimeter—meant to keep others *out* of the school, especially humans—didn't act up again, she turned back toward the main building and gently tried the handle. Sure enough, it was unlocked.

There's no way a teacher forgot to lock this up.

Slipping quickly inside, she carefully guided the door shut again without a sound and turned to sniff out the new girl's trail.

Her bare feet moved silently down the hall, and she followed Summer's scent—reminiscent of black pepper, oddly enough—as if she was back on the hunt with Johnny and the hounds.

Definitely didn't expect to be hunting down another student at school, though.

Once she turned down the next hall into the west wing, she knew the girl was up to something. Principal Glasket had made it clear this side of the main building was off-limits. Apparently, Summer still didn't think any of the rules applied to her.

The grating scrape of metal on metal echoed down the hall, followed by a short hiss of a curse. Small metal items *clinked* against each other, and Amanda paused at the end of the hall before it curved to the right again. Peering around the corner, she saw what she knew she'd find anyway.

Summer crouched on the floor beside the door to the alchemy supply room, the sign painted on the door in white paint clear as day, even in the dimly lit hall: "Alchemy Storage. Faculty Access Only." The other doors at the back of the west wing were labeled the same way—storage rooms for spell ingredients and potions, weapons, parts and devices for Mr. LeFor's Augmented Technology class, extra school supplies, training gear. The last one on the left read "In-Game Live," although Amanda had no idea what that meant.

In front of Summer was a black canvas bag that unzipped all the way to lay flat on the floor, and Summer paused in selecting another small metal tool from the assortment inside. Then she rose from her crouch and brought two different implements to the door's lock, delicately pressing them together in a series of quick twists and turns as they *clicked* against each other.

Wow. Picking a lock in a magic school. Probably a magic lock.

"You know, you'd be a lot more useful if you came to help," Summer muttered. Amanda froze, but before she could disappear around the corner again, the new girl added, "Yeah, I can tell when someone's watching me. Feels like a hot poker on my back—ow!"

The lock spat a surge of orange sparks at her, and Summer quickly jerked both lockpicks away and raised her hands as if the door could tell she was surrendering.

"Don't just stand there. Come help."

Amanda frowned and glanced at the bag of at least a dozen different lockpicks, plus a few tools that looked a lot like the tiny implements Johnny kept in his workshop. "No thanks. I'm good."

"Oh, come on. You followed me in here. That means you wanna be involved *somehow.*"

"I wanted to make sure whoever was sneaking around campus wasn't trying to hurt somebody. It looks like you probably will if you keep that up."

Summer growled and drew away again when her newest lockpick brought another spray of hissing sparks from the door the second she tried to slip it into the lock. "I don't need a babysitter, shifter girl. So now you caught me. You gonna rat me out now? Get me sent to *detention*?"

"Not if you can't break into that room. Until you do, we're at the same level of—"

"Breaking the rules? You sure do have a weird way of defining 'acceptable rebellion.'" Summer turned away from the lock and smirked as she squatted again beside her lockpick collection. "I'll get this door open eventually. With or without your help. Don't worry. Either way, I won't put a black mark on *your* record."

She snorted and went back to selecting a new instrument for her futile task.

A sinking feeling settled in Amanda's gut, and she swallowed. "How'd you get out of the dorm?"

"Please." Summer looked up at her and grinned. "You think I don't know an open-door invitation when I see one? Gotta hand it to you, though. You still didn't make it easy to find, but the mop bucket was a nice touch. You didn't even mention the break in the wards. How'd *you* find them?"

She thinks I left the door open for her. Jeeze. She doesn't give up.

Choosing not to answer that question, Amanda shoved her hands into the back pockets of her shorts and frowned at the new girl. "Well, I'm going back. To bed."

"Uh-huh. Look, if you need to cover your tracks, I get it. There's more than one way in and out of *the barracks*." Her smile broke with a wry chuckle. "So you won't be leaving me stranded. We're good." Summer nodded curtly, then returned her attention to her tools.

More than one way. She used my open door and didn't even need it. Great.

Without another word, Amanda headed silently back down the hall of the west wing, occasionally glancing over her shoulder. She didn't really expect Summer to come after her, but it wouldn't have been that much of a surprise, either.

No wonder she got kicked out of her last school. Everything's a game to her. I played right into it without even knowing. At least if she tells anyone, she'll have to explain why she was out here too.

By the time she got back to the girls' dorm—shifting one more time and carrying her clothes back inside between her powerful wolf's jaws—she was exhausted. She didn't even care that she'd put her shirt back on backward *and* inside out as she hurried up the enclosed stairwell toward the third floor and slipped quietly back into her room. The weight of the pixies' strawberry rhubarb pie in her belly made flopping down onto her bed and ready to drift off to sleep a lot easier. The thought of Summer still out there, trying to break into restricted storage rooms, made the actual falling-asleep part seem impossible.

There was no reason for Summer to go right to any of the teachers about seeing Amanda out of her room. Oddly enough, that slim possibility didn't worry her at all.

What kept her awake was the unknown of what would happen to the new girl if *she* got caught breaking the rules, especially in a place like the Academy. Because where else was she supposed to go if she got sent *here* after being kicked out of other schools? The Academy of Necessary Magic was a school too—granted, a school for bounty hunters in training—but it was also the end of the line.

I tried to warn her more than enough times.

Amanda flipped over on her bed and clutched the second pillow tightly against her chest.

Not my fault if she wants to make even more trouble for herself. I have to focus on why I'm here. Plus figure out what I'm gonna say to Ms. Calsgrave on Wednesday.

The next morning, Amanda almost forgot about her surprising find the night before as Ms. Ralthorn droned on in their first class of the day—History of Oriceran. The other freshmen didn't seem to be doing much better with their attention spans, passing notes folded up into paper airplanes or origami shapes or simply crumpled balls. Even Alex, who was usually pretty attentive—or at least always looked that way—had drowned out Ms. Ralthorn's monotone voice to focus his energy on growing a whole new root system on a small plant he'd brought inside with him from the field.

Amanda's eyelids drooped, her chin slipping off her hand where she tried to keep it propped up on the desk.

"Psst. Hey."

She slowly opened her eyes, then a wadded ball of paper smacked her in the side of the head. Frowning, she searched for the culprit and found Summer in the row behind her, three desks down.

The girl waggled her eyebrows and grinned, sparing a glance at the front of the room where Ms. Ralthorn was reading to them from a textbook. "Hey, how'd you sleep last night, huh?"

Amanda sighed, faced forward again, and stared in a daze at the teacher's lips, which were covered in a bright orange lipstick this morning and moved at a snail's pace while she read.

Grace shot Summer a confused frown, then leaned toward Amanda and whispered, "What's her deal?"

"No clue. Ignore it."

For the rest of that week, that pretty much became her new mantra. Ignore it. Amanda managed to keep her focus mostly on school and each class, refusing to respond to Summer's weirdly cryptic comments and attempts to shoot her sly, knowing glances from across the room. At least once a day, she saw the new girl huddled in private conversation with small groups of upperclassmen Amanda didn't know. They were always up against the side of a building or behind the crowds at the picnic tables during meals, and every time, Summer pulled something indecipherable from her pocket to make some kind of exchange with these other kids before they disbanded and went their separate ways.

Amanda's immediate thought when she saw it the first time was that Summer was making some kind of drug deal. However, that didn't make sense. The school had so many layers of charms and wards that kept out *illegal paraphernalia*; Principal Glasket had been clear about that the second week of the school's opening during the summer. Once Amanda saw the first exchange though, she couldn't unsee it. Then it seemed like every time they were out of class—between sessions or during meals or after dinner during their free hours before Lights Out—Summer was huddled up with another student, slipping things into each other's hands before smirking at each other and walking quickly away.

After Summer caught her staring at the last exchange and gave the shifter girl an exaggerated wink, Amanda made it a point to avoid the new girl at all costs from there on out. She couldn't let herself get distracted by what wasn't any of her business. Summer seemed intent on messing with her anyway.

The girl had even used their time in both of Mr. LeFor's Augmented Technology classes, Tuesday *and* Thursday, to rearrange her set of tools in front of her in the shape of a bucket and a door, then laughed and tried to get Amanda's attention.

"That's very...artistic of you, Miss Flannerty." Mr. LeFor peered over Summer's shoulder. He readjusted his glasses and flicked a clump of unruly red hair away from his forehead before clasping his hands behind his back. "You won't complete the circuit or get a single spark by putting the pieces *next* to each other. If you don't start taking this seriously by next week, we can always try something different."

"Oh, yeah?" The girl craned her neck to look up at him with a crooked smile. "Like better tools?"

"Hmm. I need a new assistant after hours. Right now, I'm perfecting a few modifications to my remote-control bear traps. Of course, I haven't seen many bears around campus yet, but it doesn't always have to be *bears.* Maybe you learn better in a one-on-one environment, huh?"

Summer's grin disappeared, and she quickly knocked apart her crude picture of a bucket and doorway before getting busy with the actual assignment.

That was the only time Amanda let herself respond, and it came out as a snorted laugh before she caught the new girl glaring at her and immediately tried to wipe the smile from her face.

CHAPTER THIRTEEN

The final alarm bell shrieked across the campus at 4:30 p.m. that Friday. Amanda snatched up the blue sheet of construction paper she'd been trying to *visualize* as orange in Ms. Calsgrave's class and crumpled it up into as tight of a ball as she could before standing from her desk. "I'm so done with this."

"Still nothing, huh?" Grace glanced at her paper and stepped in front of it, trying to hide it from her friend.

"Nothing. How many times did you get yours to change? Four?"

"Five." The witch tucked her short bob self-consciously behind one ear and shot Amanda an apologetic smile. "Who's counting, right?"

"I guess."

"We're free!" Jackson shouted as he slung his backpack over his shoulder. "The whole weekend to do nothing but whatever we want!"

"Dude." Alex shook his head and gathered up his things. "We did that for almost two months. This is only the first week of class."

"Boy, am I glad it's over." The wizard reached for the doorknob, but the door wouldn't budge. He jiggled it, then yanked harshly to no effect. "Hey. What's up?"

"Oh, right." Ms. Calsgrave chuckled and set down her weird black book before standing behind her desk. "I timed that as a reminder. Listen up, everybody. Make sure you're out by the dining pavilion no later than five-thirty. I'd recommend getting there a few minutes earlier, just in case. Principal Glasket is *really* excited to share a new announcement with you before dinner."

She waved at the door, and Jackson stumbled backward when he pulled way too hard on the handle again, and the door swung quickly open.

"Jeeze! No warning or anything. Come on, man." He nodded at Alex as they stepped into the hall. "I'm gonna pass out if I don't get food in the next hour."

"Good thing dinner's in an hour."

"Yeah, but they should feed us more if Mr. Petrov's gonna keep running our asses into the ground three days a week..."

Their voices faded down the hall, lost in the chaos of hurrying students and excited conversations as the other classes let out and everyone filtered outside.

Grace rolled her eyes. "I can't wait 'til he stops complaining."

Amanda snorted. "I'm not sure that's gonna happen. There's always something."

"True. Maybe he'll get bored with it?"

"I mean, there's always—"

"Miss Coulier?" Calsgrave called, and Amanda slowly turned around. "I'd like to talk to you for a minute. Do you mind?"

Grace grimaced and bumped her shoulder against Amanda's. "Good luck."

"Thanks?" She hung back as the rest of the freshman class filtered out of the room, then waited for whatever punishment she knew was coming her way.

Either she was nice on Wednesday, or I got busted for sneaking out.

"Amanda." Calsgrave raised her eyebrows, then sighed and

slowly headed toward the shifter girl's desk. "First, I want to say again how much I appreciate you coming to me after our last class to talk about what happened on Monday. It shows a lot about your character. Especially when the standard of character among the Academy's student body is...well, still developing."

"Okay." Amanda studied the teacher's blue eyes and waited for the other shoe to drop. "But?"

"What? Oh, there's no but in there at all. I simply wanted to thank you for following your conscience and tell you that I understand."

"Understand what?"

"How hard it can be for someone with your...background to stay focused in a class like mine. Honestly, you're the first...*you know*. The first like you I've had the opportunity to teach. With the way you're pouring yourself into getting down this first illusion, I know you'll get a handle on it eventually."

"Um...thanks."

"Of course." Calsgrave tilted her head and smiled. "If we get farther along in the semester and you're still struggling in my class more than you'd like, we can get you some extra tutoring. Because your attitude is most definitely in the right place."

"Yeah, okay." Amanda glanced at the open door as the shouts and raucous laughter of the free-for-the-weekend students faded down the hall. "Is that it?"

"Yep. You can go. Oh, and don't forget. Announcement at five-thirty."

"Right." She hurried out of the classroom and down the hall toward the front doors of the main building.

That was weird. Did she offer tutoring 'cause I apologized for the lightbulbs? Or 'cause I'm the only kid here who can't do any spells at all?

When she finally made it outside, she found Grace and Alex talking with some of the other freshmen and a sophomore their age who'd tested up. Vinny something, maybe. Grace saw her and left the group for a private chat. "What was that about?"

"Uh…" Amanda shrugged. "A thank you for having a conscience and an offer to tutor me in Illusions."

The witch barked out a laugh. "Seriously?"

"Yeah. I have a feeling it's pity, though."

"You don't need any of that." Grace bumped her with her shoulder. "You don't need tutoring, either. At least not from a *teacher*. Hey, if you need help, I'll do it."

"You'll teach me how to change the color of construction paper five times in two and a half hours?"

"Hell yeah. It's a lot harder than it looks so… Well, you know."

"Thanks. I guess. Where's Jackson?"

"He went to camp out at the cafeteria. I think he's trying to get the kitchen to sneak him some extra food before dinner's ready."

Amanda laughed. "Good luck with that before Lights Out."

"What?"

"Nothing." She smiled and headed toward the group of kids huddled around and speculating on what the announcement from Principal Glasket was about.

Probably another one of her long lectures on rules and how not to break them.

From the corner of her eye, she saw Summer walking across the field with Candace, Emma, and Megan. The new girl shot her a crooked smile and winked before pretending to listen to whatever the sophomore girls thought was so much more interesting.

I don't care what she thinks she's doing. I'm not helping her break into anything.

Most of the students had already gathered at the outdoor cafeteria when 5:20 p.m. rolled around. The kitchen pixies had held off on setting the large buffet table until after Principle Glasket made her announcement. That didn't mean the air wasn't thick with the smell of lemon-herb chicken wafting through the kitchen's open windows, along with the maddening scent of freshly baked bread and something with an extra vinegary sauce.

The students groaned as they waited for the principal to show up, and at 5:29 p.m., Glasket made her appearance.

"I know, I know," the principal shouted, raising her hands for everyone to quiet down. This time, she didn't make a big deal out of the process with the podium in the center field or even a mic—only her voice, which sounded hurried and distracted anyway. "You're hungry. I'm hungry. We're all ready for dinner, and I have"—she glanced at her wristwatch—"so much more to do tonight. Wow. Now that I have your attention, I'm happy to announce that the Academy of Necessary Magic has been approved as the newest team on the Louper roster. Our first match is in four weeks, which should be plenty of time for players to get the hang of the game. Hopefully. Tryouts start tomorrow morning at six, so anyone who wants a shot at making the team needs to meet out by the training arena at that time. *On* time. Mr. Petrov can answer all your questions then. That's all."

With a nod at the kitchen's open window, Glasket spun and marched smartly across the grass toward the central field and the main building beyond.

The outdoor cafeteria was silent.

"*What* did she say?"

"Louper? That's...what? A game?"

"Sounds like a sport."

"Hey, Jonathan! Sounds like your hula-hooping skills will finally be useful for something!"

A round of laughter came from that end of the cafeteria. Amanda was about to ask her friends if they knew what the heck this game was, then Summer's laugh rang out over the student body's confused voices.

"I *know*! No, no. Just wait. This game is so cool. You have no idea!"

"Huh." Grace turned toward Summer at the other end of the cafeteria and cocked her head. "I didn't know the new girl could get more excited than when she asked Zimmer about making bombs."

"Yeah, me neither," Amanda muttered.

The buffet table flashed with silver light, followed by a light *pop,* and their dinner materialized on it in huge serving dishes. She looked up at the open window and saw Fred shooting her the thumbs-up again before he turned away to focus on whatever his job was while the students snarfed down hours' worth of prepared meals.

"Yes! Finally!" Jackson darted forward through the crowd, laughing like a maniac when he reached the buffet table with no one else in line. "I can't believe it. I'm first! Hey, Coulier! Check it out. No lines!"

She glanced at him but turned to look over her shoulder as she headed toward the table. Most of the students were now crowding around Summer to listen to the new girl's even more confusing description of Louper.

"Yeah, it's awesome. So it's a virtual-reality game, right? Well, not exactly. I mean, everyone's actually on a field somewhere, wherever the teacher in charge of the match chooses. It's always different. There are headsets. You can totally be whatever. I mean, yeah, yourself, but anything else. It's like Capture the Flag too, except there's no flag. I mean, it could literally be *anything,* and you can do whatever you want to get it, and—what? No, it's not like football. What are you, crazy? Just wait. Oh, *man.* You guys have no idea what's coming. I'm telling ya. Probably the only good thing about this whole school, know what I mean?"

When Amanda turned back toward the table, Jackson was staring at the crowd around Summer with his nose wrinkled. "Is it me, or did she babble a bunch of crap that made absolutely no sense?"

"I have no idea what she said."

"Okay, good. Thought maybe I was having another episode from this concussion I got in—you know what? Never mind. Check out this *spread*." Grinning, the wizard went back to piling food on his plate, taking great care not to let any of the separate dishes touch each other. "Oh, yes! *Pie*."

Amanda shook her head and worked her way down the table as the other students slowly filtered away from Summer toward their dinner.

Grace fell in line behind her. "I don't get it. She's the only one here who apparently knows what this game is, but she can't explain it right. Everyone's *still* falling over her like she's some kind of celebrity. How does she know what Glasket's talking about?"

"She was at a different magic school last year," Amanda muttered while grabbing a chicken leg dripping with butter and lemon sauce and stabbing up a generous helping of carved chicken breast for good measure.

"Really?"

"Yeah. That's why she was so pissed about being put in the freshman class."

"Wow. So you *do* know her." Grace spooned up a heaping helping of pasta salad. "Now things are starting to make sense."

"I don't *know* her." Amanda shot her friend a sidelong glance, but the other girl was too focused on the food to notice. "I overheard the teachers talking about it."

"Ha. You overhear a lot of things. You know that?"

"Hey, we're all good at something. You can turn a yellow piece of paper violet. I can hear conversations."

Grace snorted and grabbed a fork at the end of the table. "Yeah, okay."

"Grace!" Jackson shouted from where he'd already parked himself at a picnic table. "Hey, grab me an extra piece of—"

"There's no line, Jackson. Grab it yourself."

CHAPTER FOURTEEN

That night, Amanda felt antsier than usual. Despite being as worn out as she was from the first week of classes—three days of which had started with falling off or being blasted off Mr. Petrov's obstacle course—she couldn't settle down enough to think about sleep. Not counting her brief escape for a visit to the pixies on Monday, she realized how long it had been since she'd shifted and gone out for a run.

That's what I need. A run through the swamp to get my head screwed back on straight.

The dorm had quieted down surprisingly quickly, maybe because of all the excitement about this ridiculous-sounding Louper game. That was even better. The earlier she could get out, the more time she had.

Amanda slipped out of bed and headed toward the door, listening for movement from anyone else. Nothing.

A vibrating buzz came from her dresser, and she practically leapt toward it to pull open the bottom drawer.

It had to be Johnny. No one else had her phone number. No one else had a reason to call or text her at all. Sure enough, when she pulled out her phone, his name popped up on her screen with a new text she quickly opened.

Breaking the rules wasn't something she'd come up with entirely on her own. Living with a bounty hunter and learning from one of the best had come with a few new habits she'd unintentionally picked up from him.

Just checking you're okay. Somebody's snatching up shifters round here. Reply ASAP.

Amanda fought back a laugh.

Leave it to Johnny to make up some kind of danger story to ask how I'm doing.

She quickly texted back a reply, paused, then added a smiley-face emoji at the end before sending it.

Definitely not kidnapped. Everything's good. Go catch the bastards.

Then she shoved the phone she wasn't allowed to have at the Academy back under her folded sweatpants and shut the drawer. Time to get going if she wanted to take advantage of the extra time.

She shifted *in* the supply closet on the first floor—after propping the door open again, of course—and didn't care that anyone else might find the bucket in the doorway. Someone like Summer. She'd stopped beside room 223C and had heard the new girl yawning loudly inside and shifting around in her bed. It didn't seem like Summer had any plans to sneak out tonight and try to break into anything.

So Amanda could run free as a small gray wolf under the waxing moon, and nobody would know a thing.

The second she leapt through the narrow opening in the back door of the girls' dorm, her shifter senses overtook her. More energy than she knew what to do with thrummed through her veins, and she raced toward the swamp. It was easier to pretend she wasn't on a school campus when she was splashing through the briny water, feeling the cattail reeds and ferns whipping against her face and flanks, and picking up dozens of different scents from the creatures who also called the swamps home.

The crickets and cicadas were unnaturally loud tonight, and two owls called to each other from their perches in the branches stretching far overhead.

This was where she needed to be right now. Out here, running on four paws instead of two bare feet. Where she could forget about who she was, who she'd been, and who she was trying to be.

Amanda had explored almost every campus area since first coming to the Academy for its opening ceremony in July. The warded border hugged the land closely around the main campus where they'd constructed the buildings and training arenas and outdoor cafeteria. The property also extended farther north behind the faculty building by at least another two miles. She wasn't entirely sure of the distance, but it was still plenty of space to roam around and get far away from the smell of sleeping magicals to quiet her racing mind.

She padded through the swamp beside the shoreline, stopping here and there to follow the scent of a rabbit or a squirrel. For once, she wasn't ravenous in the middle of the night when she couldn't sleep.

Better that way. Can't show up at the kitchen without clothes. Don't want to catch a squirrel and eat it as a wolf, either.

A soft *splash* on her right caught her attention, and she darted off after the sound. When a flickering line of purple light burst to life in the air two feet in front of her, she pulled up and skidded through the water to stop herself.

Another incident with the wards? Did I trigger that? Or whatever caused that splash?

The humming buzz grew louder, and smaller streaks of

purple light crackled away from her to the left and right, buzzing away like an electrical charge before a series of purple sparks popped off in quick succession. A high whine like a malfunctioning motor filled the air, joined by that weirdly sweet scent from the last time she'd seen the wards act up like this.

Amanda stepped backward through the swamp, watching the purple sparks until they vanished into an invisible line of wards again.

Weird. If that happens again, I should probably tell someone.

She turned to head north again but slightly inland this time and stopped when a different scent hit her.

Summer.

No way. She was in her room.

Still, there was no telling how long Amanda had been out here running through the swamp as a wolf. Time did weird things when she shifted.

Curious and a little annoyed by the fact that she wasn't out here alone, she turned her nose to the wind and sniffed out Summer's trail.

Whatever she's up to, it can't be good. Is she *the one messing with the wards?*

Amanda padded silently across the swamp, slipping up onto small islands of dry land before wading back down into the water again. The new girl had recently been out here, making her scent that much easier to pick up even across water. It led Amanda to an island at the northernmost tip of the Academy's campus, and when she stepped slowly through the wall of cattails at the edge, she found Summer kneeling in the center of the island.

The new girl was shaking something in a medium-sized jar, her eyes wide above an excited grin that almost made her look insane. Then she unscrewed the lid and let out a long sigh. "Can't stop *me* from finding all your hidden little secrets."

Amanda took two more silent steps up onto land to get a better view. Laid out in front of Summer was an entire array of potions, jars of different-colored powders, and a stack of something that looked like black bricks but smelled like manure.

Holding the open jar in one hand, Summer eagerly scooped up all the other ingredients in front of her and jammed them into her backpack. She zipped it quickly, slung it over her shoulder, and held the open jar of liquid glowing a dark, menacing red over the stack of smelly bricks. "This is gonna be epic."

Holy crap, she made another bomb!

Amanda shouted for Summer to stop, but all that came out was a high-pitched yelp. Summer paused for a split second, then dumped the alchemical brew she'd somehow managed to get her hands on, splattering it all over the bricks before jumping to her feet and quickly stepping back.

Still crouching in the cattails, Amanda shifted back into her human form and shouted, "What are you *doing*?"

"What?" Summer stumbled back across the grass and frantically scanned the island. "Who—"

"Make it stop! You can't blow things up here too!" Amanda darted out of the reeds, thinking only of the sparking, hissing bricks and nothing about the fact that she was running buck-naked toward an imminent explosion.

The drenched bricks threw off an enormous spray of crimson sparks. Summer lunged for Amanda, wrapped her arms around the girl, and hauled her backward off her feet. The alchemy bomb erupted before the girls hit the ground, and the force of the explosion threw them farther down the gentle slope of the island and halfway into the swamp.

The aftershock of the alchemical detonation sent a second ripple through the island. The ground trembled. A massive wall of red sparks, red flames, and waterlogged earth rose high into the air, lighting up the night sky. Then, as the clods of dirt, mud, and uprooted cattails and ferns rained down all around them, a third rumbling explosion echoed across the swamp—this time underground.

Even the constant drone of the cicadas and the crickets' chirping cut off beneath the disturbance, and the only thing Amanda could hear was the ringing in her head and the last few *plops* of earth chunks hitting the swamp water behind her.

Then she realized Summer still had her arms around her, and Amanda was still completely naked.

Summer seemed to realize this at the same time and quickly removed her hold on the shifter girl. She looked away from Amanda and stared intently at the thick column of black smoke rising from the crater she'd created in the earth.

Amanda dragged herself fully onto land, trying to catch her breath and give herself a mental once-over. *Nothing hurts. Nothing's broken. Holy crap, that was insane.*

She's insane.

She glared at Summer, who'd now propped herself up with both hands in the swamp and her legs splayed awkwardly up the incline of the island. "Are you insane?"

"What?" The new girl gave her a brief sidelong glance.

"What is *wrong* with you?" Amanda shook her head. "You got kicked out of the last school for blowing something up, and you tried it *again*? *Here*? You could've seriously hurt somebody!"

"Yeah, you really shouldn't run *toward* an explosion, shifter girl." Summer chuckled. "Figured you knew that already. Hey, good thing I was fast enough to pull you away, right?"

"I was talking about *you*."

"I'm fine." The new girl pushed herself to her feet. Saltwater cascaded from her soaked shorts and the back of her shirt to splash onto the bank and into the swamp. She pulled a soggy fern leaf from her black hair and tossed it aside. "What about you?"

"I'm pissed."

Summer finally looked down at her, frowning at Amanda's nakedness before quickly looking away again. "Well, that's *your* choice. So are clothes, apparently."

"I went out for a run." Amanda stood and shook the mud off

her hands and wrists. "Then I found you blowing up islands on campus."

"Please. This isn't campus. Technically. No one comes out here."

"You don't know that. You haven't even been here a whole *week*—"

"Look, just because you thought you were the only kid here who could sneak out at night without getting caught doesn't mean I'm stepping all over your toes here." Summer inspected her soaked backpack hanging from one shoulder, wrinkled her nose, then shrugged. "You didn't want to be part of this. Fine. Don't look at me like I'm some kind of monster, okay?"

"You stole alchemy supplies and blew up an island. On purpose."

"Yeah, and you're a shifter. Running around on four legs while everyone's asleep because you're too afraid to tell people what you are." Summer raised an eyebrow. "Maybe explosions are part of *my* nature. You ever think of that?"

Amanda stepped away from the girl and swallowed. "It's not the same."

"Really? Just because you get to change shapes means it's okay that you can't help yourself?"

She's pushing it.

The shifter girl's hands clenched into fists. "I can help it."

"Right. Like you could help *not* following me out here." Summer scoffed. "I have no idea why you're still so uptight about this. You have a bad side like me, shifter girl. Might as well embrace it."

The hell I do.

"You don't know anything about me." Amanda's voice came out as a low growl, and the tingle of an impending shift washed over her before she crushed it back down.

Yeah, she's pissing me off. I can't go full wolf on her.

Summer's eyes widened when she saw the flash of silver

around Amanda's brown eyes, and she laughed. "Whoa... See? My point exactly. Come on. Let's go check it out."

As the new girl trudged up onto the island in her squelching sneakers, Amanda fought her anger and frustration.

Why am *I so angry? Because she's right? Or because I can't help it?*

"Seriously, kid—"

"Don't call me that."

"Oh, you like shifter girl better? Sure, yeah. Whatever."

"My name's Amanda."

Summer sniggered. "Your name could be Queen Wolfie for all I care. Are you coming or not?"

"Coming where?" Amanda glared at the new girl, fighting with herself. Because now that the deed was done, she *did* want to see whatever Summer seemed so excited to investigate. And she hated it.

"Up here. Duh." Summer pointed at the column of smoke that had already died down into a few thin whisps. "Come on. You're already *here*. Might as well, right?"

Gritting her teeth, Amanda stormed up the incline to join the girl who'd now become her partner in crime. Only the crime this time was a lot more than running away from Johnny's house or letting her instincts get the better of her on a hunt or even sneaking out after Lights Out to let the wolf in her run free without fear of being seen. Now, she was complicit in blowing up school property, and if she was lucky, she *might* be able to stay at this school to chase the only real dream she could remember wanting to pursue. The only thing that made her feel useful.

"Jesus, Amanda. Don't you have any clothes?"

"Yeah, a whole dresser. None of them are wolf-sized, though."

Summer barked out a laugh, then swung her backpack off her shoulder and quickly unzipped it. She pulled out a hoodie and a pair of sweatpants, both of them soaked through. "Here. It's better than nothing."

"You keep random clothes in your backpack?"

"Listen, if you've been where I've been, running away is always an option. It sucks to run away without being prepared." Summer held the clothes out toward the other girl and looked away, shaking the soaked items eagerly. "Hurry up. We don't have all night. I wanna see what the hell's down there in that hole."

Amanda snatched up the soaked garments and struggled to put them on. They were warm and wet and baggy, but at least they covered everything.

So much for comfort. There's no way I'm not getting a rash after this.

"Let's go." Summer grinned at her and nodded at the massive crater at the center of the island. "This is the best part."

CHAPTER FIFTEEN

Both girls stood at the crater's edge and looked down into the dark hole beneath them.

"Great. You made a hole. Time to go."

"Hold on." Summer smirked. "Don't you wanna see what's down there?"

"Nope." She did—she *really* did—but the disappointment of missing out on a discovery like this was nothing compared to how pointless everything would be if they got caught and kicked out of the Academy. "Let's get back to the dorms, okay? Someone had to hear that explosion. Or at least *see* it—"

"No way. Everyone's asleep. Quit trying to be our conscience, okay? We're already here." Summer flicked her wrist, and a small orb of white light materialized in her hand, lighting up her wide grin in stark shadows as if they were telling ghost stories around a fire with a flashlight. "You know you wanna see what's down there."

Amanda didn't say anything, mostly because she didn't want to lie.

Summer leaned over the edge of the crater, lowered her hand, and let the orb slip over her fingertips to fall into the hole. It sank slowly by about six feet, illuminating the ruptured earthen walls before stopping a foot above the bottom. Now visible were two dirt-caked pillars of white stone serving as the entryway into a tunnel.

"Cool," Amanda whispered before she remembered she was supposed to be the voice of reason here.

Summer nodded, her grin widening even more. "I know, right? Let's go check it out."

"Seriously, I don't think that's a good idea."

"Why the hell not?" The new girl sat at the edge of the crater and started to climb down. "Hey, turning back now is like running away from a little rain when you're already soaking wet. I mean, yeah, technically you already *are*. But there's no point in turning down this kinda find, shifter girl."

"We don't know what's down there."

Summer's head slowly sank out of view as she descended. "Yep. That's the point."

"The whole thing could come down on top of us."

"You know how many heavy-duty explosive reagents I had to use to blow the top off this thing? A tunnel surrounded by water that's *still standing* wasn't built to crumble around a couple of kids walking through." The girl's shoes squelched when she hopped the rest of the way down, and her face was only partially illuminated by the light sphere when she looked up at Amanda. "You do you, though. I'm going in. Can't change my mind, shifter girl."

Summer dusted off her hands and turned toward the tunnel behind the white stone pillars. Her light spell bobbed along after her and cast her flickering shadow along the tunnel walls until the fading illumination was all Amanda could see.

She glanced around the silent, empty swamp, then tipped her head back to sigh at the stars.

I'm gonna regret this somehow. I know it.

Yet, she lowered herself to the edge of the hole and dropped straight down, landing firmly on both bare feet. She took off after Summer, eyes wide as she studied the tunnel walls of packed earth around her and caught up to the bobbing light up again.

Neither girl said a word as they moved down the tunnel, which dipped steadily lower underground.

There's a whole swamp above us right now. She better not have any more bombs in her backpack, or we're both drowning tonight.

After another fifteen feet, the tunnel opened into a large cavern. Eight pillars of the same dirty-white stone stood in a ring around the chamber, built as if their original purpose was to hold up all the land and water over the swamp above. Thick roots protruded through the ceiling, many of them steadily dripping water into the sizeable pool already covering most of the stone floor. In the center of the chamber was one more pillar, this one only four feet tall with a flat top carved with intricate swirls.

On the pedestal rested a dark purple crystal five inches long, glowing with dark, internal light.

"Whoa." Amanda gazed around the chamber while scratching an itch on her arm through the other girl's waterlogged hoodie. "Looks like a Roman temple or something."

"A what?" Summer waved the light orb forward with her as she stepped off the end of the tunnel and down onto the stone floor of the so-called temple. Her footsteps echoed across the chamber until she reached the large pool spreading across the area with the pedestal at the center.

"A Roman temple." Amanda didn't hesitate to step off the ledge and join the other girl, their voices echoing at least three times louder than normal. "You know, where people used to go to worship their gods or whatever."

"I don't believe in gods. Any of them."

"Okay, but you at least know what I'm talking about, right?"

Summer shrugged. "Not really."

"Did you go to *any* school before the one you got kicked out of, or are you—"

"Jesus, will you stop talking about *school* already? We discovered something awesomely epic, and you're trying to give me a lecture on architecture nobody gives a shit about."

Amanda frowned and watched the other girl wade through the two inches of water toward the central pillar. "You should leave that where it is."

"Wow, if I'd thought you'd be this much of a drag, I would've let you blow up with the rest of the island. Oh-ho, *whoa*." Summer sucked in a long, shuddering breath. "Do you feel that?"

"No."

"Hey, come here. You gotta check this out."

"Summer, this place has obviously been down here for a really long time. You think whoever built this place put a weird crystal on a *pedestal* because they wanted whoever found it to walk on by and snatch it up?"

The new girl turned over her shoulder and studied Amanda. "You're right. Better check for wards first."

"That's not what I meant…"

Summer raised both hands toward the purple crystal while muttering a spell under her breath. A faint light illuminated in her outstretched palms, but nothing else happened. She grinned. "Nothing. Looks like that rips your theory to shreds."

"What?"

"Nobody's coming back for this thing. It's been down here forever, and I'm pretty sure we're the first ones to find it after it was so nicely put on display."

"Summer…"

"No, for real. No wards. No protection charms. Whoever put it here wasn't trying to *keep* it here or warn anyone else away, either."

Amanda waded slowly through the water toward the pedestal. "Except for the fact that they built a temple underground."

"Please. Ever heard of Atlantis?"

"Oh, so you know *that* one."

"Everyone knows that one. Atlanteans exist."

"Not the way humans talk about them in stories," Amanda muttered. When she got within four feet of the pedestal, she stopped, her breath hitching in her throat. Powerful, thrumming energy rippled across her skin—like the tingling before she shifted but a hundred times stronger. And warm.

"*There* you go. You feel it now, don't you?"

She couldn't stop staring at the glowing purple stone sitting there, waiting for anyone to grab it up. "What *is* that thing?"

"No idea. Whatever it is, it's got some kinda crazy-awesome power. I know you feel it." Summer tossed her bangs out of her eyes. "Go ahead. Take it."

"What? No. You're the one who blew a hole in the ground. *You* take it."

"Pssh. Chicken." Summer snatched up the stone and hissed, her eyes growing wide.

"What? What's wrong?"

The new girl turned slowly toward Amanda with a blank stare, and her lips trembled as her mouth opened.

"Summer?"

"Ha!" Summer grinned and tossed the crystal in the air before catching it with an echoing smack in her fist. "Gotcha. Man, you looked like you were about to piss yourself, shifter kid."

Amanda puffed out a sigh and rolled her eyes. "You're the worst."

"Nah, I'd say we're tied at this point. You want it?"

"Uh-uh." Despite her answer, Amanda couldn't stop staring at the dark purple glow emanating from the other girl's closed hand.

"Suit yourself. I know a few guys who can probably tell me what this thing is." Summer slid her backpack off one shoulder and tucked the stone inside.

"In the *Everglades*? I thought you were from Virginia."

"I mean, that's the last place I was before they shipped me off on the Starbucks train to *this* sweaty armpit."

"The what train?"

Summer let out a low whistle. "For someone who knows how to slip through wards and into a different skin, you sure are clueless; you know that?"

She's making as much sense now as when she tried to explain that stupid loophole game. Or whatever it's called.

"Well. Guess we should head back up to the surface, right? Hopefully, I didn't miss any boobytraps, but just in case. You know." Summer shrugged. "Don't want the whole thing falling on our heads, right?"

Amanda turned quickly and scanned the cavern's walls as she waded back toward the mouth of the tunnel. They looked sturdy enough. That didn't mean much, and she didn't trust Summer not to screw anything else up while they were still here. So she booked it back down the tunnel toward the crater's mouth.

"Hey, wait up!" A shudder ran through the walls at Summer's shout, dislodging a clod of dirt from the ceiling. It splashed into the pool, and she grimaced. "Right. Quiet. Shifter girl. *Hey*. The light's back here."

"Shifter girl with shifter vision." Amanda's voice echoed from the mouth of the tunnel. "Thought you would've put two and two together by now."

Summer chuckled and stepped up onto the tunnel platform. "You got a hell of an attitude on you. I like it."

"Whatever. I wanna get out of here and get back to bed."

The second Summer Flannerty's fingers closed around the purple crystal in the underground temple, a low moan swept across the swamp above the girls. Trees bent in the gust of wind moving toward the island from the north, south, east, and west. The swampy waters of the Everglades moved inward with deep, thick ripples, startling sleeping reptiles from their nests when it sprayed up into their faces. A gator hissed and slithered on its thick, scaly legs into the shelter of a stand of cattail reeds.

The moan grew louder, stretching toward the nexus of its force. Its power. When the windy gust hit the invisible warded boundary of the Academy of Necessary Magic, a blaze of purple light erupted in the air. It crackled and hissed, fighting back against the presence swarming toward the island and the temple built beneath it.

Sparks flew. The wind kicked up again, howling with a voice not quite like the wind and not quite living—a voice belonging to something entirely different.

The presence burst through the confines of the Academy's wards with a deafening *crack* and sent a crackling flash of purple light zipping around the campus perimeter. If the school had any electricity running through the northernmost tip of the property, it would have shorted beneath the energy surge. Instead, the thick spray of purple sparks hit the soggy ground, the mud, the swamp water, and fizzled out with hiss after loud hiss.

The wind died. The howling faded. The presence searched anew for what was never someone else's to take.

CHAPTER SIXTEEN

"So here's the thing," Summer casually said as she waited for Amanda to get high enough toward the surface so she could start climbing herself. "If you say anything to anyone about any of this, your ass'll be as toasty as mine. Yeah, I know, *I'm* the one who blasted this awesome hole in the ground. *You're* the one who went running around on four legs in the middle of the night. Pretty sure we're breaking the same rules. So think about that before you go all goody-two-shoes on me again."

Amanda rolled her eyes and reached for the next handhold.

After this, there's gonna be a new rule about not blowing up the swamp to steal from ancient ruins underground.

"Hey, shifter girl. You hear what I'm saying?"

"Yeah, I heard you. I already told you once I'm not gonna say anything. Quit worrying about it."

"Oh, I'm not worried." Summer grunted as she pulled herself higher. "I'm making sure we're on the same page. You know, so you don't keep thinking you're better than me."

"I don't think that."

Mostly.

Amanda pulled herself up over the edge of the crater and crawled away before standing.

"Good. Because I'll tell you right now, you're not. Just because you're, like, an eight-year-old freshman who wants to be at this dumbass school for whatever reason doesn't make you magic's gift to Earth or anything."

"Oh, jeeze. Just stop. And I'm not eight."

"Okay. Well, how old are you, anyway? Nine?"

Amanda brushed the dirt and mud off her borrowed sweats and straightened. "I'm—"

She was about to say she wasn't going to talk about her age because it didn't matter. Instead, what she found on the island when she looked up through the semi-darkness beneath the waxing moon and the Everglades starlight made her freeze.

"You're what, shifter girl?"

"Shit."

Summer snorted as she hauled herself up over the edge of the crater. "Oh, come on. I wasn't trying to beat your ego down *that* hard. Christ, you're sensitive—oh."

The new girl stopped too because now they were both staring at Principal Glasket with her hands on her hips, Mr. Petrov with his arms folded, and Mrs. Zimmer tossing what looked like a clear glass ball over and over in her hand. All three of them scowled at the girls, and Glasket raised an eyebrow as she looked Summer up and down. "I should've known it was you the second I smelled smoke."

"Whoops." Summer shrugged. "Got me."

"Miss Flannerty, I thought I'd made myself clear when I told you we operate much differently here at the Academy. You apparently chose not to take that to heart." Glasket scanned the crater beside the new girl. Then her gaze fell pointedly on what remained of the weird black bricks Summer had used to fuel the explosion. "I'm starting to think you aren't capable of understanding the dangers in detonating *active explosives* on school property."

Although she didn't exactly yell, the principal's last words came out as a sharp bark. Beneath the light orb one of the teachers had summoned, Amanda clearly saw the flush in Glasket's cheeks and the vein standing out on her usually smooth forehead.

Summer folded her arms. "Is that gonna be a problem *here* too? 'Cause it's not like you have anywhere else to send me. This place *is* the bottom of the barrel."

"We didn't expect you to become a model student overnight," Mrs. Zimmer added, still tossing her glass ball. "Still, it's definitely a problem when you add breaking and entering *and* theft of school property to your already long list of violations. Do you have any idea what kind of damage you could've done with those reagents?"

"Uh...*yeah*." Summer snorted. "Why do you think I took them?"

Zimmer slowly licked her lips before pressing them tightly together and glancing at the rubble of black bricks before returning her stern gaze to the new girl. "Then we have an even bigger problem."

"Miss Coulier," Glasket barked. "This behavior isn't out of character for Miss Flannerty, but I can't wrap my head around why *you're* here. Care to explain that one?"

Amanda blinked at the principal. *I knew this was gonna happen. Should've just gone back to the dorm.* "I—"

"She was trying to stop me," Summer said.

"Trying to stop you." Glasket tilted her head and glowered at the new girl. "How so?"

Amanda couldn't help but stare at the other girl with wide eyes. *I did* not *see that coming.*

Summer shrugged. "It's pretty obvious, don't you think? I mean, here I was, minding my business—"

"You stole highly volatile alchemical explosives," Zimmer interjected.

"Yeah, we covered that. Like I said, minding my business. Then this little twerp shows up trying to be some kinda big hero, telling me not to blow up this fun little island just 'cause she didn't want me to get in trouble or some shit. I don't know."

"Language, Miss Flannerty."

"Whatever. Hey, it's not like she actually *could've* stopped me. Look at her." Everyone turned toward Amanda, who stood frozen now with her eyes wide and a hot flush creeping up her neck and into her cheeks again. "Okay, to be fair, those clothes make her look a lot bigger. But she's scrawny as hell. Tried to nag me into submission the whole time. But she didn't have shit to do with this hole."

Principal Glasket blinked quickly and stuck her hands back on her hips. "Is this true?"

"I mean..."

"Of course it's true. Come on, Glasket. Would I lie to you?" Summer's grin faded when the principal fixed her with a disdainful glare. "Yeah, I blow shit up. I don't lie about it."

"Fine. Miss Coulier had nothing to do with the explosion."

Mrs. Zimmer turned toward the principal and whispered, "Gladys, I don't think—"

"Thank you, Mrs. Zimmer." Glasket didn't take her eyes off the girls. "I see no reason why Miss Flannerty would lie through her teeth to help another student. Even when there's nothing she can say to help herself."

Summer rolled her eyes.

"However benign Miss Coulier's intentions were, she's still out of the dorms after Lights Out. Which, as I'm sure you're both aware, is a direct violation of school rules. So you're both getting detention."

"Seriously?" Summer gestured at Amanda. "You're gonna

make this runt sit in an empty room with me so we can claw our eyes out in boredom *together*?"

"She broke the rules as much as you did, Miss Flannerty." Glasket's tight-lipped smile showed the first hint of pleasure on the woman's face since she and the other teachers had shown up here. "I told you the Academy is different, and I meant it."

"Great," Summer muttered.

"You won't be spending detention in an empty room although you'll probably still want to claw your eyes out at the end of it." Principal Glasket stepped aside and pointed down the island's slope toward the main part of the campus, where the outlines of the low stone buildings were barely visible against the backdrop of the star-studded sky. "You're going straight to your rooms and will report to Mr. Petrov first thing in the morning. Five o'clock."

Mr. Petrov chuckled darkly.

Summer's eyes bulged from her head. "You're *insane*."

"You're out of line. Move it."

"Yeah, good luck trying to whip me up out of bed *that* early."

"Miss Flannerty, I told you when you got here that there are other ways of getting into your room without a key. Don't assume we can't force you out of sleep without ever having to step through your door. Go."

Glasket and Summer each held their own in an anger-fueled staring contest until Amanda finally tugged on the new girl's backpack and muttered, "Let's go. This is pointless."

"You got *that* right." Rolling her eyes, Summer let her new pseudo-friend lead her down the other side of the sloping island berm toward the swamp, which was still relatively shallow from here back to the shore of the campus' central grounds. "She thinks she's so fucking great. Running a school for the trash everyone else wants to throw away. This whole place and everyone in it can kiss my ass. Except for you, shifter girl. You're kind of okay. I guess."

Amanda ignored the warm swamp water leeching up the

legs of her borrowed sweatpants although she couldn't say she didn't enjoy the feel of the silty, occasionally slimy swamp bed beneath her bare feet. Right now, she wasn't thinking about any of it.

She turned her head toward Summer and studied the girl's profile in the low light.

"What?" Summer tossed her black bangs out of her eyes again. "Why are you looking at me like that?"

"I'm curious."

"Well, stop. You're making my skin crawl." Despite her attempt at forcing a creeped-out grimace and shudder, the girl couldn't hide her thick swallow.

She knows exactly what I'm about to ask. So just ask.

"So…" Amanda stared straight ahead again, thinking that would make the new girl more likely to answer. "Who threw *you* away?"

Summer cleared her throat. "Fuck off, shifter girl."

"Okay, then."

The new girl shot Amanda a sideways glance, and the corner of her mouth lifted in a tiny smile. "You're cool. Not *that* cool. I don't need another shrink."

"Got it."

Well, at least I know what buttons not to push until I really want something.

The teachers' low, muttered conversation filtered behind the girls as they were loosely escorted back onto the grounds and toward the girls' dorm. Amanda could still feel the thrumming energy of that weird purple crystal inside Summer's backpack. Neither of them said a word about it.

Because if we did, we'd be in a lot more trouble. Detention for sneaking out is enough.

Almost as if the other girl had read her mind, Summer glanced over her shoulder at the teachers glaring at them, then leaned toward Amanda and muttered, "You have any idea what this whole detention thing's supposed to be if we're not locked up in a room?"

Amanda wrinkled her nose. "Nobody told you about that?"

"Come on. Why would I ask you if I knew?"

"Yeah. At the Academy of Necessary Magic, AKA Bounty Hunter School…detention means hard labor."

Summer puffed out a sigh and looked straight ahead again. "Of course it does."

CHAPTER SEVENTEEN

It was still dark at 5:15 a.m. when Amanda and Summer stood outside the training arena behind Mr. Petrov's low, square building on the southeast side of campus. Amanda turned to watch a furious-looking Mrs. Zimmer storming back toward the central field and wherever she was going this early in the morning. The Alchemy teacher had shown up on the third floor of the girls' dorm to personally escort them out here with a command to wait for Mr. Petrov.

"This sucks." Summer's mouth gaped in a wide, groaning yawn she didn't bother to cover up.

Of course, when she saw it, Amanda couldn't help but do the same. Then she smacked the other girl's arm with the back of a hand. "Cut it out."

"I can't help it. Jesus, it's like you're living in another world over there. We both got the same amount of sleep. What was it? Like, five hours?"

"Try four. Or three and a half."

With a groan, Summer slowly rubbed her hands down her cheeks and rapidly blinked away the tears from her yawn. "And it's *Saturday*. These people are nuts."

"That's the worst part for you?" Amanda rolled her shoulders back and tried to draw a deep breath of the cool pre-dawn air that would only get hotter as the day progressed.

"No, the worst part was that damn alarm and all the flashing lights." Summer tossed a hand toward the girls' dorm. "I swear, they're using military torture tactics on us. Sleep-deprivation. I bet the waterboarding's next. Did you know they could set that stupid thing off in our rooms?"

"Nope. First time I've been caught blowing up school property, so..."

"Oh, come on. I got you cleared of that in two seconds. You can't use that anymore."

"Yeah, but I'm still here with you."

"Hey, I didn't make you go all wolfy to run around in the swamp. That was all you. So was trying to stop me and take over what was supposed to be *my* private business."

"I tried to stop you from setting off a bomb."

Summer snorted and turned to look down at the shorter girl, her upper lip curling in irritation. "How'd you know I was there?"

Amanda had to look away before she answered. "I caught your scent."

"Wow. You know, I had a feeling you were stalking me, but now you confirmed it."

"It doesn't work like that, and you know it."

"Honestly, I have no idea how shifters work. Never seen one up close and personal before *you*."

Amanda rolled her eyes. "Stop talking about me like I'm some kinda circus freak."

"Well, maybe if you stopped sneaking around like some kinda circus freak, there wouldn't be so much hype."

"Seriously." She turned to glare up at the older girl. "This is—"

The door to the combat building burst open and *clanged* against the outer wall.

"Look alive, ladies," Mr. Petrov barked as he lugged a cart outside after him. "This isn't recess, and it sure as hell isn't gossip time. I'm as happy to be up this early coddling the two of you as you are to be standing here in my arena. Although I'm pretty sure you won't feel any better about it by the end of the weekend."

Summer groaned. "The *whole* weekend?"

"Twelve hours each day, Miss Flannerty." Petrov dropped the wagon's handle and dusted off his hands. "If *I* were in charge, I'd have you two on repair duty for a week. This was the compromise with Principal Glasket. So this is what you get. Still plenty of a lesson to be learned this way."

"On repairs?" Amanda glanced at the buckets and the ends of long handles sticking out of the wagon.

"No. I don't care who you are or where you've been. There's no amount of useful repair work to get done in only two days." Petrov grabbed one of the wooden handles and yanked the tool out of the wagon to reveal a crusty-looking mop head. His beady eyes glinted as he grinned viciously at them. "You two get to clean the hell out of this place. Human-style. Better get to work."

The mop sailed through the air and landed in the grass at Amanda's feet with a *thud*. She grimaced and cocked her head. "What are we cleaning?"

"As much as you can in a twelve-hour shift. Outbuildings first. Don't want you two running off to the dorms thinking you can sneak out from under *my* gaze. Start right here. Kitchen and refectory are next. I doubt you'll get farther than that today."

Summer folded her arms. "We're not allowed in the kitchen."

"I didn't say *in*, did I?" Petrov pointed at the wall of the training building, and a bright shard of yellow light bloomed from his finger. When he slowly lowered it like a claw, the yellow light turned like a blade against the concrete and shaved off a thick layer of dirt that crumbled into the grass. What lay behind it was a lot brighter—almost white compared to the rest of the building. "I want these walls to look like that top to bottom. Don't forget the gutters."

"We can't clean the walls with a *mop*," Amanda muttered.

"You can clean them with your tongue for all I care, as long as you get the job done. I'd get hopping if I were you. You'll get an extra weekend of detention like this for every square foot that isn't crisp and clean by the end of your…shift." Petrov waggled his eyebrows at them and turned toward the training building's open door, leaving it wide open. The scrape of metal chair legs across the concrete floor echoed after him, then he appeared in the doorway with the chair in one hand and a mug of coffee in the other. He sat, sipped his coffee, and widened his eyes at the two freshmen gaping back at him. "That wasn't a joke."

"Damnit." Summer shot Amanda a scathing glance and stomped toward the wagon.

Pressing her lips together, Amanda followed the other girl, distracted by the first chirps of the birds waking up as black sky gave way to the blue-gray right before dawn. *I can't believe this is happening.*

Summer rifled through the supplies in the wagon, then shouted, "I don't see any gloves."

"No gloves. No smocks," Petrov called from inside. "That's the deal."

"Oh, great. If we don't die from exhaustion or poison by chemical fumes, we'll get our skin burned off." Summer snatched up a wire-bristled scrub brush and a gallon jug of bleach. "What the hell are we supposed to use the Pine-Sol for?"

"I don't know." Amanda picked up some kind of porous mitt with bristles on the palm and wrinkled her nose. "To make it smell good after?"

The other girl snorted. "Have you ever actually *smelled* that stuff? It's the exact *opposite* of fresh."

Amanda shrugged. "So what goes first?"

"What, you've never cleaned a house before?" Summer was clearly joking, but when she looked up at the younger girl, a light of realization flickered behind her eyes before she glanced at the open door of the training building and lowered her voice. "Wait, seriously?"

"I mean, I…used to clean my room."

"Oh, yeah. Real tough life, shifter girl." Summer lugged the bleach and the wire brush toward the wall. "You have a maid do your laundry and dusting too?"

Amanda sniffed and grabbed an unlabeled gallon jug. If it was in the bucket, it had to be *some* sort of cleaning solution. *I'm not talking about my home life before it...disappeared.*

"Wow." The bleach thumped onto the grass, and Summer turned to stare at the younger girl. "Your silence is pretty condemning; you know that?"

"Can we get to the cleaning part so we can be done with this? I really don't want to keep adding weekends because you were too busy asking personal questions."

"Relax. He wasn't serious about that."

Petrov cleared his throat. "Wanna bet?"

"Shit." Summer unscrewed the lid of the bleach, tentatively sniffed from a foot above the opening, and jerked her head away. "Ugh. That's way stronger than I remember. Don't let it touch you."

Amanda had already sidled down the wall to put distance between herself and the acrid stench of bleach and something else that didn't quite smell like bleach. "No problem."

She opened her jug, which didn't smell nearly as strong, and poured a thin stream of it onto the wall. A thick river of grime washed away beneath the pour. "Wow. How much you wanna bet he stayed up all night throwing dirt on the walls so we'd have something to do?"

"Nah. Half an hour tops." Summer poured the bleach and

started scrubbing, then nodded toward the open door blocking Mr. Petrov from view. "He gets to use magic all he wants. We don't."

Amanda forced herself to breathe through her mouth only and started scrubbing. *Not like I could use magic anyway. I can't even* envision *a different-colored piece of paper.*

Half an hour later, at least thirty students who'd gotten up early on a Saturday to show up for Louper tryouts crowded the training arena. Apparently, Summer was the only kid here who had a clue what the game entailed, and her explanation had done nothing to inform the Academy's upperclassmen all vying for a spot on the team.

Amanda jumped when Mr. LeFor's voice rang out from beside the obstacle course. "All right, listen up. You're here to try out for the Louper team. If you don't already know what it is, forget everything you think you know about high school sports."

"We get to tackle the other team, right?" one bulky senior shouted, snorting and guffawing with his buddies as they shoved each other around.

"Sure." LeFor looked them up and down. "Ancestors help the poor kids playing against you. It's more than tackling though. You get to use your magic if you want. Or the abilities of any other race besides your own. Because while this is a physical and magical game, it's also mental, emotional—"

"Yeah, when we bash them into the ground so hard they start *crying*."

"—and *virtual*," LeFor finished, giving the violence-oriented seniors a warning glance as they sniggered and pummeled each other again. Nobody seemed to notice.

At that last part, Amanda turned from the two-foot section of wall she'd scrubbed halfway clean over the previous thirty minutes. *Virtual? I thought Summer was making that up.*

LeFor slung the large duffle bag off his shoulder and unzipped it to pull out a pair of bulky goggles with a criss-crossing strap attached to both sides. Except the goggles didn't have any lenses and the solid black plastic covered where they'd go. "Virtual headsets. With a few magical upgrades to sync them with the game rules and the viewing links. These are *our* prototypes, of course, but by the time we have our first match next month, the Academy's Louper team will be playing with top-of-the-line, fully enhanced gear. I can promise you that."

"How the hell are we supposed to see in those things?" a junior shouted over the semi-impressed muttering.

"That's why you're here. To learn how." LeFor ran a hand through his spiky red hair and smirked, looking incredibly pleased with himself. "The best eight scores by the end of the weekend make the team. Six starters. Two backups, just in case."

"In case of what?"

"Well, you never know. Especially at *this* school."

"Wait, there are, like…" A short, stalky sophomore Amanda didn't know counted the heads of the students gathered for tryouts. "At least twenty of us out here. And only *eight* make the team?"

"The best of the best." Mr. LeFor grinned. "You'll compete against the in-game avatar *and* each other during tryouts. Scores are partially based on teamwork and cooperation, so of course, that's who we want on the team. So line up! I only have six headsets right now. We'll have to rotate in sessions."

As the Augmented Technology teacher called out the first six students' names to receive their gear, Amanda found herself paying more attention to the wizard's explanation of the rules and how the players' avatars worked than to scrubbing the wall of the training building.

I still have the record for making it the farthest through the obstacle course. Bet I could blow those guys out of the water in that game.

Almost as if he'd read her mind, Mr. LeFor looked up at her after handing out the headsets and raised his eyebrows.

She returned to the wall with a heavy sigh and kept scrubbing, shooting Summer a sidelong glance.

As soon as we clean these stupid walls after her stupid choices.

CHAPTER EIGHTEEN

If they'd thought starting their days in Combat Training was exhausting, scrubbing magically dirt-caked walls for twelve hours on Saturday took it to a whole new level. Waking up at 5:00 a.m. on Sunday to do it all over again was worse.

To top it off, Amanda and Summer had to suffer through listening to Mr. LeFor's instructions about the Louper game while the students trying out for the team blundered their way around the training arena trying to get the hang of the headsets.

Fred brought them lunch from the kitchen and winked as he handed Amanda her tray. "Halfway there, girl. And you can recover tomorrow. You know, make sure you don't end up here again next weekend, right?"

"Trust me. I'd rather be out there in that arena with a headset on." She took the tray from him and nodded at the field.

The large, burly pixie chuckled. "I bet you would. Hey, don't forget to use a napkin."

With another wink, he left the freshman girls to their detention—and all fifteen minutes that Mr. Petrov gave them for lunch—and headed behind the training building toward the kitchen.

Amanda wolfed down the plain sandwich and the sprig of grapes, then picked up her napkin and found a square of dark chocolate fudge beneath it. With a laugh, she popped the whole thing in her mouth right before Summer looked up at her from her lunch.

"What was that?"

"Nothing."

"You got a secret pixie admirer or something?"

"No." A chunk of fudge popped out of her mouth, and she fumbled to catch it and shove it back in again.

Summer snorted and rolled her eyes. "Whatever. Think you can finish this last section on your own? I'm gonna go start on the kitchen."

"Yeah, sure." The fudge went down in a painful lump as Amanda swallowed and watched the other girl shuffle off with her wire brush and newly refilled jug of bleach. Then she returned her attention to the Louper tryouts, where the second rotation of kids had ended their practice match and pulled off their headsets to hand them to the next in line.

I still have five minutes. Might as well make a move now.

She took a huge drink from her water bottle—at least Glasket hadn't prohibited them from hydrating while they spent all day in the sun and the muggy heat—then hurried across the training arena. "Mr. LeFor?"

The red-haired wizard looked at her with a small, tight smile. "Just a second, Miss Coulier. Garber! If I see you put that headset on upside down one more time, I don't care *how* fast you are. You're out. Get it right and line up. I'll reset the field in a minute."

Amanda rubbed her palms on her jean shorts and stared at the six upperclassmen putting on their gear, all of them much taller and bulkier than the other kids trying out.

LeFor smiled at her again although he was too distracted not to glance back at the new tryout team every ten seconds. "What can I help you with, Miss Coulier?"

"I want to try out for the Louper team."

The teacher snorted out a laugh, then cleared his throat when he realized she was serious. "Oh. I, uh… I'm not sure that's an option for you."

"Why?" She folded her arms and glanced at the kids in the training arena, ready to finally say what she'd been wondering for the last day and a half. "Because I'm a girl? Or because of what I am?"

Mr. LeFor swallowed, and his smile disappeared. "Why would you think that?"

"Because there aren't any girls trying out. Or…" She lowered her voice and gestured toward herself. "You know."

"I'll give you points for your creative assumption, Miss Coulier, but the *real* reason is that you still have detention to finish."

Amanda's mouth popped open at that. Then she quickly looked away. "Oh. Well, what about next weekend?"

"Sorry. Tryouts are this weekend only. We start practicing and training next weekend, and I need to keep the team on the same page if we want any chance at all of competing with the other schools. It's not an option right now."

"What about tonight?" She stepped toward him. "I only have five hours left of this, and I don't mind trying out on my own. You can score me against everyone else and pick the team tomorrow."

"Not enough in-game avatars to make it a fair challenge for you without other teammates, Miss Coulier. We're on a tight schedule with this, so—"

"Time's up, Coulier!" Mr. Petrov barked from his chair inside the training building's open door. "Get back to scrubbing."

"*Please,* Mr. LeFor."

"Don't ask me again." The Augmented Technology teacher gave her a sympathetic frown and lowered his voice. "Maybe next year you won't be so eager to break the rules during the first week of school. We'll have tryouts again next fall."

"But—"

"All right, guys!" LeFor clapped his hands and walked away from her. "If you aren't ready in three seconds, that's a mark against your overall score."

"Coulier!"

Amanda whirled around to see Mr. Petrov standing in the open doorway now, pointing firmly at her supplies. "Yeah, I get it. Lunch break's over."

She stomped back toward her bristled glove and cleaning solution.

They have no idea what they're missing out on. I could be the best player on the team if they gave me a chance.

Half an hour later, she was only too happy to pick up her supplies and sling them with her across the grass toward the kitchen building where Summer had already gotten to work. Sure, Mr. Petrov could still keep an eye on them through one of the back windows of the training building, but the guy had seemed a lot more interested in watching the Louper tryouts in his training arena. Even if he seemed more amused by the other kids' cluelessness than impressed by whatever they could do on the field.

Amanda set down her cleaning supplies and wiped the sweat off her forehead with the back of her hand.

I could sit in a quiet room and daydream all day, no problem. No wonder they think manual labor is better detention. I'm never doing this again.

"Psst!"

She straightened and turned around, scanning the lawn and the pavilion in the outdoor cafeteria.

The sounds of other students shouting and running around in

the central field and in and out of the dorms' common rooms mixed with the encouraging shouts from the Louper tryouts, but whoever was trying to get Amanda's attention was much closer than anyone else.

"Hey!"

She spun and saw Summer poking her head out from around the corner of the kitchen building.

The new girl's eyes were wide, and she glanced toward the training building before waving Amanda forward. "Come here, shifter girl. You gotta see this."

"*Oh,* no. No way." Amanda picked up the scrubbing glove. "I'm not falling for your crap again."

"It's not crap, okay? Come here."

"No. Do *you* want to be here again next weekend because we didn't get these walls clean in time? Because you're over there screwing around? 'Cause I don't—"

"Christ, Amanda. We have over four hours left to get this done, and I already got a head start." Summer sighed and rolled her eyes. "That doesn't matter. You *really* wanna see this."

"Why?"

"You can't—ugh. Because I think I figured out what a certain purple thing does, and I'd *really* rather not talk about it across an entire wall. Come on!"

Purple thing.

"The crystal?"

"Yeah, that one. Now shut up about it and get over here."

Amanda took her cleaning supplies with her in case Mr. Petrov or anyone else was watching the first two students since the Academy's founding to get detention. When she rounded the corner and joined Summer behind the kitchen building, her cleaning supplies thumped into the grass, and she stared at the humming, glowing purple crystal in the other girl's palm. "Somebody's gonna see that."

"No shit. Act natural and try not to look suspicious." Summer scrubbed absently at the dry, dirt-covered concrete wall with one hand and held the stone in the other by her hip. "It's a *battery*. Can you believe it?"

"Not really, 'cause I have no idea what you're talking about. Battery for what?"

"For *magic*. Come on, that's kind of a no-brainer. *This* pretty little thing is the answer to all our problems."

"Are you serious?" Amanda could hear the pixies moving around inside the kitchen and muttering in low voices as they worked on dinner, but fortunately, none of them heard the girls talking outside. Or if they did, they didn't care. "How does it work?"

Summer grinned. "Easiest thing I've ever done. Apparently, you hold the thing and do magic. It's *perfect*."

Frowning at the other girl, Amanda slowly shook her head. "That doesn't answer any of our problems. That's casting spells with a rock in your hand—"

"No, it's not. Look." Summer tightened her hand around the crystal, then inhaled and pointed at the wall. A yellow light rose from her finger, and as she drew a downward line in the air, a flat blade of yellow light scraped along the wall, peeling off chunks of caked dirt and leaving a perfectly clean surface behind it.

With the swamp at their backs now, there wasn't anyone around who could have caught the barest glimpse of them, but that didn't stop Amanda from glancing all over to double-check. "Are you crazy? We can't do magic to finish this."

"Yeah, we can, shifter girl. With *this*."

"Mr. Petrov said—"

"Screw what he said. Mr. Petrov thinks we'd follow those rules because we don't know cleaning spells."

"*You* obviously do." Amanda stared at the clean strip on the wall.

"No, I don't." Summer's grin only widened. "I've never used a cleaning spell in my life. Pretty pointless when I'm about to move on to the next place anyway. I don't know that spell."

"Then how—"

"I *thought* about what I wanted to do—and did it."

That made Amanda pause, and she looked slowly down at the purple crystal. Standing so close to it made its tingling, buzzing energy wash over her that much more strongly. "There has to be a catch, though, right?"

"Not as far as I've seen. Seriously, we could use this thing for literally *anything* here. Finish the obstacle course. Cast whatever spells we want. Hey, I bet you could even use this on the Louper team. You'd be a hell of a player to go up against."

"LeFor won't let me try out."

Summer snorted. "Well, whatever. Shit, I mean, if you had this thing in Illusions, you could re-color a stupid piece of paper like *that*."

The girl snapped her fingers, and Amanda tried to shut the whole idea down in her mind.

This is cheating. Isn't it? Or maybe it's a little extra help to learn what I came here for so I can graduate. Like a tutor. Except it's a rock.

"Okay, well, we have to practice with it in private so we know how it works before using it in class."

"Duh." Laughing, Summer pumped her fist at her side. "I *knew* you'd be into this."

"Hey, only until I can figure out how to cast spells on my own."

"Oh, *sure*. Then you can hand it over to me, and *I'll* be the only one using it. Man, the look on Glasket's face when she sees me getting top grades in *everything*." Summer pointed at the wall again and scraped off another swath of dirt and grime in one magical swipe.

"How about the look on Petrov's face when he sees we finished all this *before* five-thirty?"

"Ha! That bald asshole won't know what to do with himself. Priceless!"

Amanda flinched and scanned the area around them again. "Maybe keep it down, though, huh? No one ever sounds that happy in detention."

"I like the way you think, shifter girl."

CHAPTER NINETEEN

Mr. Petrov was as confused as they thought he'd be when they returned the cleaning supplies twenty minutes before their time was up. He dismissed them gruffly, and the girls tried not to break out laughing as they headed toward the center field, looking back to see the teacher inspecting the pristinely clean walls in complete bewilderment.

That night, despite getting out of more detention by the skin of their teeth, Amanda and Summer met again after Lights Out and slipped through the hole in the dorm's wards to practice with the purple crystal. They made sure to take it far away from the campus' main buildings although they didn't return to the uncovered ruins of whatever temple had housed the crystal for so long.

"Please tell me you didn't bring anything else for blowing stuff up," Amanda muttered as Summer unzipped her backpack.

"Not this time." The new girl smirked as she withdrew the crystal. "If we get good enough at using this thing, I might have to change my specialty away from magical bombs."

"To *what?*"

"Whatever the hell I want. Here." Summer handed her the

crystal. "I've been hogging it. You get the first practice run tonight."

I can't tell if she's serious or screwing with me.

Amanda slowly took the purple crystal, and the buzz of its concentrated magic thrummed up her arm and into her chest. "Wow…"

"Go ahead. Any kinda spell." Summer grinned and gestured at the broad swath of open land and the swamp around them. "Maybe start with something small."

Out of all the things she could have chosen to focus on with this newfound power, the only spell that came to mind was the one she'd been struggling all week to nail down. With the crystal resting in her open palm, Amanda turned toward the cattail reeds and thought of changing their color. The crystal buzzed with a sharp sting that wasn't exactly unpleasant, and the cattails shimmered. Then each dark brown, fuzzy capsule of fluff turned a bright neon green and glowed in the darkness.

"Wow." Summer folded her arms. "Okay, impressive, I guess. I honestly expected you to do something a lot…cooler."

"I did it," Amanda whispered. "Holy shit, I *did* it! I cast an illusion! It worked!"

"Yeah, maybe keep it down, though, huh?" A surprised chuckle escaped the new girl as she looked around the empty, secluded area at the edge of the campus' boundaries. "Someone might think you're out here getting murdered."

Amanda let out an excited squeal and spun to face the other girl. "I can do *magic*. Like real, actual magic that—"

"Um…shifter girl? You might wanna—"

"—works and does exactly what I want!"

As her voice rose again, the neon green cattail heads glowed brighter, and a low hum rose from the reeds before the cattails exploded in a burst of glittering green. Clumps of white fluff flew around the girls and fluttered to the ground, some of them dropping with a light *plop* into the swamp.

"Whoops."

"Okay, now that you're all high on magic..." Summer snatched the stone from her and turned away with a smirk. "We'll trade off."

"We can use that thing in class."

"Yeah, that's what I said. Not every class, though. We should figure out right now which one of us gets this thing when. Like, I get it in Alchemy."

"What? No way." Amanda tried to scowl at her friend, but her incredulous smile still broke through. "You already know how to blow things up. You'll take all of us down with you if you do that in class. If Zimmer doesn't kill you first."

"That's not how it works, shifter girl. You need this thing in Illusions. It's only fair I get it in Alchemy."

Amanda couldn't help but stare at the glowing purple stone. "Why don't we practice with this thing right now and worry about who gets it later? It's not like we have all night."

Summer grinned. "We might if I cast a time loop—"

"No! Don't even—just no. You can't mess with time like that when you have no idea what you're doing."

"Relax, shifter girl. I'm only messing with you." Laughing, Summer turned toward the swamp and scanned the thick tree trunks bending sideways, their branches hanging low over the water. "I'll stick with what I know. For now."

Amanda bit her lip and watched the other girl cast another spell with magic that wasn't her own. *What she knows could be anything. Still, this will be a hell of a way for me to learn more.*

Over the next five weeks, they traded the stone back and forth, sneaking out less and less at night to practice with it because they had plenty of time to use it in class. Eventually, they settled into a rhythm of passing the crystal off between classes when it came time for either girl to use it. Summer had it during Alchemy and Combat Training—although even with the crystal in her pocket, she couldn't get farther along on the obstacle course than Amanda—and Amanda took the crystal during Illusions and Augmented Technology. Neither of them cared about who had it during History of Oriceran, which didn't require any skill, magical or physical. The only ability needed to make it through Ms. Ralthorn's droning lectures was a mastery of not pulling their hair out in boredom or falling asleep, and the purple crystal didn't help with either of those.

Amanda still hung out mostly with Grace, Jackson, and Alex during her free time after long days of class and all the physical activity Mr. Petrov could squeeze out of them first thing in the morning. None of her friends seemed to notice a difference in her after all the secret time she spent with Summer. They *did* see her sudden improvement in spells, particularly in Illusions.

Ms. Calsgrave asked her to stay back after one such class and stared at Amanda for a good twenty seconds before saying anything. "You've improved quite a bit in the last few weeks, Miss Coulier."

"Just hard work, I guess." She shrugged. "I really wanna be here."

"Clearly. If you're still interested in private tutoring, my offer still stands."

"I'm good, thanks. Probably needed to get used to *envisioning* stuff, you know?" Amanda booked it out of the classroom without waiting for the teacher to say anything else and found her friends waiting for her in the hall.

"What was *that* about?" Grace asked with a confused smile.

"Guess she wanted me to know that she knows I'm getting better at spells."

"Yeah, you're good, all right." Jackson leaned toward her, narrowing his eyes in a mocking attempt to look suspicious. "A little *too* good. How the hell did you make that rock look like an apple on your first try? I had to work on it the whole class."

"You couldn't even get it to look round," Alex muttered.

"Shut up."

Amanda shrugged again and headed down the hall. "Takes practice, I guess. Hey, we should go hang out at the kitchens 'til dinner. I'm starving."

"As long as you let me copy off your homework assignment for Ms. Ralthorn."

Grace shot Jackson a disapproving frown. "Are you serious?"

"I mean, yeah. Don't tell me you remember anything she says during the most boring class ever invented."

"Of course not." The witch smirked. "I take notes."

"Oh, well, then I'm copying off *you*."

She and Summer had an unspoken agreement that they wouldn't start hanging out after class or during free time, mostly to keep everyone else from getting too suspicious. No one would believe that a skinny twelve-year-old girl no one knew was a shifter and the fifteen-year-old freshmen who'd been kicked out of one magic school already had become friends. Plus, they didn't want to draw any extra attention from the teachers, who'd all been keeping a particularly close eye on them since their first infraction and detention sentence—especially Principal Glasket.

Amanda still slipped out of the dorms twice a week to shift and run around on her own or to visit the kitchen pixies when her almost insatiable hunger wouldn't let her sleep. Fortunately, no one had discovered the hole in the dorm's wards—or if they had, no one had bothered to seal it back up. She was still the only shifter at the school, after all. She was also determined not to get into any more trouble when she snuck out to do what shifters did.

Sometimes, Summer would show up at some of Amanda's favorite spots to sit and stare up at the moon or listen to the swamp in the middle of the night. Now that they had enough practice with the stone under their belts, they didn't need to use it nearly as much outside of class. Most of the time when the new girl came to find her like this, they only sat together. Neither one of them had much to say because they'd already run out of things that didn't include talking about their past or where they'd been before coming to the Academy.

She never told Summer to leave her alone, even if that was what she wanted. Still, whenever Amanda picked up Summer's scent around campus during her runs, she made it a point to avoid the other girl. Just in case.

By the time the end of September rolled around, the entire school was gearing up with an excitement Amanda didn't understand. She had no idea what homecoming was, even after Glasket's announcement, until Brandon Everly caught up to her after class the Thursday before and practically cornered her in the hallway.

"Amanda." The half-Crystal shuffled from foot to foot and scratched vigorously at his hair. The flecks of ice falling to his shoulders and tinkling across the floor were apparently some part of a nervous tick.

She tried not to make it too obvious when she glanced down the hall and saw Grace staring at them. *What is Brandon doing?* She hoped her gaze sent the message across, but Grace only shrugged.

"Um...I was...uh..."

"You okay?" Amanda wrinkled her nose at the nervous kid looming at least a foot over her.

Brandon cleared his throat. "Yeah. Totally. Do you, uh... wanna maybe..."

"Call someone to take you to the med ward?"

At the same time, he blurted, "...go to Homecoming with me?"

"What?"

"What?"

They stared at each other, and thin streams of mist rose from Brandon's cheeks.

Like the fog that pours off dry ice.

She wrinkled her nose. "I'm...not sure what you're getting at."

"Like, as my date." Brandon swallowed thickly. "You know, to the dance."

"Oh. Um..." Another glance at Grace didn't help her at all. *I don't want a date. I'm twelve.* "I mean, I wasn't planning on going for the dance. More like for the food, so...I guess I'll think about it?"

"Yeah, okay." Brandon turned away from her, his nervous half-Crystal mist fading despite the deepening blush. "No pressure or anything. I figured I'd ask."

"Cool. Thanks." She snuck away from him, seizing her opening to slip away from the wall and hurry toward Grace with wide eyes.

"Wow." The blonde witch snorted and looked over her shoulder to shoot Brandon a gleaming grin. The minute he saw her, he spun and booked it through the sea of students heading out to the central field, pushing through them to move aimlessly in the opposite direction. "He asked you to Homecoming, didn't he?"

Amanda grimaced. "I think so..."

"What did you say?"

"That I'd think about it."

"Oh, man." Grace slapped a palm against her forehead. "No wonder he looked like he was ready to crawl into a hole and die."

"*What?*"

They pushed open the front doors of the main building and headed out toward the main field. "Amanda, if a guy asks you out to a dance, the worst thing you can do is *not* give him an answer."

"Why?"

"Because they can't handle it." Grace snorted. "Look, Homecoming's in two days, right? Now he's gonna spend the next two days wondering what your answer will be. But he's not gonna come back and ask you *again*. He'll be waiting for you to come to him and tell him because he doesn't wanna seem desperate."

"Well, then I'll tell him tomorrow."

"No. You can't do that either. That's even worse."

Amanda stopped on the grass and frowned. "I don't get it."

"If you talk to him again before Homecoming, he'll get all excited and think you're gonna say yes. Are you?"

"Be his date to a dance?" Amanda scrunched up her face. "No."

"That's why it's worse." Grace grabbed her arm and led her across the field toward the outdoor cafeteria. "'Cause he'll be all excited again, then you say no, and you basically end up crushing his soul *twice*. I don't know if he can handle it."

"Sure he can. It's only a dance."

"Not when he asked you to it."

Amanda rolled her eyes. "Come on. It's so much worse to be waiting around and wondering when I'm gonna tell him no. I can tell him in class tomorrow—"

"No, you can't. Now you have to avoid him like the plague until Saturday. Then when everyone shows up at the dance, and you haven't said anything, he'll get the hint."

"That's *so* mean."

"That's how high school works, okay?" Grace's grip tightened on her arm, and they stopped so the witch could turn toward Amanda and look her straight in the eyes. "So here's your first lesson about dating."

"Ew."

"Well, now you know. Next time someone asks you out, and your immediate answer isn't yes, tell him no. Sometimes you have to be a jerk to save them from a lot more misery later. Don't worry. You'll learn how to—"

"Coulier!" Jackson called from the middle of the lunch line. "I saved you a spot. Get over here."

Grace headed toward him without a word, and Amanda stayed where she was for a moment, trying to process everything the older girl had told her.

Dating? Yeah, right. That's the last thing I wanna do. I should tell Brandon thanks but no thanks to his face.

Deciding that in her mind didn't make her feel any better about any of it.

When she reached Jackson in the line stretching away from the buffet table, the wizard grinned and slapped a hand down on her shoulder. "Thought you were gonna take forever. Here. You're in front of me."

"Dude." The sophomore behind Jackson glared at him and gestured at the girls. "You said *one*."

"Oh, yeah. Sorry, Grace." Jackson shoved her playfully away. "I held a spot for Coulier. You gotta go to the back of the line."

"What?" Grace's blue eyes widened.

"That was the deal," the sophomore said. "Back of the line."

"Jackson..."

"You didn't even *try* to help me in Augmented Technology this morning."

"No, I didn't let you cheat off my test."

The wizard clicked his tongue. "Should've thought of that before you covered up all your answers. Just lost all your friend privileges for...I don't know. As long as I feel like it. Go on."

He pointed at the back of the line, and Grace rolled her eyes before stalking off to take her place behind Alex.

"You too, huh?" the half-Wood Elf said dully.

"Did *Amanda* let him copy her answers?"

"No." Alex shrugged. "I think he likes her."

"Well, he better not ask her to Homecoming."

"What?"

"Never mind."

CHAPTER TWENTY

The day before Homecoming was even worse. None of the students could keep their heads on straight, and the teachers were equally distracted. That was unbearably apparent in their last class of the day.

Amanda had only been half-listening to Ms. Ralthorn ramble on and on about whatever the woman thought was important about the history of Oriceran, not even trying anymore not to drift off into boredom-inspired dozing. Until the teacher mentioned the kemanas.

"As I'm sure you all know, these kemanas were created centuries ago by ancient magicals who crossed through the gates straight from Oriceran. They knew all too well that when those gates eventually closed, it would cut off the magicals who stayed here on Earth from their original magic sources on the other planet. As far as we know, these ancients are the ones who created the giant crystals powering each kemana on Earth. Including the one beside which this school was built."

Amanda whipped her head up off her stacked arms on her desk and quickly wiped the line of drool that would have eventually made it out of the corner of her mouth.

"These crystals are, of course, our only truly sustainable source of magic on this planet," Ralthorn continued. "While we know very little about their true origins beyond a few educated guesses or the occasional historian professing their undying beliefs about the way they work, we *do* know their purpose here."

The teacher didn't say anything else remotely interesting after that, but Amanda's mind was already racing. She was vaguely aware of Summer turning around and shooting her a wide-eyed glance before the girl thrust her hand in the air.

Ms. Ralthorn was too engrossed in her lecture notes to notice, so Summer shouted, "How big is the smallest crystal?"

"And it's—I...I'm sorry?" The teacher looked up from her notes and finally scanned the class to see Summer's raised hand right before she dropped it onto her desk with a smack. "The *smallest* crystal?"

"Yeah. In the kemanas."

"Well, I..." Blinking furiously at the unexpected interruption, Ralthorn removed her reading glasses and gazed blankly at the back of the classroom. "Honestly, I've never been asked that before. I do know they're all fairly large."

"You mean way bigger than anything that could be picked up and carried off, right?"

Amanda stared at Summer's profile, finally realizing what the other girl was trying to get at.

No, we didn't find a kemana crystal underground. I think. I don't even know what a kemana really is...

"Miss Flannerty, there is no conceivable way on either world that a kemana crystal could ever be *picked up and carried off*." Ms. Ralthorn scowled. "Beyond their enormous size, the crystals have literally been built *into* each kemana and are firmly rooted in their locations, both by time and ancient magic. The idea that they're transferrable is...ridiculous at best and life-threatening at worst. So throw that idea right out of your head. Don't even try it."

"What?" Summer barked out a laugh. "I never said *I* wanted to—"

"As I was saying." The teacher returned her reading glasses to the bridge of her nose and kept going. "The kemana crystals harness and store magic from Oriceran while also fueling magic reserves on Earth. This—"

"Where's the closest one?" Amanda blurted.

Ralthorn drew a deep breath, then looked up at her. "The closest what, Miss Coulier?"

"Kemana. You said there was one next to the school."

"Yes. The location of every magic school on Earth is chosen based on an area's proximity to a kemana."

"So where is it? 'Cause we're kind of in the middle of nowhere." Amanda's mind raced as she tried to figure out where one of these hidden magical cities could be. *Unless that temple was a dead, empty kemana with a shriveled-up crystal inside, we're not close enough to any major city.*

"Well, it's... Now let me see." Ralthorn opened the center drawer of her desk and pulled out a large three-ring binder before dropping it on her desk with a loud *thump*. The few students whose attention hadn't been caught by Summer's interruption of the teacher's lecture jumped and jerked their heads off their desks at the sound. "Obviously, our closest kemana is in the Everglades. Although that doesn't narrow it down by much—ah. Yes. Here it is on the map. Right by...hmm."

"By what?" Amanda almost shrieked it as she leaned forward on her desk.

Ms. Ralthorn looked sharply up at her. "Watch your tone, Miss Coulier."

"Sorry."

"Thank you. Our closest kemana marks what looks like the final corner of a square between the Academy, Everglades Town—"

"You mean Everglades City?"

"Yes, excuse me. Everglades City. And Miami." The teacher's frown deepened. "I'm sure that was to create equal access to magicals on the east and west ends of Florida's peninsula. Admittedly, I haven't seen a kemana removed from major cities quite like this. Then again, the locals here seem rather unamused by the idea of traveling from these remote parts to Miami..."

Amanda couldn't help a snort. *Because of all the tourists, I bet. Johnny's not the only one who hates them.*

"Be that as it may, the kemana is still entirely accessible to magicals in this area of the world. Including students at the Academy of Necessary Magic."

"Wait; *what?*" Tommy sat up perfectly straight at his desk. "We get to go there?"

"Not *you.*" Ralthorn took off her reading glasses again and lifted her chin to gaze at the half-wizard at the back of the classroom. "Not this year, anyway. I believe the other three grades will be making a school-sanctioned trip sometime this semester, if not in the spring. Then, only upperclassmen and the occasional excelling sophomore will have open access to enter the kemana outside school hours."

Tommy scoffed. "Figures."

"It's an *earned* privilege, Mr. Brunsen—"

"If *we* haven't earned it," Jasmine said from her desk in the front almost directly centered with the teacher's desk, "none of the other grades have either. We all got here at the same time."

"True, Miss McVar. But we have to start somewhere, and these are guidelines set out by other magic schools across the country—"

"That's such bullshit," Summer muttered. Everyone stared at her, including Ms. Ralthorn, but the girl either didn't notice or didn't care. "The whole point of this place is that it isn't like every other school. You're grooming us to be bounty hunters, not pencil-pushers at some stupid magical desk job. Right?"

The teacher's smile tightened into a grimace as her eyelids

fluttered. "Those are not the only two options for young, graduating magicals—"

"I'm right."

"I don't make the rules, Miss Flannerty."

"Yeah, I know. Glasket can't make up her mind about which rules matter and which ones are a load of crap."

"That's quite enough!" Ralthorn's chair screeched behind her as she stood, and she slammed a hand down on her desk. Crackling lines of orange light snaked across the surface of her desk, and a brighter orb of warning orange grew over the back of her hand. She didn't seem to realize what she was doing until Summer folded her arms and raised an eyebrow. Then the teacher cleared her throat and slowly removed her hand. Her magical warning faded. "This class is History of Oriceran. Not Debate Club. Not a speculative disassembly of current school policies. When this class is *over,* feel free to take your complaints to Principal Glasket although you're more likely to waste both your time and hers in the process. Now, if you don't mind, I would very much like to move on with today's lesson."

No one said a word, and even Summer managed to hold back whatever she was bursting to say in reply.

She's gonna get kicked out if she doesn't stop. At least out of the class, if not the school.

Amanda tried to settle back into her chair again but couldn't get comfortable. How had she not known about a giant magical city in the middle of the Everglades powered by a crystal with magic straight from Oriceran? Did Johnny know about it?

"There's an incredibly long and rich history of not only Oriceran magicals making their way through the gates to Earth but Oriceran artifacts as well. Some of them, of course, are purely cultural, and getting into those details would be an entirely different class on the subject. Most of these artifacts, however, have magical properties that remain intact after passing through the realm between the gates. A kemana in Wisconsin showcases a selection of some of the very first-known artifacts that were brought across, and some magical historians believe these artifacts may predate the formation of the kemanas themselves. And the crystals that power them, of course."

"Why Wisconsin?" Evan asked.

"We can't be sure of the answer to that, Mr. Hutchinson." Ralthorn finally sat and readjusted her reading glasses. "At the time they arrived in that part of the Continental U.S., it wasn't the Continental U.S. There is, of course, some speculation of a more concentrated community of magicals way back when who'd chosen the region as some form of landmark. Of course, that kemana is partially beneath what we now call Milwaukee. It's become something of a hub for displaced magicals now trying to find their way through society like the rest of us. Of course, as all of *you* know, there are displaced magicals *everywhere—*"

"Because we lived underground doesn't mean we didn't have anywhere else to go." Corey grunted and folded his massive, shockingly hairy half-Kilomea arms.

"Well, of course not, Mr. Baker. But there *is* a certain level of—"

"Discrimination?" Grace asked. "Because that's what it sounds like."

Ms. Ralthorn frowned. "I'm not discriminating against anyone, Miss Porter. Merely stating conclusions that have already been drawn based on gathered data over the last several decades."

"What about shifters?" Summer piped up. The classroom fell silent.

"What about shifters, Miss Flannerty?" Ralthorn said it slowly, trying not to lose her composure as her freshmen actively engaged in her class for the first time since the semester started.

Amanda automatically sank lower in her chair and stared at her desk. *No, no, no. Did she seriously have to bring that up right here in front of everyone? It has nothing to do with anything.*

Summer shrugged. "I mean, everyone else pretty much discriminates against shifters, right? I bet there's a bunch of them running around *Milwaukee.*"

"That's an entirely different subject," Ralthorn barked. "There's still some contention around the idea of whether or not shifters should be considered magicals at all. If you ask me, they're not. As a general rule, they lack any inherent understanding of magic itself despite being the only race who can actively shift their entire form at will. Of course, it's still an ongoing debate. Mostly perpetuated by shifters, of course. There's something of a radical group of them who recently banded together to—"

"Wait, wait, wait." Summer snorted and held up a hand to stop the teacher before breaking into a wide grin.

Amanda wanted to sink through the floor and disappear. *Why does she love this so much?*

"Miss Flannerty—"

"No, hear me out for a sec. So you're trying to say right now that if some shifter kid showed up at this school and wanted to get in, you'd turn them away because they're not *magical* enough?"

Amanda closed her eyes.

"Well, that would be—" Ms. Ralthorn stopped abruptly and stared straight ahead at the back wall of her classroom. One eye twitched behind the narrow frames of her reading glasses, and she cleared her throat. Her gaze flickered briefly toward Amanda. "That would most likely be a decision made on a case-by-case basis."

Summer leaned forward toward the teacher, her devious grin growing still wider. "Even at a school that takes in a bunch of homeless kids no one else wants? Are you *sure?*"

Ralthorn's mouth popped open, her lips soundlessly working before she found her voice. "This is—"

"Can we drop this whole thing?" Amanda blurted, staring at

Summer despite feeling all the other students' confused gazes on *her* now. "I mean, we're gonna miss lunch if this keeps going."

"Ha." Behind her, Jackson folded his arms and muttered, "Right there with you, Coulier. Wait, you won't *keep* us here through lunch, right? I can't skip a meal—"

"No, Mr. Pris. Still, if we're to stay on track with the syllabus for your first semester, I would very much like to return to my lesson plan for the day." Ralthorn swept her gaze across the room and let it linger a little longer on Summer than anyone else. "*Without* interruptions."

Summer shrugged and slumped back in her chair.

During the rest of the interminably long class, Amanda tried to ignore what felt like all the other students' eyes on her. *They have no idea what I am. Jackson didn't pick up on it. He's only worried about food.*

When she shot Grace a quick sidelong glance, the witch smiled at her, nodded toward the droning Ms. Ralthorn, and playfully rolled her eyes.

Or if they do know, nobody's gonna say anything. At least I know how Ralthorn feels about me being here. Jeeze.

When class was finally over at 4:30 p.m., and the alarm bell made all the thoroughly bored freshmen jump in their seats, Amanda was the first to grab her backpack and head for the door. However, Ms. Ralthorn asked her to stay back, and she couldn't pretend to ignore the request because she'd been looking right at Ralthorn when she'd said it.

The witch waited for the classroom to empty, drumming her fingers on the desk while Amanda stared at the floor.

"Miss Coulier—"

"It's fine." Amanda shook her head. "I get it. It's not like I expected *everyone* to want me here."

"I want to apologize." Ralthorn cleared her throat. "I've been studying Oriceran and *our* shared origins almost my entire life, looking at things from a purely academic perspective. Obviously, it doesn't help my awareness that I don't see many…"

"Magicals like me?" Amanda met the woman's gaze.

"Shifters. Correct. Honestly, I'm a little embarrassed to say you're the first I've met face to face. And you're so, well…*normal.* It's easy to forget what you are."

Amanda opened her mouth, realizing her lips were moving on their own despite a complete lack of words coming out of them. *What the heck am I supposed to say to that?*

"Okay, well… Maybe you should—"

"Do more research on modern shifters on Earth? Yes, that's the exact idea I had when I asked you to stay behind. I promise to share with you anything I find that may end up being useful to you. Enjoy your lunch, Miss Coulier. I'll see you at the match tonight."

"Right." Amanda turned with wide eyes and headed for the open classroom door. *I have no idea what just happened. I only hope nobody else picked up on how seriously weird that was.*

CHAPTER TWENTY-ONE

All through lunch, as Grace and Jackson got into an argument about what constituted *decorating* for the Homecoming dance the next day, Amanda couldn't stop thinking about the purple crystal, which she still had with her after her turn to use it in Augmented Technology class that morning.

Somehow, after Ms. Ralthorn's blunder about shifters, using the crystal to power the magic she had seemed more important than ever. She'd come to this school to learn everything she needed about becoming a bounty hunter like Johnny—*better* than Johnny. Now, she had to be *the best* in the entire school, so she could go right into the job as soon as she graduated.

Kicking bad guys' asses and protecting kids like me. The ones everyone forgets until they go too far. How many people feel like that about shifters?

The answer didn't matter. She was here, no matter what Ralthorn or any other teacher thought about having someone like her for a student at the Academy. With the crystal, she'd be able to ace every single class, and no one would be able to turn her away. Or hurt her like she'd been hurt over the last four months.

She looked up and saw Summer studying her from two picnic tables down. The older girl smiled and waggled her eyebrows.

After returning the gesture, Amanda quickly turned back toward her friends and pretended to listen to Jackson's confusing description of some party he'd gone to when he was eight. *I have to figure out how to get Summer to let me keep the crystal. Or only let her use it when I don't need it until I can handle doing magic all on my own.*

That night, the entire student body gathered in the central field to watch the Homecoming Louper match between the Academy's Florida Gators—their new mascot—and the Kentucky Wildcats. It was the team's second match of the season, which stretched out through the year's duration and ended with the championship right before the end of spring semester.

Amanda had wanted to try out for the team, but every time she'd asked Mr. LeFor to reconsider, he'd turned her down. Now, as Principal Glasket finished her opening speech about Homecoming and the Florida Gators' skilled team, she realized she didn't want to be here to watch the game. *What's the point if I should've been on the team in the first place?*

It was cool to watch the team get teleported out of the main field—virtual-reality headsets and all—to the match's undisclosed location. Then the blown-up projection of the match field and all the players' virtual avatars took up all the space in front of the stage and podium, and Academy students cheered and roared for their team as the game kicked off.

I need to get out of here.

She stood from her chair, and Grace looked up at her in concern. "What's wrong?"

"Gotta get some air."

"We're already outside."

"And privacy."

"Aw, come on, Coulier." Jackson glanced at her, then returned eagerly to the projected screen to watch the game. "You're gonna —yeah!" He threw a fist in the air. "Kick his virtual ass, McGuire! Don't let him get away! Coulier, you're gonna miss all the action. Seriously, I had no idea a game as awesome as this existed. Hell, a few headsets back in LA would've made all the difference in the world while we were—look out!"

A collective groan rose from the student body as one of their team members got shoved off a rock outcropping by another player and fell into the pond below him on the field. The second he splashed into the water, his avatar disappeared from the screen, and the player was sent out of the match's virtual-reality world to wait until the game was over.

"I need a minute." Amanda sidled down the row of chairs as kids around her screamed at the game, pumping their fists in the air and grimacing at the magical battles being fought in front of them. "Enjoy the game, though. I'll see you later."

"Yeah, and we're gonna win!" Jackson screamed.

When she finally got away from all the noise, Amanda walked aimlessly across the campus until she reached the kitchen. She couldn't see Fred or any of the other kitchen pixies through the windows, but the smell of steak and asparagus and mashed potatoes meant they were hard at work cooking everyone one heck of an after-game meal.

She passed the kitchen, ignored her growling stomach, and stuck her hand into the deep pocket of her cargo shorts to feel the purple crystal's clean-cut edges.

"Not a big fan of watching a game you can't play, huh?" Summer said behind her.

Amanda spun and stared at the girl. "I guess. I mean, it's a cool game and everything. I'm not really in a screaming-at-the-team kinda mood."

"What about a *Homecoming* mood?"

She snorted. "Yeah, right. I don't get the point of that either."

"Eh, it's something fun to focus on, I guess. Or at least that's what all the teachers think it's supposed to be."

"You don't like it either?"

Summer stuck her hands in the pockets of her zip-up hoodie and gazed out at the swamp as they ambled away from the campus buildings toward the open space ahead of them. "More like I'm indifferent."

"I figured you'd be pumped about watching the game. You were pretty excited about it when Glasket said we were starting a team."

"Yeah, then I blew up an island, went down into a buried temple, and found a shiny rock that helps us both use magic we don't actually know. So…kind of a tough act for a game to follow. Even Louper."

Amanda cocked her head in concession. "Fair enough. If Mr. LeFor would let me try out for the team, I'd probably use this thing to help me play."

"The crystal?"

She pulled the glowing purple stone out of her pocket and held it toward Summer. "Not like I need it right now anyway."

"Nah. You can keep it over the weekend. Practice and everything, right?" Summer turned away from the stone. "As long as I get it back before Combat Training on Monday."

"Yeah, okay. Thanks."

They wandered across the grounds toward the campus' northern edge, and the shouts and cheers from the student spectators faded away behind them.

"So what about the whole dance thing?" Amanda asked.

"If you're asking me to Homecoming, shifter girl, I'm gonna have to say no."

"Wait; what?" They both burst out laughing, and Amanda shook her head. "I meant are you going?"

"I know what you meant. I don't know yet. This kinda thing

at my last school wasn't my thing. I guess things here are as different as they're ever gonna get." Summer picked at a tall fern and shrugged. "I'll probably show up to see what kinda disaster it turns into. Kids like us don't exactly mix well with school dances."

"Yeah, probably not." *I've been to plenty of fancy parties that might as well have been dances.*

The memories curdled into twisted knots in Amanda's gut, and she didn't think about it before she opened up and started talking. "You know, back in New York, my parents used to take us to a whole bunch of parties. Seemed like there was a different one practically every weekend. I hated it. Always having to stand there in a dress and smile until my face felt frozen like that and laugh at these stupid jokes about politics and accounting that never made any sense."

"Yeesh." Summer wrinkled her nose. "Sounds like hell."

"Kinda."

"So what'd you do? Finally stopping laughing, and your parents shipped you out here?"

"Not exactly." Bending to grab a stick, Amanda straightened and swung it aimlessly at the ferns and the cattail reeds. *I need to stop talking about them before I won't be able to.*

"Huh. Okay. Then at least tell me what happened to the other one."

"What?"

"You said, 'My parents used to take *us*.' More than just you, shifter girl. Where'd the other one end up?"

Claire. Her name was Claire.

"Uh..." A strangled, hesitant groan escaped her. "I don't wanna talk about it."

"Right." Summer frowned at her. "I mean, you're the one who brought it up, but whatever."

"I was trying to say I hope this Homecoming thing isn't anything like those parties. That's all."

With a snort, the other girl folded her arms and turned to face the rising shouts of triumph coming from the center field. "This is a magic school for juvenile delinquents, shifter girl. It won't be anything like your fancy New York parties. Kinda weird to say, but I'm pretty sure that's a good thing."

CHAPTER TWENTY-TWO

The Florida Gators didn't win their second match for the school's first Homecoming Louper game. The Kentucky Wildcats took the victory, but it didn't seem to put a damper on the excitement buzzing around the entire campus at the Academy. Because the next day, they still had the Homecoming party and dance. Amanda should've been more excited, but she couldn't see the point.

What she wanted was to be alone for a while after lunch because Ms. Ralthorn had said something yesterday that had stayed with her.

"There's something of a radical group of them who recently banded together..."

The teacher had been talking about shifters, and that unfinished sentence had kept Amanda awake a lot later than she'd wanted the night before until she realized there *was* something she could do about it.

Now, she sat on her bed with Johnny's black service box and her cell phone—both of which were considered contraband—and figured the best place to start without raising any red flags at the Academy was the internet.

Not sure how many legit hits I'll get for searching 'radical shifter organizations,' but it's worth a shot.

Before she could type in the search, Grace knocked on her door. "Amanda?"

She shoved her phone and the black box under her pillow. "What?"

"Hey, come on. You can't lock yourself up in your room. We should get ready for the dance."

"Yeah…I don't know if I'm even gonna go."

"That's the dumbest thing I've heard you say. Come on. Open up."

Amanda rolled her eyes, grabbed her devices, and chucked them back into her dresser drawer before closing it and heading to the door. The last thing she needed was for Grace to find them. Not that she thought the witch would run to the teachers about it, but Amanda preferred her secrets.

When she opened her door, Grace was already grinning with her arms spread wide. "There's no way you're missing out on your first school dance. Not if I have anything to say about it."

"What's the big deal anyway?" Amanda scratched her head as the witch barreled into her room and gazed around. "I don't get it."

"Have you *seen* what the teachers are doing with the decorations in the central field?"

"No…"

"Well, when you do, you'll understand. Look, Amanda, this is a *magical dance.* I promise you've never seen anything like it. We need to make sure that no one's seen anything like *you* before, either."

"What?"

"Exactly what I said. You had no idea how to say no to Brandon Everly when he asked you to go with him, so I guess you also don't have any idea how to get ready for a dance like this. Am I right?"

"I mean, it's not exactly my first party—"

"Yeah, but this isn't a birthday party. This is high school." Grace went right to the sliding door of the long, thin closet and thrust it open. She scanned the three hangers inside, which held Amanda's heavier sweaters, and her shoulders slumped. "You have the emptiest closet I've ever seen."

"Most of my stuff doesn't need to be hung up."

"Please don't tell me you keep your nice clothes in your dresser." The witch turned round to scowl at Amanda. "That's the worst thing you can do to a dance dress."

"I don't have any dance dresses."

"Yeah. Right." With a snort, Grace headed straight for the dresser and jerked open the top drawer. "Huh. You like shorts and tank tops a lot, don't you?"

"We're in Florida."

"No skirts? Jumpers? Nothing?"

Before Grace could make it to opening the bottom drawer with Amanda's illegal technology resting right on top, Amanda leapt toward the dresser and pulled her friend away. "Hold on."

"What's wrong? I'm here to help you pick out the best thing to wear."

"Grace, I don't *care* what I wear to this thing. I'll go, okay?"

"Yeah, but you have to dress up. It's Homecoming. Sure, it's probably gonna be different than all the other schools, but we still have a chance to get all fancy. Take a break from all the hardcore learning and dragging our butts around that stupid obstacle course—"

"I don't have anything fancy." Amanda swallowed and looked at the floor. "So…"

"What?" Grace shot her a confused smile. "You mean you've never worn a dress?"

"No, I've worn dresses plenty of times." *I hate them.* Amanda sighed. "Look, before I came here, I was living with Johnny—"

"Yeah, yeah. The big bad bounty hunter. What does that have to do with anything?"

"I'm saying I don't have anything from before I went to stay with him, okay? Pretty much everything I own is in that dresser."

"Oh." Grace glanced around the room and tucked her short blonde bob behind one ear, finally realizing part of what Amanda was trying to get at—that everything connected to her old life in New York before Johnny Walker and before the Academy had stayed in her past. "Yeah, I didn't have a whole lot to bring with me from LA, either. They didn't take you out to get anything before you got on the train?"

Amanda barked out a laugh. "What train? People keep talking about it, but I have no idea what it is."

"The magical train." Grace stared at her. "The one that runs underground to every Starbucks. How do you *not* know this?"

"I mean, I was already staying in the Everglades." *Plus, my parents weren't big on interacting with other magicals.* "That's how all of you got here?"

"Most of us, yeah. Except for Summer, obviously. Do you know where she's from? I don't mean her last school."

"Nope."

"Well, whatever. I don't care about *her*. I care about getting you into a dress for the dance. Come on." Grace snatched up Amanda's hand and pulled her into the hall. "We're gonna find something that fits you. Oh, hey. Annabelle's your size."

"Annabelle's a dwarf."

"Yeah, and I bet she has an extra dress she'd let you borrow. Seriously, Amanda, I'd be the worst friend in the world if I let you sit out on this one. Trust me. You're gonna love it."

As it turned out, Annabelle and Amanda wore the same sizes. The dwarf girl didn't hand over her *best* dress—she wore that one herself—but she had a black and green striped mini-dress she and Grace both squealed over when they held it up against Amanda's shoulders. "Oh my God, this is perfect."

"It'll look *so* much better on you than on me," Annabelle added. "You need to wear this."

"I'm not really into dresses, guys."

The other girls looked at each other and giggled.

"It's a *dance*. Wear the dress, Amanda." Grace stuck her hands on her hips. "What are you gonna do with your hair?"

"Um…brush it?"

"Wrong answer." Annabelle darted out of her dorm room and headed down the hall. "Margaret has some of the *best* ideas with hair. I don't know how she managed to bring almost an entire salon with her, but we're gonna use it. Be right back."

"An entire salon." Amanda wrinkled her nose.

"I'm pretty sure she stole it," Grace muttered. "*And* the duffel bag with the Endless enchantment on it."

"The what?"

"You know. The enchantment that makes things, like, bigger on the inside." Grace shrugged. "She only has one bag, but you should see her room on the second floor. There's *way* more stuff in there than what she could fit in that bag. That's what *I* wanna learn how to do before we graduate. Cast those kinds of enchantments."

Amanda smiled and nodded, but her mind instantly went to the purple crystal resting in her backpack down the hall. *I bet I could make an enchantment with that thing. Then I'd have to explain to everyone how the girl who couldn't change the color of construction paper suddenly knows high-level enchantments.*

When Annabelle returned, she had Margaret with her. The other girl carried her Endless duffel bag in one hand and smirked when she looked Amanda up and down. "We're gonna make you look so amazing. I can't even stand it."

"You don't have to—"

"Don't worry about it. You know what? Don't even talk." Margaret laid the duffel bag on the floor in Annabelle's room and grinned. "Let us do all the work. You're gonna love this, I promise."

Amanda shot Grace a hesitant grimace, but the witch was way too excited about the youngest freshman's *makeover* to pick up on it. So Amanda resigned herself to being fawned over by three other high school girls who insisted they knew more about what she wanted to look like than she did.

Just like Mom. Oh man, this is like getting ready for the governor's gala all over again.

Yet, trying to tell these girls about how much she'd hated being done up like this for her parents' parties—and how much her sister Claire had loved it—would only bring up more questions she didn't want to answer. So she changed into Annabelle's striped dress and sat on the dwarf girl's bed so they could do whatever they had in mind for Amanda's *grand appearance* at a stupid Homecoming dance. She swallowed the lump in her throat, trying to push down the memories one more time.

I'd give anything to see Mom and Claire getting their nails done and Dad shaving in front of the mirror. Can't think about that now, Amanda. They're gone, and you're not. Move on.

When the girls finished dressing Amanda up like a living doll, they squealed and giggled and wouldn't stop talking about how amazing she looked. Then they scrambled to get themselves ready for the dance.

The teachers had ordered everyone to stay off the central field until the official start of the dance at 7:00 p.m. although the outdoor cafeteria was fortunately still open for dinner. Grace wouldn't let Amanda leave the dorms to get food. "Are you kidding? It has to be a surprise. I'll go get you a plate. Stay here. Oh! Margaret, what about that eye shadow—"

"Nope." Amanda raised both hands and shook her head. "I'll wait here for food, Grace, but I am *not* wearing makeup."

"Why?"

"That's where I draw the line. Not my thing."

"She looks amazing without it," Margaret agreed. "Don't you dare leave the dorms until we're all ready to go to the dance together, got it?"

Laughing at the ridiculousness of the other girls' excitement, Amanda finally agreed and stayed in the building. However, she went back down the hall to her room instead of waiting in Annabelle's. Part of her hoped Summer was in her room right across the hall, but the door was closed, and she couldn't hear anything through it over the excited chatter of the other girls on the third floor as they all got ready for the dance too.

One night. It'll be over tomorrow. Then everyone will go back to normal, and I can focus on getting better at magic.

CHAPTER TWENTY-THREE

Although everyone else was dressed up as much as possible—including the guys—she still felt ridiculous when she walked out of the girls' dorm with Grace's arm linked through hers.

"Don't look so nervous." Grace grinned at her. "You look amazing."

"Thanks. I guess. You too."

"Really? Thanks. This is the first time I've gotten to wear this dress. I wish I had better shoes, but it's not like they were gonna let us go out for a shopping trip."

"Not like we have any money to go shopping with either," Annabelle added.

"Please." Margaret laughed and playfully rolled her eyes. "We never had to *buy* anything in LA."

"Yeah, but no one knew who we were in LA. Now we have files at an official magic school with our names on them. You wanna have a bunch of theft on your record forever?"

The students filed out of the dorms in one giant horde and headed for the central field, which was officially open now that the dance was starting. The teachers had sectioned it off from the dorms and the kitchen with a massive archway of twisting vines spanning the entire length of the field. Hanging from the archway was some kind of shimmering fabric that hid everything behind it from view, and a banner of deep blue and emerald green fluttered at the top of the archway—Homecoming at the Academy of Necessary Magic.

"This is it." Grace bit her bottom lip in excitement although it didn't get rid of her grin. "What do you think the theme is?"

"They didn't give us a clue," Margaret said. "I guess some kind of nature theme, judging by the vines and the colors."

"There's a theme?" Amanda asked.

"Yeah, there's always a theme. At least, that's what Evi said. *She* went to school in..."

Amanda tuned out Annabelle's chatter when she caught sight of what lay beyond the archway as a group of students passed through the fluttering curtain ahead of them. When it was their turn, it took everything she had not to whisk her arm out of Grace's and run through the curtain on her own.

Then they passed beneath the archway and into what looked like a completely different world.

The teachers had transformed the field to look like the bottom of the ocean. Magical lights floated through the air, casting flickering blue and white to mimic light refracted through water. A banquet table with piles of cakes, cookies, brownies, and a huge bowl of turquoise punch was at the far end of the field. The dance floor in the center reflected the same watery lights, and the bright pinks and oranges on the surface that made it look like coral had to be one of Calsgrave's illusions.

Lining the field to show the dance floor's boundary were huge strands of artificial kelp eight feet tall, enchanted to float slowly back and forth as if they grew out of the ocean floor instead of the grass in the swamp. Amanda couldn't find the speakers pumping out lilting instrumental music with the occasional sound of rippling bubbles and a far-off whale song between the melody, but the sound completed the Homecoming theme's feel.

The students milled around the center field, most of them heading straight for the dessert table and the punch. When everyone made it through the archway, a puff of dark blue glittering smoke erupted over the stage—which had been decorated with similar strands of kelp, another archway, and four pillars of what looked like white stone but was probably Styrofoam. Or another illusion.

The music died, and Principal Glasket stepped through the glittering blue smoke wearing a gown that looked made from seaweed and seafoam. She'd even painted her face not with regular makeup but with glittering blue and green to make her skin and neck look like glistening scales covered them. The principal spread her arms, and she didn't use a microphone this time to address the student body. Her voice amplified across the field, also with a watery-sounding echo.

"Welcome to Homecoming," she said. Some students cheered and whooped and whistled. "We want all of you to enjoy yourselves as we kick off the first of many dances and celebrations like this at the Academy of Necessary Magic. As you can see, the theme we've chosen this year is Atlantis. The underwater city of Earth legend, of course. Not the original home of Atlantean Oricerans.

"Now, I have a few announcements to make before we get down to the festivities. First, I want to thank your teachers and the rest of our incredible staff at this school for helping to create such a magical night for us. Yes, pun intended. Although our Louper team didn't bring home a win during the match yesterday, I also want to congratulate our team. Their training is starting to pay off, and as human tradition also dictates on Earth, Homecoming is partially to celebrate our athletes, no matter the sport or skill. Oh, and there's no curfew or Lights Out tonight—"

The students broke into raucous cheers.

"However, that doesn't mean you have a free pass to run around like a bunch of crazies tonight. Have fun!"

Someone turned the music back up, and the students returned to their small groups of friends for conversations. Only a handful tried to dance to the watery music playing from what must have been Mr. LeFor's hidden speakers somewhere.

Amanda finally slipped her arm from Grace's and pointed at the dessert table across the field. "You want a cookie?"

"Not right now, thanks. *You* obviously do. Go ahead. I'll find you later when it's time for the *real* dancing."

Annabelle wrinkled her nose and glanced around the field. "Someone should change the music. This is supposed to be a dance, right? Not an underwater expedition in costumes."

Margaret snickered. "Yeah, I think Glasket spent too much time behind a research desk before they gave her this job. Hey, Mikey!"

"Yeah?" A short boy with spiky black hair approached them, his eyes darting in every direction but at the girls themselves.

"Somebody's gonna take care of the music, right?"

"Yeah. Pete's on it. He'll have it fixed in no time. As long as LeFor didn't move the controls again."

Amanda took the opportunity to slip away from Grace and the others and made her way across the coral-looking dancefloor toward the banquet table. She grabbed two chocolate chip cookies and stepped away; otherwise, she'd end up snatching the whole plate.

"Look at you in a dress."

She spun and puffed out a sigh when she saw Summer approaching the table. "Why are you always sneaking up on me?"

"Not always. Only when you're distracted." The girl leaned over the end of the table and grabbed one of each different kind of cookie she could reach from there.

"So what made you show up?"

Summer shrugged. "Wanted to see what all the hype was about. Didn't expect *you* to get so dressed up."

"Yeah, well, it was easier to be someone else's makeover guinea pig than have to explain why I didn't want to."

Cookie crumbs fell from the other girl's mouth as she looked Amanda up and down. "I like it. Kind of…fancy badass."

"Ha. Thanks. You too." She nodded at Summer's all-black outfit—a pleated mini-skirt with studs, a tank top with only one strap and a giant bow on the back, and tall combat boots. "Especially the boots."

"I figured they're the perfect mix of 'Fine, I'll be here' and 'Nobody talk to me.'" They both laughed, then Summer nodded toward the stage decorated with fake seaweed and the four white columns. "*That* looks familiar."

"At least there's no pedestal with a purple stone on it. Then we'd probably have to 'fess up to taking the thing."

"Nah." Summer crammed another cookie into her mouth. "They have no idea. I plan to keep it that way. You should too."

"Trust me. I'm not telling anyone."

"I believe you, shifter girl."

"Coulier!" Jackson jogged toward her with his hand in the air. Summer looked the wizard up and down, rolled her eyes, then took off around the perimeter to watch the rest of the dance on her own. Jackson watched her briefly, then chuckled. "What's up with *her*?"

Amanda shrugged. "I think she showed up for the cookies."

"Yeah, me too." He wouldn't stop staring at her as he said it, and he didn't reach for any of the desserts on the table behind her.

"You okay?"

"What? Yeah. Of course, I'm okay. I just…I mean, you're wearing a dress."

She laughed. "It wasn't my first choice—"

"You look great. I mean, good. You look…whatever." Jackson leapt at the table and crammed a fistful of fudge squares into his mouth. Then he said something else unintelligible through the mouthful.

"What?"

He circled a finger in the air and rolled his eyes as he chewed.

A harsh squeal burst from the invisible speakers, and the warbling instrumental music cut out. Two seconds later, the quick, heavy bass of a new song blasted across the field, followed by an electronic melody growing steadily louder.

"Yes!" Jackson swallowed. "That's what I'm talking about!"

The other students cheered as the first EDM track got everyone moving to the music. Then the electronic voice came through with a string of cussing repeated with the new rhythm.

Principal Glasket looked horrified as she stood beside the stage with the other teachers. "What is this? Who chose this music?"

Mr. LeFor looked at her with wide eyes. "It wasn't me."

"We can't play *this* at a school dance, Edward!"

"*I* know that."

"Well, *fix* it."

Blinking furiously behind his thick-rimmed glasses, LeFor ruffled his red hair and stormed off toward the main building.

Jackson elbowed Amanda in the side. "Looks like Glasket expected this party to be PG, huh?"

She turned toward him and burst out laughing when he grinned at her and danced wildly to the music, flinging his arms in every direction. "You're right. Those moves are *not* PG."

"I meant the lyrics, Coulier. Although my moves are pretty badass. Come on. Let's dance."

The memory of trying to get Johnny to dance with her and Lisa at a local Everglades party over the summer made her snort. *No point in being* that *much like Johnny.*

"Yeah, okay." She grabbed another cookie and followed him onto the quickly crowding dancefloor.

Grace joined them and had a good laugh at Jackson's moves too. "What are you *doing?*"

"Letting it move through me." He thrust a finger into the air and nodded. "You gotta *feel* the—"

The music shrieked again, stopped, and moved on to a different song. It was still electronic dance music, but this time, there were no lyrics. No one seemed to mind the switch, and the dancing continued.

Amanda caught sight of Pete darting toward the field from the back of the main building and booking it toward the dance floor. He pumped a victorious fist in the air before glancing over his shoulder. Apparently, Mr. LeFor hadn't yet figured out that the culprit had already escaped.

"See?" Grace shouted at her over the music. "This is fun, right?"

"Yeah, now that there's real music."

"Hey, I heard there was gonna be a pie-eating contest later." Jackson whirled around with his crazy dance moves to scan the field. "I'm so down for that. No idea what the prize is, but I bet it's epic. Coulier, you could totally win that."

"I'm good on pie, thanks." Amanda ate the rest of her last cookie and almost sprayed it all over when Jackson's next energetic spin on the dancefloor sent him knocking into a group of senior girls trying to get to the dessert table.

"Hey! I'm dancing here!"

"Go dance somewhere else." The girls shoved him back onto the dancefloor, laughing and rolling their eyes as they finally got to the desserts.

"Psh. No appreciation for skill, huh?" Jackson wiggled his way toward the center of the dancefloor, and the other students moved away to give his flailing arms and legs a wide berth.

Grace shook her head. "The whole 'ignorance is bliss' thing definitely applies to him."

"At least he's having a good time." Amanda went to brush her hair out of her face, remembered Margaret's styling efforts, and dropped her hand as she gazed around the field. "That's what this whole thing is about, right?"

"Hey, you're *finally* getting it!" Grace leaned toward Amanda and whispered in her ear, "Did you hear about what Kevin Archer has planned for later?"

Amanda shook her head.

"I heard he smuggled some kind of magical booze in when the seniors went out to the kemana last week."

"Seriously?"

"Who knows? Might be fun to watch, though."

Amanda didn't have anything to say to that. Sure, most of the other students had spent a long time being practically homeless and having to break the rules a lot to survive. She wondered why they were *still* trying to break the rules when they'd all been given a second chance here at the school.

Yeah, and I break the rules too, don't I?

A faint glimmer of purple light beyond the dance's magical barrier caught her eye. It flickered behind the west wing of the main building, right where the wards around the campus were supposed to be. A brief burst of purple sparks shot into the air and quickly disappeared.

What is *that?*

Grace caught her frown and looked in the same direction, but the purple light was gone. "What's wrong?"

"Nothing. I thought I saw something."

"Yeah, maybe you shouldn't drink anything but that blue punch over there if you already see things."

"Very funny."

CHAPTER TWENTY-FOUR

"Mr. Derbyshire!" LeFor barked. "I did *not* give you permission to—"

"It's fine, it's fine. Really. I got this." Pete waved off the Augmented Technology teacher and hopped up onto the stage. "This one goes out to all the kids who have no idea what they're doing with their life!"

The students cheered.

"Mr. Derbyshire—"

"Wait." Pete spread his arms and grinned. "I guess that's pretty much all of us, right? Wait for it..."

The skinny kid hiked up his skinny jeans, then pointed in the air as the last track faded away. When the new one began—some kind of remix, as far as Amanda could tell—he stomped his foot on the stage and nodded.

The other kids cheered and bounced around on the dance-floor, pumping their fists in the air.

Amanda turned toward Grace. "What's this?"

"You don't know Dagger Head?"

"Who?"

"Only the best magical DJ on the West Coast! Just wait. It gets better."

Amanda glanced at Pete, who was now doing some kind of shuffling dance across the stage before Principal Glasket pointed at the ground for him to get off. The witch still couldn't hide her small, partially amused smile when Pete took a flying leap into the closest students on the dancefloor and went right back to dancing.

So maybe not everyone's *getting in trouble for breaking the rules. Maybe there* are *no rules during Homecoming. Probably not the best idea with these kids...*

Another round of cheering went up when the rhythm of the song changed. The students jumped around in a sea of bobbing heads and pumping fists, then somebody screamed at the other side of the field.

"Yeah! It's awesome!" Pete shouted in reply.

Amanda turned toward the scream but couldn't see a thing through all the bodies. So she darted away from the dancefloor to get a better look.

"Hey, where are you going?" Grace asked.

"I heard something."

"Amanda! Hold on!"

She slipped through the other dancing bodies, and someone else screamed this time. When she stepped out onto the grass and headed farther away from the dance to look across the campus, the silhouettes of four students were visible in the darkness. They raced toward the central field, stumbling over themselves and turning to look over their shoulders.

"Everybody look out!" one of the junior boys shouted. "Get out of the way!"

Over the music and the cheering and the stomping feet on the dance floor, nobody heard him but Amanda.

"Get out!" Candace Jones screamed. "They're heading right for the field!"

Amanda took off toward them, and the farther away she got from the magical lights floating around the dancefloor, the more her vision adjusted to the dark. One of the four kids hurrying toward them was limping, clutching his leg, and the other one kept grabbing his friend's wrist to help him forward.

"Hey, what happened?"

"We were screwing around." The injured kid grimaced, his hands slippery and covered in his blood. "I had no idea they were so—"

An angry squeal rose from the swamp at the edge of the campus, and the four kids barreled past Amanda toward the dancefloor. "Watch out! Everybody look out!"

Then she saw the enormous wild boar burst through a wall of cattails, heading right for the center of the field.

Only one. That's easy enough—

Two more darted after the first, squealing and grunting and churning up large clods of dirt behind them as their toed hooves moved with desperate speed across the grass. Four more followed, and she didn't wait to see how many more boars raced toward them from the swamp. She spun and booked it toward the dance.

"Look out! Hey!" She waved her arms over her head. "There's a bunch of—"

Someone else screamed when three more wild boars burst through the shimmering curtain hanging from the archway and charged right into the field full of dancing kids.

"What the—" Mr. Petrov leapt aside when one of the beasts charged him, then pointed at it and let off a red dart of light. It struck the boar in its hindquarters and sent the thing skidding across the grass, squealing and writhing to get back to its feet. Then it charged again.

"No, no, wait!" Amanda shouted. "That'll make them—"

The dessert table flew sideways and crashed to the ground, scattering cookies and brownies and other desserts into the dancing crowd. More students screamed and shouted and fled in every direction. The teachers tried to find the wild animals in the darkness, summoning their attack spells that stood out like beacons, illuminating their faces.

They won't be able to see anything like that—

"Amanda!" Summer shouted.

She spun to see the giant boar with huge, stained tusks lowered as it charged.

There wasn't any time to think about it. She shifted and leapt aside, landing on the grass on all four paws as the boar barreled right into her clothes before stumbling and crashing to the ground with a shriek.

"We're being attacked!" Corey shouted, raising both his large, meaty hands in the air and barreling through the other panicked students. "Someone's trying to kill us!"

Then everyone completely lost their shit.

Spells flew in every direction. Kids stumbled over each other and the scattered dessert. The glass punch bowl skittered across the dance floor and shattered. The teachers shouted for everyone to calm down, but they didn't sound calm at all.

Amanda ignored all of it and focused instead on the scent of almost a dozen wild boars running loose across the campus, all of them as terrified as the students and teachers, and no one else knew it.

She darted after the closest boar charging toward a wide-eyed junior girl who stood there, frozen. With a snarl, she leapt at the thing and snapped at its back legs. The boar squealed and darted sharply to the left before racing off toward the swamp again. Amanda spun and took off after the next strongest scent.

"Holy shit, it's a wolf!"

"Get out of the way, man. That thing will bite your face off!"

"I *hate* the Everglades!"

With a snarl, Amanda leapt through the scattering students and barreled into the side of a mud-splattered boar charging

Principal Glasket's turned back. The beast squealed and rolled twice across the grass before scrambling up again and taking off for the main building. It ran head-first into the glass door, writhed around again, and got up one more time to make a swerving, unbalanced race back into the swamp.

Glasket spun and stared at Amanda with wide eyes and her mouth hanging open.

The gray wolf darted off again to snap at a much smaller boar squealing and running in circles. As soon as it took off away from her, something heavy and hard rammed into her hind legs and sent her skittering across the grass. When she righted herself, the biggest beast of them all was already charging toward her with a growling grunt, shredded strips of her borrowed dress dangling from one of its tusks.

She snarled at the thing and waited until the last second.

"Miss Coulier!" Glasket shouted and launched a fireball at the boar. It glanced off the top of the thing's back and did little more than singe the thick, bristly hairs on its hide before it swung both deadly sharp tusks toward the gray wolf waiting for it.

Amanda leapt aside and twisted in midair to snap her jaws down around the boar's backside. Its rear legs gave out, and it screamed before she let it go. That didn't stop her from racing off after it, snapping and snarling until the thing disappeared through a stand of mangroves at the edge of the swamp, snapping off branches and leaves before it splashed into the shallow water.

Then she turned back and trotted in a wide circle around the central field and the dancefloor, sniffing the air and panting. *There better not be any more.*

There didn't seem to be.

The music still pumping from the invisible speakers echoed across the campus, and when an electronic musical explosion sounded, it startled the last boar from where the thing had been rooting around in the scattered desserts. It squealed and scurried off, bashing against the side of the overturned banquet table before zigzagging back toward the water's edge.

There. Now they're gone.

Only then did she notice that the entire student body was staring at her—the small gray wolf standing fifty feet outside the decorated dancefloor. Nobody said a thing.

Uh-oh.

Amanda sat on her haunches and licked her muzzle, searching the stupefied faces all turned toward her.

I can't shift back.

"Mr. Petrov," Glasket muttered.

"Huh?"

"Hand me your dinner jacket."

The Combat Training teacher stared blankly at her. "You want—"

"Right now, Stanley. I'm pretty sure that animal raced off with the last of Miss Coulier's clothes on its tusks. Give me your jacket!"

The wizard leapt into action and peeled off his jacket before she snatched it from him and hurried across the field in her seafoam dress, her heels clicking harshly on the dancefloor. The students had already started to whisper to each other in surprise when she reached Amanda with her lips pressed firmly together.

"Did you know she was a *shifter*?"

"Did the *teachers* know?"

"She's even scrawny as a wolf."

"Watch. I bet she'll bite Glasket's hand off."

"Dude, shut up."

Glasket lowered herself to the grass in her fancy underwater-theme gown and held out Petrov's long dinner jacket in both hands. "That was very well done, Miss Coulier. Surprising to see, of course, but you handled the issue."

Amanda stared at the teacher and let her wrap the jacket

around her back. It smelled like Mr. Petrov's overwhelmingly strong cologne with an undercurrent of old, stale coffee.

"I'll have to ask you to change back now," Glasket whispered. "To put everyone else a little more at ease, if you don't mind."

With a low whine, the girl shifted back into her human-like form and immediately grabbed the edges of Petrov's jacket to wrap them tighter around herself. "Sorry."

"Don't be sorry, Amanda." Glasket slowly stood. "I don't think anyone else here had any idea how to handle the situation. What happened?"

"There were some kids—oh. He's hurt."

"Who?"

"One of the kids. I think they scared the boars and—"

"Principal Glasket!" Candace shouted. "Principal Glasket! Rob's hurt!"

Glasket stormed toward the group of students who'd tried to warn the rest of the school as Amanda rose to her feet and turned away from the dancefloor, mostly so she could finish buttoning the dinner jacket that didn't cover as much as she wanted.

"Hey." Summer approached her, looking over her shoulder at the stunned students now crowding around Candace and the other kids as Rob wailed in agony, and Principal Glasket told him to suck it up at least until Nurse Aiken could have a look. "You could probably make a getaway now while that giant baby howls up a storm. I left my backpack on the other side of that weird arch thing."

"You still have an extra set of clothes in there?"

"Always."

With a tight laugh, Amanda kept her head down and quickly walked off with Summer. "That was weird."

"No, that was awesome. Seriously." They skirted around the archway, and Summer grabbed the extra sweats from her backpack, holding them out and looking away while Amanda quickly pulled them on. "Leave it to this place to get attacked by a bunch of pigs—"

"Boars."

"Whatever."

"They were scared. I think Candace and those other kids stumbled onto their den and freaked them out. Which was stupid."

Summer burst out laughing. "You sound like you've chased around a bunch of wild boars a few times."

Amanda smirked. "A few, yeah. I'm pretty sure those panicked. A bunch of dancing kids and loud music didn't exactly help." She clenched her eyes shut and shook her head. "Now everyone knows what I am."

"Oh, come on." Summer tossed Petrov's jacket aside and thumped Amanda on the back. "It was gonna happen sooner or later, right? Might as well make the reveal in badass style as you did."

"I guess…"

They stared at each other, and her shifter hearing picked up the muttered conversations of the students as they all talked about her—the shifter girl.

"Miss Coulier?" That was Principal Glasket. "Did anyone see where she went?"

"Behind the curtain," someone replied.

Summer shook her head. "Screw 'em. You don't have to—"

"No, it'll be worse now if I keep hiding and try to pretend this never happened." Amanda shot the other girl a tight smile, then stalked off toward the curtain in the archway again. Pulling the hood of the zip-up sweatshirt over her head was probably as close as she would get to having any privacy tonight. *Now I'm definitely the odd one out at this school.*

CHAPTER TWENTY-FIVE

"Hey, there she is!"

Amanda had no idea who shouted it, but the second she stepped through the curtain, a cheer rose from the students. Stopping in surprise, she looked up to see most of the kids scattered around the field grinning and nodding at her, clapping or whistling or watching her with approval.

Definitely not what I expected.

Her smile felt tight and not precisely genuine. She caught a fleeting glimpse of Principal Glasket guiding Rob toward the main building to see Nurse Aiken. The kid limped and groaned, and Candace and the other two kids who'd snuck off from the dance with him huddled together on the dancefloor, scowling.

"Coulier!" Jackson jogged toward her, looking her up and down with a mixture of awe and apprehension. "Holy shit. I mean, yeah, I guess we all expected you to be something awesome, but a *shifter*? You should've said something."

"Why?" Grace asked, beside him. "It's none of your business. Or any of us ours."

"Well, it kind of is now, huh?" He gestured at the other

students, most of whom had now gone back to dancing on the dessert-strewn floor as the music continued. A few still watched Amanda with eager grins, whispering to each other when they thought she wasn't looking. She could hear most of what they said.

Of course, they don't think I fit in here. Nobody does. I'll prove them all wrong.

She even heard Mr. Petrov muttering to Ms. Ralthorn as he leaned toward her. "What the hell was that dwarf *teaching* her?"

"I heard there was a lot of hunting involved. Which would explain all *this*."

"That was pretty awesome, though." Jackson stepped toward Amanda and clapped a hand on her shoulder. "You look like yourself again when you're not in a dress. Hey, how'd you learn to do that?"

"Do what?"

"Chase giant pigs away from people."

Summer snorted and folded her arms. "They're boars."

"Same thing, isn't it?"

Amanda shot him a crooked smile. "Not exactly. I just—"

"Check it out." David Grady sniggered and walked toward her and her friends, surrounded by the other Louper players who never left his side since Mr. LeFor had named him team captain. "We have a magical sheepdog to round up the pigs and send 'em back home. *That's* why you're really here, isn't it?"

She knew he was trying to get to her. Right now, after the boars crashed the dance and she'd revealed her biggest secret to everyone all at once, she didn't want to get into it with another kid.

No point in fighting.

"Whatever." She turned around and headed back toward the archway.

"Hey, I didn't say you could go, *shifter*," David snarled, summoning a blotchy spell of flickering orange light in his large hand. "'Cause now we need to set some ground rules. Can't have you running around wolfing out on us all the time. Gives you a pretty unfair advantage."

"Because you're failing your magic classes doesn't give her an advantage," Grace retorted.

"Nobody asked you." David pointed at her, then gestured toward the dance floor. "Go take your fancy ass back to the party before you break a nail or something."

Grace glared at him.

"I'm going to bed," Amanda said. "Grace, it's fine. I don't care."

"Yeah, well I do," David shouted. "There's a reason nobody wants to keep shifters around. You don't belong here."

Now there was a crowd growing at the far end of the field where the junior Louper player wouldn't leave her alone. A larger number of students were sniggering at her now, pointing, laughing, whispering to each other about whatever they thought she *really* was.

"If you're trying to fight me," she told David, "it's not gonna happen."

"Of course not. You still need a collar. Maybe a nice fenced-in yard out here so you can run around without—"

"Will you shut the hell up already?" Summer stormed toward the huge half-Kilomea junior. "Whatever you're trying to do, you're making yourself look even more like an idiot. I thought that was impossible until right now."

David looked her up and down and snorted. "You a shifter too?"

"What? No. I'm not an insecure assbag who thinks he's better than everyone because he plays on the only Louper team in existence that hasn't won a single game yet."

The other team members looked at their captain in confusion, and even David looked confused for a second to find a girl who hadn't been with them in LA standing up to him like this. He tried to chuckle and folded his arms. "What're you gonna do about it?"

"I'm telling you to shut up and leave her alone."

"Make me."

With a sigh, Summer glanced at Amanda and shrugged. "Yeah, okay."

She jumped toward the half-Kilomea and shot her hand out toward him, launching a brilliant burst of strobing yellow light. He yelped and raised a hand to shield his eyes, also blocking his view of Summer darting in to land a surprisingly hard uppercut to his gut. David grunted and crashed to his knees.

"Hey!" one of the sophomore players shouted. "You can't—"

Summer punched him in the face and shoved him into the other team members.

"My fucking nose!" Blood poured between his fingers clamped down over his face.

She spread her arms and stared at them. "Anybody else wanna start being a dick all of a sudden? 'Cause I promise I'm really good at dealing with assholes."

The kid with the bloody nose groaned before racing across the field. David struggled to his feet, gasping, and glared at the black-haired girl. "You're an idiot if you want a shifter for a friend."

"Say that again. I dare you."

"Summer." Amanda grabbed the girl's arm and gave it a warning squeeze. "Let it go. I don't wanna spend another weekend scrubbing walls."

"Naw, this guy has it coming." Summer pulled her arm away and jerked her chin up at David. "Are you gonna run away from this like your friend or what?"

He snorted and rubbed his sore stomach. "You're pathetic."

Still, he turned and stalked back toward the other kids revving up with the dancing again now that the wild boars were gone and Amanda looked like a girl instead of a wolf.

"Yeah, and you won't make it through the first *five* minutes of the next Louper game," Summer shouted after him. "I have a bet going already!"

Jackson ran a hand through his hair and stared at her, his mouth gaping open. "I can't believe you hit him."

"Yeah, well, someone had to." Summer turned toward Amanda, breathing heavily and casting angry glances at the backs of the retreating Louper players. "Hey, where's the thing?"

"No."

"Come on. I could use that and knock his dumb ass back to California. He has no idea who he's messing with. Go get it."

"What's the thing?" Grace asked.

"Nothing." Amanda shook her head. *We can't use the crystal we stole from a temple to fight other students.* She hoped Summer could see all that in her gaze as she stared at the other girl and slowly shook her head.

Summer sneered at her. "Whatever. This dance sucks." She blew past Amanda and threw the shimmering curtain aside before stomping through the archway, presumably back to the dorms.

Amanda stuck her hands in the pockets of Summer's zip-up hoodie and wrinkled her nose.

"Wow." Jackson chuckled. "Someone's *really* on Team Shifter, huh?"

Grace smacked his arm. "Why would you say something like that?"

"What? Summer's been a jerk since day one, and now all of a sudden she's punching Louper players in the face because they wanted to fight Coulier. What gives?"

"Maybe she doesn't like bullies." Amanda shrugged.

"Nah, that's not it. She's up to something—"

The music turned off, and Principal Glasket stepped up onto the stage. "Well, that was certainly an unexpected addition to the festivities tonight."

"Turn the music back on!" someone shouted.

"Yeah, we're still dancing!"

The witch blinked furiously as the students started chanting for the music again. Then she rolled her eyes, flicked her hand, and the pumping bass blared through the invisible speakers again. The kids roared their approval and got back to dancing.

"Hey, you think those pigs ate all the cookies?" Jackson didn't wait for a reply. "I'm gonna go find out."

Grace stepped toward Amanda as all the other students at the Academy went back to acting as if nothing had happened, despite the destroyed dancefloor and the overturned table and a handful of students still casting wary glances around the field, looking for more wild boars. "You know, you could've told us."

"I know." Amanda sighed. "It's not something I wanna talk about all that much."

"Sure. I get it. You did a good job of keeping it a secret this whole time, though. I mean, not like it mattered."

"Thanks, I guess."

"So…you and Summer are friends too now, huh?"

"Maybe?" Amanda shrugged. "I didn't expect her to start punching people for me."

Grace barked out a laugh. "Yeah, it's not like you need help defending yourself, right?"

"Grace!" Annabelle waved the witch toward their other group of friends on the dance floor.

"Come on. Let's forget about the whole thing."

"I think I'm gonna go for a walk, but thanks."

"Okay. Hey, don't worry about Annabelle's dress." Grace grinned. "She'll love being able to say a boar ripped it up at a dance. See ya."

The witch raced off to the other kids, and Amanda stood there with her hands in her pockets, frowning at the whole thing.

How is everyone so cool about this? I mean, I guess they're all used to pretty crazy stuff happening in LA. Or whatever.

Slowly, she turned to head back through the curtain in the archway, glancing over her shoulder in case anyone else was still watching her and wanted to finish the fight David had tried to start. Nobody did.

Maybe I don't have to keep hiding.

CHAPTER TWENTY-SIX

Over the next month, Amanda split her free time between meeting with Summer to practice with the purple stone—which they were getting a lot better at using for their classes when they needed it—and being approached during the day by random students who wanted to talk to her about being a shifter.

Where did she come from? When was the first time she shifted? Did she wolf out during the full moon? Could she remember what she did when she was a wolf and not a girl? Did her clothes always come off?

She stuck to answering the questions with two- or three-word sentences. When it became clear that she wasn't into telling the same stories over and over or being bombarded by curious magical kids, the onslaught eventually stopped. Ms. Ralthorn was a lot more careful about what she decided to talk about in History of Oriceran, and Mr. Petrov watched Amanda intently during Combat Training as if he expected her to shift while she ran the obstacle course and use that to her advantage. She didn't. Somehow, that felt like cheating. Mostly, she didn't want to have to go back through the course afterward to pick up her clothes.

She still got the occasional pat on the back in the halls, and a lot more students smiled at her and nodded when they saw her, apparently excited to know a shifter who could fight off wild boars and not get hurt.

The weirdest thing was that Summer refused to talk about that night at Homecoming and always deflected whenever Amanda brought it up.

"Don't get all sentimental on me, shifter girl. I'm not trying to be your hero or anything. Trust me. I like punching idiots almost as much as I like blowing stuff up."

Amanda almost opened up to the other girl a few times about her parents and her sister Claire, but then she thought better of it.

No one wants to hear a sob story. Especially these kids. Everyone has their own, don't they?

The temperate Florida climate meant that the start of fall didn't feel like it the way it did back in New York or most other parts of the country. At least the sweltering heat had decreased as the days grew shorter. Then it was the end of October, and everyone started talking about Halloween.

Pumpkins and dragon-shaped scarecrows appeared in random places around the campus. Mr. Petrov strung up a stuffed dummy from the obstacle course to make it look like a hanged man—making Blake Cameron scream bloody murder the first morning they found it—and said anyone who knocked it down while trying to run the course would also be running laps for two hours after dinner. Day by day, there were more Halloween and fall-themed decorations placed around the school —ghosts, cobwebs, corncobs, and some gadget of Mr. LeFor's that floated in and out of every building and leapt around corners to scare anyone who was there with a pre-recorded howl.

The most visibly excited teacher was Ms. Calsgrave. During their last day of classes before Halloween, she'd stopped her lesson on casting illusions on oneself to change the subject to something completely different.

"As you all know by now, it's almost Halloween."

One of the freshmen in the back raised both hands, wiggled his fingers, and attempted a spooky groan.

"Yeah, yeah. Very funny. Your terrifying qualities put all the fake monsters to shame, Mr. DeVolos." Calsgrave stood from her desk and swept her gaze across the students' faces, her mouth turning up in a knowing smile. "And yes, because Halloween is tomorrow, that does mean no classes. You get a three-day weekend. We'll have another party with games and a *huge* dinner the kitchen's been planning for weeks now. Lots of pie. All the usual Halloween stuff."

"You don't expect us to go trick-or-treating, do you?" Evan asked.

The teacher grimaced. "That wasn't part of the plan, Mr. Hutchinson. We don't have stations for you to walk around and grab candy. No, Ms. Ralthorn and I have something a lot more meaningful in mind."

Grace leaned toward Amanda with a smirk. "This is gonna be good. Whenever she says *meaningful,* she's talking about something completely whacko and out there."

"You mean like that debate she got into with Jasmine about too many illusions darkening your conscience as much as too many lies?"

The blonde witch snorted and pointed at Amanda. "Yeah, like that. What kind of teacher argues *against* what they teach?"

"Now, what some of you may not know is that Halloween is only one name for this incredible power day of the year. Yes, while it's all fun and games and dressing up and scaring people—and trick-or-treating, if you're still in elementary school—there is a deeper, *older* reason to celebrate this day. Anyone heard of Samhain?"

"Sow?" Corey snorted and rolled his eyes. "You're not bringing those stupid pigs back, are you?"

Calsgrave blinked at him in confusion. "I'm sorry?"

"No worries, though," Tommy shouted, turning in his chair to grin at Amanda. "We have the shifter girl who rounds up pigs like it's her job, right Amanda?"

"They were wild *boars*, dummy," Grace shouted back at him. "Did you see those tusks?"

Amanda smirked and stared at her desk. *At least someone's picking up on the differences.*

"No, no, no, Mr. Baker." Calsgrave giggled and waved off the odd turn of conversation. "S-A-M-H-A-I-N. It's the Celtic name for the holiday, and many other Earth cultures have their name for it and ways of celebrating. Beyond what you know as Halloween for costumes and candy, *Samhain* is the day of the year where the veil between the world of the living and the spirit world is thinnest."

"You mean spirits like...dead people?" Blake squeaked, shrinking in her chair.

"Yes, Ms. Cameron. Traditionally, Samhain has been one of the most potent days of the year for connecting with our ancestors' spirits. Not simply the generic version of ghosts."

Tommy snorted. "That's boring."

"Well, you're entitled to your opinion." Calsgrave tapped her fingers on the desk. "So here's what Ms. Ralthorn and I have come up with for this year's Samhain celebration. I've been working with channeling spirits and connecting with ancestors for quite some time. Among all the other activities planned for you during the party tomorrow, I'll also have a booth set up to perform these rituals with each of you. It will count as part of your grade both in this class and in History of Oriceran."

"What?" Summer wrinkled her nose. "Ghosts have nothing to do with school."

"Ah, but they have everything to do with *you*. Also, I prefer the term spirits, Miss Flannerty. Now, while our *magical* ancestors are originally from Oriceran, we all have ancestors who've been living on this planet for generations. They're waiting right behind the veil to reach out and speak to each of you. Hopefully with a clear message, but you'll still get credit for sitting down with an open mind and attempting these ceremonies. It's an important step in each of you learning how to harness your magical abilities and strengths to become the best version of yourselves." Calsgrave cleared her throat and failed to hide another private smile. "No matter what you end up doing when you eventually graduate from the Academy."

"Do we have to, like, make a sacrifice or something?" Jackson asked.

Everyone turned in their seats to stare at him, and Ms. Calsgrave laughed until she realized he was serious. "No, Mr. Pris. The only sacrifice you'll make is your time and whatever reservations you have about sitting down with me during the celebration tomorrow. I *don't* want to see anyone trying to make a joke out of that by trying to torture small animals and blaming it on me, Ms. Ralthorn, or this assignment."

The classroom fell silent.

"Why would any of that happen?" Amanda asked.

The teacher shook her head. "Don't worry about it."

The alarm bell blared across the school, and everyone hurried out of the classroom to head out for dinner, talking about Halloween and the next party of the semester and what they were going to dress up as without access to regular costume shops.

Summer caught up to Amanda in the hall and elbowed her in the ribs. "Is it me, or did that sound like Calsgrave has experience with someone blaming her for animal sacrifices?"

"I have no idea."

"She has that book with the creepy pentagram on it too. I bet she has some kind of satanic ritual for us to help her with, and she won't be able to get any of us to do it without saying it's for class credit."

Amanda stared at her, then they both burst out laughing.

"Seriously, though. You gonna hit up her special ancestor booth?"

"Probably. I mean, we're getting graded on it."

Summer rolled her eyes. "I think it's a load of crap. My *ancestors* weren't anything special. I doubt they'd want to come back to tell me how I'm walking in their footsteps. It'd be cool if my grandma showed up, though. She'd probably end up cursing out all the teachers and trying to throw ghost plates at everybody or something. She did that a lot when she was alive. With real plates, I mean."

"Hey, at least you knew your grandparents." Amanda drew a deep breath of the cooling fall air as they stepped outside and headed across the central field. "Mine died when I was a baby. I don't have any aunts or uncles either, and my parents never really talked about *their* parents, so..."

"Wait, they're *both* only children?"

"Yeah." *They were. They're not anything anymore.*

Summer exaggerated a wince. "I bet *that* was a power struggle."

"What?"

"Nothing. Are you? An only child?"

"No." The same harsh, rigid lump that showed up whenever she got too close to talking about her family formed in Amanda's throat now. She shook her head. "What about you?"

"No." Summer's smile disappeared, and they both stared straight ahead as they made their way toward the outdoor cafeteria. "I *am* the youngest, though. Of four. Pretty sure I was a mistake. My parents had three kids all two years apart, and when they thought they were done, bam. I showed up when my brother Paul was sixteen, and they had to start all over again."

"Wow. That's a long time."

"Yeah. Haven't seen my brothers or sister in...a long time." A tense silence fell between them, then Summer snorted. "Hey, at least they won't show up at Calsgrave's séance, right? What a shitshow *that* would be."

"Yeah. Probably."

Still, Amanda couldn't help but wonder which one of her *ancestors* would attempt to communicate with her "from beyond the veil," if that was a real thing. Maybe it would work at Ms. Calsgrave's table tomorrow. Maybe not. They were getting graded on whether or not they sat with the teacher to attempt it, so that was what she'd do.

CHAPTER TWENTY-SEVEN

The Halloween celebration turned out to be a lot more exciting than Homecoming. The kitchen pixies had laid out an incredible spread on *two* banquet tables in the central field, which someone had decorated with hay bales and corncobs and stuffed scarecrows beneath magically floating strings of white lights stretching from one end of the field to the other. Some kind of screechy violin music that was probably supposed to sound scary came through the invisible speakers, and there were plenty of activities set up to keep people busy—bobbing for apples, pumpkin-carving, and a pie-eating contest this time. There was also a costume contest, which the sophomore class was particularly excited about because apparently, they'd been planning their costumes together for weeks.

Black candles floated around the field, flickering in and out as they moved over the party. Amanda didn't dress up, but she and Grace had a good laugh over trying to figure out what everyone else was supposed to be with the few supplies they'd had at their disposal to make costumes.

"Okay. Billy has to be a..." Grace squinted as they sat on one of the hay bales and stuffed their faces with honeyed ham and steaming-hot dinner rolls. "A computer."

Amanda snorted. "He's missing a few parts. That's cardboard, right?"

"I think so. Oh, jeeze. Of course, Candace would go for skanky nurse."

"Hey, look at Mr. Petrov." Amanda pointed at the banquet table as Petrov turned, his bald head covered in fake blood with a phony ax sticking through one side of his head and coming out of the other.

"Ew. Hey, how does that even work? Aren't those things usually headbands? He's bald, and there's no... Yeah, I don't see a headband."

"I bet it's an illusion."

Grace scoffed. "Figures. Of course, he wouldn't put any effort into a costume."

"Dude, get off me." Alex struggled to shove Jackson away from him as the wizard pushed him across the field toward the pumpkin carving. "They're gross. I don't wanna do it."

"Come on, man." Jackson saw the girls sitting on the hay and winked. "You should see what he can do with wood carving. Listen, Alex. I'll scrape out the seeds and all the goo, okay? You carve the damn thing. Make it good. I'll split the prize with you fifty-fifty."

"*And* give me your extra dessert for a week."

Jackson stared at the half-Wood Elf, then shrugged. "Yeah, sure. Sounds fair to me."

Someone screamed beside the main building, and a group of seniors cracked up laughing when their successful attempt to scare the crap out of Blake sent the girl running back toward the dorms. Amanda rolled her eyes. "That's mean."

"At least it's not more wild animals crashing another party. Hey, are you gonna go sit at Calsgrave's table?"

"Uh...yeah. It's part of our grade, right?"

"Okay. Let's go." Grace grabbed both of their empty paper plates and chucked them into a trashcan decorated with a sign that said, "Toss the Remains in Here." A fake skeleton hand flopped over the side of the trashcan.

The line in front of Calsgrave's table wasn't long; only four other freshmen stood there watching the "ancestor ritual" their Illusions teacher conducted with each one of them. Ms. Ralthorn sat beside Calsgrave, eyeing the entire process with a mix of eager curiosity and poorly masked skepticism.

"Doesn't look like Ralthorn believes in ghosts," Amanda muttered.

"She's probably trying to figure out how to make it make sense with all her *historical facts.* Oh, look. Brandon's up next. You think we'll see any Crystal ghosts?"

Amanda snorted. "Can they shed ice too?"

Calsgrave's muttering was too low for even Amanda to hear, mostly because the witch wasn't saying the full words but imitating the sound of some kind of incantation. She grabbed Brandon's hands and closed her eyes. "Now we're going to call your ancestors to join us. Close your eyes with me, Mr. Everly. Open yourself to communication."

"Uh..."

"It's okay. I'll guide you."

Two black candles floating over her table flickered and sputtered out when a wind kicked up. Brandon's eyes flew open, and he stared at the candles. "What does that mean?"

"Huh. Maybe they're trying to reach you."

"Or maybe it's getting windy," Summer said from the back of the line. "You know, 'cause we're outside."

"Can I go now?" Brandon muttered, staring at the candles.

"Sure." Calsgrave released him and called for the next student in line.

Jasmine's *connection* with her ancestors took less than thirty seconds. The girl burst out sobbing when a white light flickered in the air in front of her. "That's her. That's my Aunt Cheryl."

Even Ms. Calsgrave looked surprised by the immediate response. "Are you receiving a message from her?"

"Yeah. She...she... Oh my God, I'm so sorry!" Jasmine lurched from the chair and raced out of the field, bawling her eyes out.

"Well. Sometimes the messages are that powerful." Calsgrave opened her black book with the pentagram on the cover and flipped through a few pages before shrugging. "Haven't seen a reaction like *that* in a while. Next!"

"You think this is gonna work?" Summer asked.

Grace turned in line and cocked her head. "You sound skeptical."

"I mean, yeah. We're trying to talk to our dead relatives at a *party*."

"You never know until you try it. Right, Amanda?"

Amanda glanced back and forth between her friends—who didn't consider *each other* friends—and tried to hide a smile. "I mean, I'm doing this because it's for a grade—"

"Miss Coulier." Calsgrave waved her forward. "You're up."

"Wish me luck." With an exaggerated hop in her step, she approached the table and slid into the chair across from Calsgrave. "Let's do this."

"All right." Calsgrave and Ralthorn exchanged an amused glance, and the Illusions teacher stretched her hands out over the table to reach for Amanda's. "Take my hands. Relax. Try to clear your mind. Think about reaching out to communicate with—"

"My ancestors. Yeah, I know." Shifting around in the chair, Amanda wiped her palms on her pant legs and took the teacher's hands. "Do I have to say anything specific, or..."

"Nope. We have everything we need right here, and I'll direct the energies so they flow through you. Ready?"

Whatever that means. "Sure."

Calsgrave closed her eyes and muttered the same wordless

chant under her breath. Amanda cracked her eyelids open and studied the table covered in black velvet and lace, white candles, and an actual crystal ball half-buried in more cloth. "What's the crystal ball for?"

"Sometimes it helps with remote viewing."

"What?"

"Shh. Focus on your ancestors." Calsgrave took up her chanting again, and Amanda gently closed her eyes.

This doesn't feel like a real thing. I could blow out a huge sigh, and she'd say spirits were trying to get through.

Before she could laugh at her thought, a cold tingle raced up her hands and into her arms. Calsgrave gasped and released Amanda's hands, her eyes flying open. "Oh. That was… Ms. Ralthorn, hand me that unlit candle if you would."

"Of course." Ralthorn grabbed the thick silver candle from a crate behind the table and handed it over.

"What was that?" Amanda asked, studying her hands.

"Extremely energetic activity, Miss Coulier." Calsgrave's eyes were wide with excitement as she offered the girl a box of matches. "Someone really wants to speak with you."

"Huh."

"Light the candle. Hurry."

After a glance over her shoulder—where Grace nodded in encouragement and Summer rolled her eyes—Amanda struck one of the matches and lit the silver candle.

"Now, focus again on making that connection," Calsgrave muttered. "This is wonderful. Excellent work. We definitely want to keep going."

"I didn't do anything."

"That little flare between our hands says otherwise, Miss Coulier." Calsgrave nodded. "Try again. Focus a little more this time."

This is nuts. Amanda closed her eyes and drew a deep breath. *Okay, ancestors. Whoever you are. I've never met you, but if you're trying to show up and give me a message, now's pretty much the only time I—*

The flame on the silver candle erupted and grew to a full foot in height, making Ralthorn leap back in her chair with a shriek. Now more students were getting interested in Calsgrave's ritual table, and they slowly made their way toward Amanda's not-so-private séance with whatever ancestors made the candle freak out.

"What's going on?"

"Keep going." Calsgrave stared at the massive flame. "This is—"

A thick pillar of green-gray smoke burst from the silver candle, rising high and fanning out to create a roughly circular cloud in the air. Amanda instinctively reached into her hoodie pocket to feel the purple crystal there and instantly regretted it. Because the second her fingers touched the buzzing surface of the magic-amplifying stone, it amplified the message from her ancestors with full force, not only for her to receive but for everyone watching to see for themselves.

Green light flickered inside the thick cloud as the silver candle sputtered and shot flames higher above the table. A strong gust of wind kicked up, ruffling the pages of Calsgrave's open black book until she slammed it shut. Then a howl rose from the green-flashing smoke before three faces appeared in it.

No.

Amanda felt like her heart would explode when she saw the faces of her parents and her sister Claire in the thick cloud. They did not look happy to see her.

Blood matted both of her parents' hair, their eyes sunken and dark as they turned to fix their daughter with warning stares.

"Oh my..." Calsgrave breathed. "These spirits are not at rest, Miss Coulier. Ask them what they want."

Of course, they're not at rest. They were murdered.

Amanda immediately let go of the purple crystal in her

pocket, but it didn't reverse the effects of this visit from her dead family members. "W-what do you want?"

"Danger," her father said, his voice breaking through the cloud as if from miles away instead of three feet in front of her.

"Grave mistake," her mom added, lifting a finger to point at Amanda.

"You must fix it."

"Before it's too late."

"Don't waste any more time."

Amanda swallowed and couldn't find her voice. *This* was what her parents' spirits came back to tell her? That everything she was doing was a mistake? "I don't get it. What mistake?"

One of the students gathered around the table gasped and pointed at the silhouette of Amanda's sister within the cloud. "Holy crap, that's *you*! It's Amanda!"

Right on cue, the image of Amanda's twin sister Claire solidified within the smoke, and Amanda stared in horror. She hadn't had a chance to see her sister like this the night the crime ring known as the Boneblade broke into her house and murdered her family. She'd had a bag shoved over her head before those assholes knocked her out, tied her up, and took her across New York. Now she saw her sister's face, eyes wide in terror, hair also matted with blood, and the side of her face singed from some asshole magical's fiery attack.

"Take it back," Claire said.

The wind howled and kicked up, making everyone around the table stumble against each other.

"Before it's too late for you!" Claire screamed. "It's too dangerous—"

"Okay!" Ms. Calsgrave stood abruptly and shoved everything off the table—the black cloth, the silver candle, and her black book. The second everything toppled into the grass, the candle's flame snuffed out. So did the thick cloud of smoke that had channeled Amanda's most immediate family members—not her ancestors. The wind died instantly, and Calsgrave dusted off her hands. "I think we've had quite enough of that. Thank you, Miss Coulier. Next!"

"Um…" Grace stared at the now bare table in front of their teacher. "Are you sure that's a good idea?"

"Well… Maybe we'll take a fifteen-minute break." Calsgrave smiled weakly at the students standing in line. "Go have a piece of pie or something. Miss Coulier, can I talk to you for a moment?"

Crap.

"Okay." Amanda stood and watched Calsgrave stalk off toward the main building.

"Amanda, that was nuts," Grace said breathlessly. "Was that real?"

"Yeah, I think so."

"Why were you in that smoke all bloody and—"

"I don't know. Gotta go. Sorry." She met Summer's gaze and nodded for the girl to come with her as she turned to follow Ms. Calsgrave.

"Damn, shifter girl." Summer grinned at her. "You have some seriously fucked-up ancestors."

"Those were my parents," Amanda muttered and whipped the crystal out of her pocket to hand it over. "I think this had something to do with it. I forgot I had it. So just…take it, okay?"

"Uh-huh." Summer absently let the crystal drop into her palm and stared at her friend. "Did you say your *parents?*"

Amanda swallowed thickly and pointed at the main building. "I should go. Don't tell anyone else."

"Yeah, I don't even know what I'd say…"

The shifter girl jogged away from the field, trying to drown out the dozens of conversations from the shocked and confused students about what they'd seen. She could hear all of it.

I can't tell them that wasn't me. Then I'll have to get into the whole thing about my family and having a dead twin and how the heck I ended up here afterward. How did this happen?

She finally reached Ms. Calsgrave, who'd stopped outside the main building's front doors to get them far enough away for a private talk. The teacher seemed a lot more pulled together now that she'd had a moment to herself.

"That was a powerful message, Amanda."

"You said this was for connecting with our *ancestors*."

"I did, and it is. Your parents happen to fall into that category."

"A little warning would've been nice."

Calsgrave shook her head and drew a deep breath. "I'm sorry I didn't stop to consider the fact that would happen for you. Honestly, that was the clearest interaction I've seen with spirits from the other side. Do you have any idea how that was possible?"

Amanda stuck her hands in her pockets and tried to make her frown look convincingly clueless. "Nope."

Summer has the crystal, so the teachers can search me all they want.

"Okay. Well, it would make sense that you had such a strong connection tonight because of how recently your parents passed. Who was the girl? The one who looked like you, only..." Calsgrave didn't have to say "dead" or "bloody" or "terrifying." All that had been clear to everyone who'd seen the spirits of Amanda's murdered family members.

"That was Claire," Amanda muttered, trying to swallow that thick lump in her throat again. "My twin."

"I see." Calsgrave's mouth popped open, and she struggled with finding something else to say.

"Sorry about crashing the Halloween party. Samhain party. Whatever."

"No, don't be sorry. That wasn't your fault. I... Well, honestly, I had no idea anything quite like *that* was possible. If you'd like to talk more about what happened—"

"I don't, but thanks." Amanda stared at the grass and kicked the sole of her sneaker back and forth across the blades. "I'm gonna go lie down or something."

"Sure. Of course. I'll be at my table for the rest of the night. If you need anything, you know where to find me."

"Yep." She tried to smile at the teacher as Ms. Calsgrave set a gentle hand on her shoulder, then the woman walked quickly back toward the central field to pick up where she'd left off.

No one else is gonna have anywhere near the same kind of connection. *Wish I'd found a dead body instead of seeing Mom and Dad like that.*

Trying to push the image of her parents and sister out of her mind, Amanda took off through the buildings and headed for her favorite spot behind the outdoor cafeteria. At the very least, she could hang out beneath the mangroves and think of something else—anything else—before heading to bed. It would probably be impossible to get to sleep.

CHAPTER TWENTY-EIGHT

She stayed out there by the edge of the swamp through the rest of the Halloween party, listening to the conversations and the dancing and laughter slowly die out as the students turned in for the night or headed somewhere else in small groups. No one came looking for her until almost midnight, and the only one who tried turned out to be Summer.

Amanda heard her coming although the other girl tried to be quiet and sneaky. "I'm fine."

"Oh, yeah. Obviously. You came out here to spend the rest of a Friday night with some trees and stinking saltwater."

"There's some mud too." Amanda grabbed a handful of the thick mud at her side before slopping it back onto the bank.

"Fun." Summer stopped beside her and lowered herself to the ground.

"Did you do the whole 'talk to your family's ghosts' thing too?"

"Yeah. I mean, I didn't touch the crystal at the same time, so I'm pretty sure I'm the only one who saw or heard what I did."

"I had no idea that would happen."

"I know."

The girls sat silently for a moment, listening to the wind through the cattails and the occasional skitter and *plop* of some nocturnal creature moving through the swamp.

"So what the hell was all that about with the ghosts?" Summer asked. "Like, some creepy future version of you if you don't 'fix the mistake?'"

She tried to make a joke out of it, but Amanda could only sigh morosely and shake her head. "That was my sister."

"Whoa. For real?"

"Yeah. Claire." The shifter girl clenched her eyes shut and swallowed. "I thought ghosts or spirits or whatever only looked like that in movies."

"Calsgrave said they weren't at rest yet, right?"

"Yeah."

"What…" Summer tossed her bangs out of her eyes and stared out at the dark swamp. "What happened?"

Amanda twisted to look up at her. "If I tell you, you can't tell anyone else. I haven't actually… I mean, I haven't talked about it. 'Cause it's—"

"Shitty?"

A wry chuckle burst from the shifter girl's lips. "Yeah, you could say that."

"Don't worry about it, shifter girl. If anyone can handle shitty, it's me. I was raised on it, so…"

"Okay, okay." Amanda wrung her hands in her lap and wrinkled her nose as she studied the dark shadows of the trees playing across the moon's reflection on the water. "My family was killed in May."

"This last May?"

"Yep."

"Jesus."

"Some crime ring or gang or whatever. I guess they found out about my family. That we're shifters. I'm pretty sure they tried to take Claire *and* me, but my parents fought back. Didn't help. I'm the only one who made it out after that, and it wasn't 'cause I ran away."

"Damn."

Amanda shook her head. "Next thing I knew, I woke up in this gross basement. Like, in a cell. Bunch of other girls passed out in other cells. Kidnapped. I almost escaped once."

"For real?" Summer's eyes widened. "How'd you do that?"

"Shifted and tore a guy's throat out. Crashed the van we were in."

"Holy *shit*." The other girl playfully slapped Amanda's shoulder with the back of a hand. "I *knew* you were badass."

"I guess. Still got caught again, though. Turns out these guys were kidnapping girls from all over the place to sell us. Obviously, that didn't happen to me."

Summer didn't have anything to say to that but kept listening.

"Johnny's the one who found me before I ended up somewhere horrible. He and Lisa. She's a Fed."

"Magical?"

"Yep." Amanda stripped a handful of grass from the earth and chucked it at the water. "Then he kinda took me in. So that's where *I'm* from. I haven't been back to my old house since those assholes mur—since they did what they did to my family. I knew they were gone. I wanted to stay with Johnny, and he let me. Then I wanted to come here."

"Shit." Summer ran a hand through her hair and let out a heavy sigh. "I had no idea."

"Yeah, most people don't. I kinda wanna keep it that way."

"I totally understand. I would too." Summer smirked. "Makes you *way* more badass than I ever expected, though."

"Feels more depressing than anything else, honestly."

"Yeah, but you're not depressing. You're here. Those weenies out in the field were screaming their heads off because actual ghosts showed up, and you sat there like it was no big deal."

Amanda shrugged. "I'm pretty sure I was in shock."

"Ha. Yeah, probably."

"So what did you see with *your* 'ancestor-ritual' thing?"

Summer grimaced and leaned back to prop herself up with her hands in the grass. "My grandma. You know, the one I said would probably cuss everyone out and start throwing shit."

"Is that what happened?"

"I mean, you know… Yeah. She basically told me a bunch of crap about how much of a failure I am and no wonder my parents don't wanna talk to me and I should go blah, blah, blah. I'm the only one who saw it, though. Told Calsgrave I saw some beautiful lady with flowing locks saying she was here to guide me toward my life's purpose. She ate that up like candy."

Amanda snorted, then they both cracked up laughing.

When they quieted, Summer tilted her head back and forth. "Not nearly as crazy as having my whole family murdered, though."

Hearing that sentence out loud made Amanda freeze. No one had said that before—that they'd been *murdered*. Not Johnny, not Lisa, not even Amanda herself. Because that finally made it officially real.

"I'm trying to move past it, you know?"

"Who wouldn't?"

"That *is* why I came here, Summer. Why I actually wanna be here. I *have* to get better at everything there is to learn here so I can make sure the same thing doesn't happen to some other kid. Who knows? Maybe my family's spirits will fizzle out and quit being so creepy at Halloween parties."

Summer snorted. "That's probably a good start. So you *are* into this whole bounty hunter thing, huh?"

"Yep. That's exactly what I'm gonna do when I graduate."

"I mean, it's cool that you know. Not like I had much choice coming here, but hey. There's still plenty of time for me to figure out what I wanna do after school. Still haven't made up my mind about the whole bounty hunter thing yet. I'm pretty sure I'll end up doing something in explosives. Probably."

Amanda tried to shoot the other girl a warning glance but burst out laughing instead. "Follow your passions, I guess. Right?"

"Yeah, right down into a secret temple under the swamp."

After the Halloween party, Amanda was more hesitant to touch the stone she and Summer had found. She still took it for Illusions and Augmented Technology, but it stayed in her pocket, and she had to actively force herself not to stick her hands in her pockets too.

Thin veil between worlds or not, I'll never be able to focus and get better at magic here if I get another visit from Mom, Dad, and Claire. Who told me I'm making a mistake. Did they mean I'm not supposed to be at the Academy?

Besides the occasional run as a wolf after slipping through the hole in the dorm's wards—and even those were short and vigorous, spending all her extra energy so she could get to sleep—the only other effective way to distract herself from thinking about her family was watching Louper practice. Oddly enough, watching the team train with the headsets as their magical avatars helped calm her down and focus her mind. Mr. LeFor took notice of the young shifter girl sitting against the wall of the training building to watch the small projection of the team's virtual field, but he didn't tell her to leave. David, the team captain, didn't say anything to her about it either, most likely because Summer had made her point at the Halloween party and also because Amanda wasn't disturbing the team's practices.

This way, Amanda learned everything there was to learn about the game without actually putting on one of those headsets and stepping into a practice herself.

I could. I wouldn't have to train nearly as hard as any of the other players here. I know all the rules.

Plus, she had access to Mr. LeFor's training by listening in and watching.

When the team's fourth Louper match rolled around, Amanda was the first student spectator sitting in her seat in the central field to watch the projection. The players huddled around Mr. LeFor for their coach's pep talk about the upcoming game—how winning didn't matter so much as improving their game scores, stats, and skills. "Still, try not to get yourselves kicked off the field in the first fifteen minutes, okay? That's all I want you guys to focus on this time around."

The seats slowly filled as the students came to watch the game. Only about half of them showed up this time. It was a Friday night, after all, and the Florida Gators hadn't won a single game yet. Amanda had told Grace, Alex, and Jackson that she wanted to watch the game and start getting involved, but her friends were among those who didn't feel like it was worth it to sit through another game as they watched their rough-and-tumble new team fall to another loss.

"Besides, I'm trying to finish that writeup for Ralthorn," Grace had said, glancing awkwardly at Jackson and Alex. "You know, describing how our little *talk* with our ancestors on Halloween ties into our personal history as a magical. I think it's a stupid assignment, honestly, but I don't wanna fail."

"Yeah, me neither," Jackson had added, scratching his head and avoiding looking at Amanda. "Maybe we'll join you for the next game."

Both of them had left dinner early, and Amanda couldn't help but ask Alex what was going on with them.

The half-Wood Elf shrugged and tossed his long brown ponytail back over his shoulder as he leaned over his bowl of soup. The loud slurp from his spoon didn't buy him much time. "They're a little freaked out about the whole dead family thing."

"What?"

"You know. That you didn't tell any of us first."

"Are *you* freaked out about it?"

He looked up at her with his bright green eyes and slowly shook his head. "They'll get over it."

That was what Amanda kept telling herself as she sat on a folding metal chair in the center field before the next Louper match. *They'll all get over it. So will I. I didn't come here to make everyone else feel comfortable. I came here to be the best.*

Her hand almost went into the pocket of her loose sweatpants, but she stopped herself before her fingers got anywhere close to the purple crystal resting against her thigh.

The Master of Ceremonies' voice came through the magical-virtual projector, announcing the start of the game between the Academy's Florida Gators and the New Orleans Crawfish. As the team broke their huddle and strapped on their headsets, David turned and immediately found Amanda sitting in the crowd. The half-Kilomea upperclassman sneered at her and jerked the headset down over his eyes.

"You'd think he'd enjoy having any die-hard fans at all," Summer said behind her.

Amanda jumped in her seat and turned to glare at the girl before she laughed. "*Still* sneaking up on me?"

"Only when you're—"

"Distracted. Yeah, I know." Amanda nodded at the empty chair beside her. There were a lot more empty chairs beside her these days—at the picnic tables, in class, and now in the center field during Louper games.

With a smirk, Summer stood and slipped through the row of chairs to sit beside her friend. "I bet you'd make the best player on the team with how much you've been hanging around them lately."

The shifter girl snorted. "If Mr. LeFor ever lets me put on a headset. I mean, I'm pretty sure I have one of the highest grades in his class already. It's not like I'm gonna break the gear or kick the whole team out of the game so I can hog the spotlight."

"The spotlight's kinda your style, though, isn't it?"

"Not on purpose."

"Players, take your places and prepare to enter the playing field," the Master of Ceremonies announced, her voice warbly through the projection as it came through from an undisclosed location for this particular match.

"He might let you practice eventually," Summer muttered. "I don't think you'll ever play a game."

Amanda frowned at her. "Why?"

"Reason number one? You're a girl. Number two, you're a shifter, and now everybody knows it, so..." Summer grimaced and shrugged. "I guess the Academy's trying something different from the other schools."

Gritting her teeth, Amanda looked back at the Louper team, each of whom flickered out of existence as they were teleported to the new game field for the match and appeared as their avatars on the projection. "I knew it."

"Oh, yeah?"

"You know, I *asked* him if those were the reasons he wouldn't let me try out for the team. LeFor told me it was because we had detention that weekend. Lied right to my face."

Summer puffed out a sigh and shook her head. "Yeah. They tend to do that."

"Teachers? Tell me about it."

"I was pretty much talking about the entire world, shifter girl. Everybody lies right to our faces. Especially when we're the kind of magical kids nobody wants around."

A cheer went up from the students who'd bothered to attend the match. Amanda stared at the game projection as it panned out to give a wide-angle view of all twelve players on the new field as they found their teammates and took off together to find the prize, whatever that happened to be.

Everyone lies. Maybe that is *the truth. I lied. By omission, sure, but now my secrets are all out, and it still doesn't matter.*

She could hardly pay attention to the match now that she had Summer's oddly insightful statement to mull over in her head.

"No, Montgomery!" LeFor shouted at the projection. "You have to *dodge* his attack and—" The man slapped a palm to his forehead, knocking his glasses to the ground. "There goes another one out for the whole game. Fifteen minutes and thirty-four seconds. At least he made it that far."

LeFor bent to retrieve his glasses and quickly fumbled to right them again on his face.

Spells flashed across the projection as the players battled each other, trying both to knock the other team out of the game and find the hidden prize that ended the game early and won the match for the team that got their hands on it.

Amanda's gaze swept over the projection, but she wasn't paying attention until she saw a glimmer of silver light in the corner. "Oh, wait. There it is."

"What?" Summer glanced at her until Amanda pointed at the projection.

"Bottom right corner. It's a...I don't know. Looks like a giant leaf."

Summer squinted at the projection, then her eyes widened. "Shit. Look at that. You got a good eye for this."

"I mean, it's *glowing*." If she could have screamed at their players to head toward the silver leaf, she would have. However, the projection only worked one way. "If Lenny doesn't get there first, it's game over."

"It'll probably be game over for our team every single match of every single year." Summer slumped back in her chair and shook her head. "I was excited to have this game here, but our players suck."

"Go, go, go!" LeFor shouted as Lenny darted beneath an opponent's fireball blast and headed for the glowing leaf.

"*Or* maybe they're getting better." Summer shrugged. "He's gotten pretty fast! Damn, we might win this."

The students watching the game cheered their player on, and Lenny Burke's avatar leapt toward the glowing leaf, his arm outstretched. Before he could touch the prize, the projection sputtered and went out.

"What happened?"

"Hey, we're still watching!"

"Did we win?"

Now the students were shouting in confusion and anger. Mr. LeFor scowled at his device that kept track of his team's stats and stabbed it. "I don't—"

All six team members were teleported back into the central field simultaneously, without the Master of Ceremonies' announcement of a winner. They whipped off their headsets and looked around.

"What happened?" LeFor shouted. "Did you end the game?"

David shook his head and dangled his headset in front of their coach. "It went black. Nobody won the game. Like, it just turned off."

"Mr. LeFor." Glasket stood from her chair beside the stage. "Is there something wrong with our gear?"

"Of course not." LeFor stabbed his device again. "I have no idea what happened."

The principal frowned and pulled out her cell phone. "I'll see what happened."

Amanda scanned the players' faces—all of them looked confused and pissed, mostly because they'd been on the verge of winning their first game before something knocked them out of the match.

When Glasket returned to the stage and slipped her phone back into her pocket, she raised her hands for the students to quiet down. "I spoke with the dean of the other school. It seems there's been some kind of malfunction within the game system itself. No one won. Until we can figure out what happened, we've both agreed to forfeit the game and call this match a draw."

The students groaned.

"Are you kidding me?" David roared. "We would've won. We should get the points for that."

"It's already agreed on, Mr. Grady. Plus, the system won't reset the game, so there's no more playing anyway."

The team captain snarled and chucked his headset to the ground.

"Hey!" LeFor shouted. "You pick that up right now. Do you have any idea how much time it takes to recalibrate a broken—"

"They're all broken. We're always gonna lose." David glared at the coach, then turned and stomped off across the field toward the dorms. The rest of the team glanced at each other in confusion, then slowly headed after their hulking captain, frowning and scratching their heads as one by one they dropped their headsets into LeFor's duffel bag for their gear.

Amanda watched the teachers approach each other to talk about what happened, and none of them looked sure about how to proceed. Her shifter hearing picked up the conversation easily enough.

"I have no idea what could've done this."

"She said there was some kind of interference with the system. Is that possible?"

"It shouldn't be. This game has been around for a while."

"Well, we need to figure out what happened. If someone got their hands on the system, even long enough to insert a virus or to shut down the game, we'll have a lot bigger problem on our hands than a disappointed student body." Glasket took off toward the faculty building while pulling her phone out again to make more calls.

Amanda leaned toward Summer. "Something's wrong with the gear."

"Ya think?"

"I think it's—" She stopped when a flicker of purple light caught her eye, right behind the faculty building. It was the wards again, and in the confusion around the malfunctioning game, no one else noticed. The scent of sulfur and that odd sweetness hit her again.

"You think it's what?"

"I don't know." Amanda turned to look at Summer and raised her eyebrows. "I'm pretty sure we can find out. Later."

Summer smirked. "As long as we don't get caught again, right?"

CHAPTER TWENTY-NINE

They met in front of the main building that night after Lights Out. Amanda had already shifted back and put her clothes on again, and she reached the front doors as Summer pulled two lockpicks from them. "See? Told you I knew what I was doing."

Amanda glanced around in the darkness, but they were alone. "Think you can get that to work on the gear room?"

"Are you kidding? I can open almost any door, shifter girl. As long as it's not the alchemy supplies."

They slipped inside and silently made their way toward the west wing and the hallway lined with locked doors of supplies for each of their classes. When they reached LeFor's room, Summer withdrew her lockpicks again and got to work.

Five minutes passed, then ten. Amanda leaned against the wall beside the door and stared at the end of the hall. *Someone's gonna find us if she doesn't hurry up.*

"Are you sure you can do this?"

"Hey, you said you were sure you could figure out what's going on with the headsets. I'm sure I can open a damn—" A flare of orange sparks rippled up Summer's arms, and she lurched away from the door. "Really? Come on. Since when did he start putting wards on *this* lock too?"

"Probably since someone messed with the game." Amanda only hesitated for a moment before reaching into her pocket and pulling out the purple crystal. "Here. This will work, right?"

Summer scowled at her, but it transformed into a smile instantly the second she saw the crystal. "You're getting a lot better at being badass. You know that?"

"Just use it." She wiped her hands on her sweatpants and scanned both ends of the hall again. "Hurry."

"No one's gonna come looking for us, Amanda. Relax." Summer closed her fist around the crystal and pointed at the lock. A flash of white and orange light rose around the door. Then the lock popped open. "We're in. Good thinking."

I'm surprised she didn't think of it first.

Both girls hurried into LeFor's supply and gear room and gazed around at the shelves of tech pieces and miscellaneous gadgets the teacher apparently thought were too important or dangerous or both to leave in his classroom.

"Man, think of all the things we could build with this stuff." Summer grinned and pointed at the extra magical weapons on the top shelf. "Hey, if we reprogrammed those, we could fly through the obstacle course no problem—"

"That's not why we're here." Amanda reached the duffel bag with the Louper headsets and pulled it off the table. "I want to see what happened with the game."

"Yeah, and maybe reprogram it a little, right?" Summer snickered and finally gave up when the other girl shot her a warning glance. "Yeah, yeah, okay. I get it. You think you can figure out how to use that thing?"

"Definitely." Amanda pulled out LeFor's device. It was kind of like a tablet that allowed him to view the team's in-game stats and keep an eye on everyone at once, even when they weren't front and center in the projection during the game. "Johnny's big on stuff like this."

Summer rolled her eyes. "This again?"

"I'm only saying I learned a few things. There's always a way to figure out what happened. I have to find the—" She stopped and grimaced at the screen. "That's weird."

"What?"

"Nothing but a huge error message." Amanda tapped different spots on the screen. "Like, even to open the data on this."

"So the gear's broken. Big deal. Maybe it's not anything we can—"

The walls and floor shuddered around them, sending some of the smaller devices toppling off the shelves.

"Hey. What are you doing?" Amanda scowled at her friend.

"What? I'm not doing this."

A warning buzz grew outside in the hall, and the girls looked at each other before racing to the door and stepping into the corridor. All the locks on the supply doors were glowing, throwing red and orange sparks in the air.

"You have the crystal, Summer." Amanda pointed at the locks and their malfunctioning wards. "You sure you didn't try to—"

"Why would I want to unlock every single door in the west wing, huh? That's stupid."

"Then what's going on?"

"How the hell should *I* know? It's not like—"

A new alarm they hadn't yet heard at the school flared to life —a shrieking, warbling scream that made both girls instantly clap their hands over their ears.

"Security breach," a robotic voice roared. *"Unidentified intruder detected. Security breach."*

"What the hell?" Summer gazed around the hallway. "Since when did they have a freaking robot keeping eyes on the place?"

"I mean, it's supposed to be a Quantico for magical kids, right?"

"That's the dumbest thing I've ever heard, shifter girl. This thing's gonna wake up the whole damn school. We need to get out of here."

Amanda didn't try to argue with her. They raced down the hall toward the front of the main building. *Unidentified intruder? If it was us, I'm pretty sure that wouldn't be the robot's choice of words.*

Right before they reached the front double doors, a massive crackling explosion rocked the campus. Both girls stumbled against the doors before Summer finally pushed one open, and they staggered out onto the grass. "What was *that*?"

"I don't know. It's—"

Another explosion interrupted her, and both girls turned to see the invisible ward line around the school going up in a blaze of purple light and flames and showers of sparks. One by one, like detonated bombs every six feet, the wards burst and popped, lighting up the night with blazing purple flashes.

Amanda looked at Summer with wide eyes.

The other girl shook her head. "This isn't me. I swear."

"Well, *you're* the one who keeps blowing things up!"

An enormous gust of wind kicked up and blew them both backward. The howl that rose above the sporadic explosions in the wards sounded almost like a voice—growling, furious, and coming closer by the second.

"Something's wrong."

Summer snorted. "Yeah, really great insight into the obvious."

A dark cloud kicking up sprays of water and reeds and dirt barreled toward the campus out of the swamp, rising and groaning and bringing with it an even more powerful wind as the intruder alarm still blared across the school.

Amanda took off toward the dorms again.

"What are you doing?" Summer shouted after her.

"Do you wanna get caught out here in this and get detention again? I don't!"

Before they reached the dorm, there was already a crowd of

groggy students emerging from both buildings, rubbing their eyes and grimacing at the alarm.

"Someone needs to turn that thing off."

"What the hell's going on?"

"Man, how are we supposed to sleep with all this noise?"

Amanda turned and stared at Summer. "Something's been happening with the wards. The ones around the school."

"You know this how?"

"It's been happening all semester."

"Everyone back inside!" Ms. Calsgrave raced toward the doors with a large cloth tote slung over one shoulder, her hair whipping around her face. "Get back to your rooms and stay there!"

"What's happening?"

"Ms. Calsgrave, did someone break in?"

The Illusions teacher ignored the questions and waved back toward the dorms. "We'll answer your questions later, but for now—"

The wards around the school exploded again behind the dorms, and the students lost it.

Calsgrave gritted her teeth and raced out into the center of the field. Behind her were Mr. Petrov and Principal Glasket, both of them still in their pajamas.

"Everyone get your asses inside!" Petrov roared.

The other students had no problem following his orders as they all scrambled back toward the dorms.

The dark cloud that had built out in the swamps now made its way like a cyclone across campus toward the central field, right where Ms. Calsgrave knelt in the grass and hurriedly pulled out a bunch of different tools—candles, cloths, crystals.

"Miss Coulier. Miss Flannerty." Glasket came up behind them, trying not to look worried as the dark storm ripped up the smaller trees at the edge of campus and hurled them back into the swamp. "Everyone needs to get inside."

"What's going on?" Amanda asked.

"Yeah, who's this unidentified intruder?"

"We'll handle this, girls. Our top priority is keeping our students safe, and that includes you."

Amanda stared at Calsgrave trying to assemble what looked a lot like the setup she'd had at her ancestral séance table at Halloween. "She thinks it's a spirit?"

"We aren't sure."

Amanda turned to Summer and held out her hand. "Give me the crystal."

"Yeah, take it. I don't want it."

The buzzing, tingling stone settled in Amanda's hand, and she took off toward the field and Calsgrave.

"Get inside and—Miss Coulier! Stop!" Glasket shouted. "Amanda!"

"I can help!" She raced toward the Illusions teacher with the crystal buzzing in her hand as the wind kicked up even harder. Calsgrave didn't notice her arrival until the shifter girl slid across the grass on her knees. "You think it's a spirit, don't you?"

"Miss Coulier, in all my years of communing with the dead and unseen forces, there are only two times I've seen something as powerful as this." The woman fumbled to arrange her crystals as the wind whipped at both of them. "This is the second."

"The first was with my parents. Right?"

Calsgrave pressed her lips together and shot the girl a brief sidelong glance. "You do seem to attract rather powerful entities."

"I have no idea why. Maybe I can stop it." Amanda opened her hand to reveal the purple crystal.

The teacher frowned. "What is that?"

"It helps with magic. What do you have to do?"

"I'm going to banish this entity out of the school. It's triggered the wards and alarms—"

"I'll try to hold it off." Amanda leapt to her feet and took off toward the building storm cloud howling its way out of the swamps.

"Amanda, stop! You can't—"

The woman's words were lost in the wind as Amanda darted forward. *If I could bring my family back for everyone to see with this stupid rock, I can do something with whatever* this *thing is.*

A younger oak tree split and cracked under the gale, shedding long branches and a spray of splintered wood before the storm tossed it across the field. Amanda ducked beneath the flying branches and kept running toward the cyclone. *I have to figure out the right magic to use. Or visualize it.*

She skidded to a stop in front of the wards when they burst again with purple light and spraying sparks. The dark cloud roiled toward her, and she clenched the stone even tighter as she held it out toward the howling entity.

The dark light of the crystal flashed in her hand as she imagined banishing whatever this was from the campus and away from the students and teachers. *Come on!*

The light flashed brilliantly, blinding her for a moment, and the storm only kicked up with even more force. Then a face appeared in the dark cloud—a man's face, distorted and elongated and furious, churning in the air.

"Take it back!" the entity screamed, and its mouth opened impossibly wide as the storm barreled toward her.

Trees uprooted all over the campus, tossed aside as the wards went haywire and lit up the entire school in a blaze of purple light and sparks and sulfur.

Take it back? That's what Claire said.

The ground trembled, and the pissed-off entity became a massive fist of wind and dirt that crashed down toward her. Amanda leapt aside and stumbled to her knees as the ghostly fist pummeled the earth, sending up huge chunks of grass and dirt. The thing roared.

Spirits. And this stone. I shouldn't be trying to do magic with this thing at all.

As the cloud reared back to attack again, Amanda shifted,

scooped up the crystal between her jaws, and darted away around the edge of the field toward the northern tip of the campus.

That was the mistake. Taking this crystal. Not me.

Calsgrave stared at her with wide eyes as the small gray wolf raced around the field. "Amanda! It's not safe!"

The students gathered inside the common rooms of the dorms stared out the open doorways, watching the dark entity moan and howl and charge across the campus after the wolf with the purple crystal in her mouth.

Amanda raced as fast as she could, her sides heaving. She ran wide around the buildings, hoping the angry spirit wouldn't barrel right through the dorms or the kitchen and send students and faculty flying.

I knew this was a bad idea. Now I have to fix it.

CHAPTER THIRTY

The spirit chased her back to the northernmost tip of the campus boundaries. By the time Amanda reached the island where Summer's first explosion had unearthed the underground temple, swamp water, mud, and flying debris coated her. Trees groaned and splintered all around her. The wind coming after her pushed her even faster until she skidded to a halt in front of the crater in the ground.

Take it back. No problem.

She meant to dive into the tunnel and return the crystal to that pedestal in the ruins, but the spirit caught up to her before she could leap.

An animalistic growl split the air, and the wind pummeled into Amanda and tossed her across the ground.

She yelped and rolled, and the crystal flew from her jaws, toppling toward the hole.

No, no, no. Wait. I have to put it back.

"Mine!" the entity roared, gaining on her as she struggled to her feet.

She tried to find the crystal, but it was gone now. Maybe lying at the bottom of the hole and hopefully not buried in the mud at the bottom of the swamp. She turned to face the thing and snarled. *I can't fight it with magic or my teeth. Plus, I don't have what it wants anymore.*

She heard the teachers shouting her name as they raced after her, and she darted toward the opening to check for the crystal. There it was, pulsing with dark light at the bottom. Amanda leapt down, bashing her flank against the earthen wall but escaping another huge ghost fist crashing down onto the island.

The crystal skittered across the dirt, but she picked it up again in her jaws and raced down the tunnel toward the underground temple.

Take it back. Take it back.

When she reached the open chamber, the entire place shuddered and trembled around her. Her paws splashed through the water, and she shifted back into her human form as she reached the pedestal, spitting the crystal out into her open hand. Then she slammed it down on the pedestal and stepped away. "Sorry. I'm sorry, okay? I didn't know."

The howling wind whistled through the tunnel behind her. Before she could turn to face the angry spirit, the gale pulled her off her feet and sucked her back through the corridor. Her arms and legs bashed against the walls, and she scrambled to find a handhold on anything that would keep her from being thrown from the tunnel's end. However, when she reached the opening leading to the surface, the powerful entity tossing her around drew her up and out and spat her back down on the island.

"Amanda!" Glasket shouted while splashing through the water. A flash of white light rose from the principal's hands.

Amanda saw the ground racing up to meet her but didn't have time to do anything before she hit the earth and everything went black.

The next time she moved, her entire body flared to life as one massive ache. She tried to push herself up and found soft sheets and a mattress beneath her instead of the hard ground of the island she'd expected. Then she opened her eyes to the blazing overhead light.

Where am I?

It took a moment for her to get her bearings again, but then the dizziness finally stopped, and she realized she was lying in a bed in the med ward.

Great. I hope I didn't break anything.

With a groan, she sat up and looked herself over. The bruises on her arms—at least the ones she could see—were already starting to heal. She stretched her neck out from side to side and smacked her parched lips.

"Oh, good. Look who's awake." Nurse Aiken scurried across the room with a plastic cup of water in hand. "Here."

"Thanks." Amanda's voice was raspy and barely more than a whisper, but she downed the whole glass of water anyway and tried again. "Thank you."

"Mm-hmm." The dwarf nurse with huge brown curls pinned high on her head set the cup down and stuck both hands on her hips. "This might be the only time I tell a student it's a good thing they're a shifter. Anyone else would've spent a week in my care before they could sit up like that. You've healed quickly."

"Yeah. That happens." Amanda ran a hand through her hair and grimaced at the tightness of her muscles. "Is everyone okay?"

Nurse Aiken scoffed. "That depends on how you define *okay*. Is anyone else hurt? Not nearly as much as you were. For the most part, I think they're merely confused and scared. So sure, I'd say everyone's all right. Especially now that you're awake. Can you walk?"

"I think so." Amanda pushed herself to the edge of the bed and slowly stood on shaky legs.

"Good." Aiken let out a disgruntled huff. "Then you'd better make your way to Principal Glasket's office. She's waiting for you to show up and explain yourself."

"Oh. Right now?"

The nurse pointed at the open door, and Amanda shuffled across the room. "Am I in trouble?"

"That's for Principal Glasket to say. Still, I wouldn't keep her waiting if I were you."

Great. I just woke up from being knocked out by a ghost, and now I'm getting sent to the principal's office.

Gritting her teeth, Amanda made her way through the med ward's empty halls and out into the main corridor, where she turned toward the center of the building. No, she hadn't had to go to Glasket's office before this, but she knew where it was. Front and center at the top of the second-floor staircase.

When she finally reached the office, the door was slightly open, and she glimpsed Glasket sitting behind her desk. The principal gave her a sharp glance, then waved her forward.

"Come in, Miss Coulier. Good to see you up and walking around so soon."

Grimacing more in apprehension than pain, Amanda pushed the door wider and stepped inside.

Ms. Calsgrave sat in a chair beside the principal's desk, and only one of the chairs in front of Glasket was empty. The other one held Summer.

"Oh."

"Have a seat." Glasket gestured toward the empty chair. "We have a lot to discuss."

Amanda sat and shared a glance with Summer, who scowled at everybody and everything. "Is everyone okay?"

"They are. That was some quick thinking. Of course, we would've been better equipped to handle the situation if either of you had told us about your little discovery out there in the swamp." Glasket folded her hands on her desk and raised her eyebrows, glancing back and forth between the girls. "Let's hear it, then."

"I already told you," Summer said. "I blew up the island, we found that temple underground and the stone, and I took it. What else is there?"

"Yes, Miss Flannerty. Your recap was more than enlightening enough. Thank you. I'd like to hear the story from Miss Coulier this time."

Amanda cleared her throat. "That's what happened."

"And the crystal?" Calsgrave asked.

"Yeah, we used it."

"Uh-huh." Glasket sat back in her chair. "In the last twenty-four hours since a powerful entity breached the Academy's warded boundary, Ms. Calsgrave and I discovered what you two stumbled upon. The owner of that stone more or less created that *temple*. You're lucky the owner isn't alive to press charges for ransacking a magical's grave and essentially looting their tomb."

"Yeah, I figured out what it was during the chase." Amanda glanced down at her lap. "I put the stone back."

"You did. Not a moment too soon, either."

"That artifact called the magical's spirit back into this realm," Calsgrave continued. "It almost destroyed this school in the process. You should've turned the soul shard over to us the second you found it. Do you understand?"

Neither girl said a word.

"Ms. Calsgrave asked you a question," Glasket barked.

"Yes, I understand," Amanda muttered.

"Got it," Summer added.

"Good." Glasket cleared her throat. "Now that we know what happened, we've sealed the temple, and neither of you is to return to that part of the swamp."

"Wait; what?" Summer whipped her head up to stare at the teachers. "That crystal is super powerful. It channels *magic*. You guys should at least keep it. Study it. Hell, figure out how to make more so we can—"

"And risk the wrath of that unsettled spirit sweeping through this entire campus with its vengeance? Again?" Principal Glasket shook her head. "Absolutely not, Miss Flannerty. You uncovered a magical's resting place, and the *only* thing we'll do with it is allow that magical to continue to rest. Is that clear?"

Summer rolled her eyes but didn't say anything.

"Of course, none of us at this school were aware of such temples and tombs beneath the grounds. The Everglades have been here for quite some time, and it's impossible to discover everything within them. Or beneath them." Glasket looked at Calsgrave and nodded.

"That's why we'll be extra careful with how we move forward," the Illusions teacher added. "Taking a much closer look at the grounds and paying special attention to what we find, where it is, and how we interact with it. Needless to say, there will most likely be more discoveries as you two progress through your classes and move onto the next three years of your academic career at this school."

"You're not kicking us out?" Amanda asked, her heart fluttering in her chest.

"No, Miss Coulier." Glasket's smile was tight. "However, you *have* earned yourself another round of detention. Both of you."

"*What?*"

"Oh, come on." Summer scoffed. "She *saved* the school. You saw what that thing did—"

"Yes, and that *spirit* would never have arisen to take back what belonged to it if either of you had come forward with your discovery," Calsgrave admonished. "If Amanda wanted to get points for saving the school, she should have told us about what you'd found that first week."

"So you want all the students to turn into snitches here, then. Is that it?" Summer folded her arms and glared at the teachers.

"No." Glasket shook her head. "We want you to learn the difference between keeping necessary secrets and divulging them. Between secrets that protect others and those that do far more harm than good."

The principal looked directly at Amanda then and raised an eyebrow.

Yeah. All my secrets too. Like being a shifter and having a murdered family and almost being sold into slavery.

"Your detention starts today since Miss Coulier is well enough to be up and about after last night's escapades."

"More scrubbing buildings, huh?"

"That's part of it. You'll also be scouring the campus boundaries and double-checking the *reinforced* wards around the school. Three times a day at a minimum. If any of us catch you doing anything but cleaning or checking the wards, you'll only add more time to your punishments. Most likely more punishments too. You'll do this every day for the rest of the semester, which I believe is about four weeks."

"This is stupid."

"Yes, Miss Flannerty." Glasket looked like she was about to burst out laughing. "At least you'll have plenty of time to think about how *you* can be smarter. You're dismissed. Mr. Petrov has the cleaning supplies out and waiting for you. Plus instructions on how to double-check our new wards."

The principal gestured toward the door, and both girls stood to make their way outside.

As they headed down the stairs, Amanda muttered, "At least they didn't kick us out."

"I don't think that's a good thing this time."

CHAPTER THIRTY-ONE

As the semester came to a close, the other students' excitement was palpable. Of course, Amanda and Summer didn't get to take part in it nearly as much as they wanted because they were still scrubbing walls and checking wards.

One good part about Amanda's actions the night the spirit attacked the school was that it had made the other students more comfortable around her. Most of the other kids either stopped to thank her or told her she was pretty okay. Some of them, like Candace and David and several upperclassmen, continued to ignore her, still treating her like the misfit among misfits.

She could deal with that. Amanda wasn't at the Academy of Necessary Magic to fit in with all the other kids. She promised herself to keep her head down from now on.

If any of them knew what I've been through this year, I still don't think they'd quit staring at me like I have two heads.

During the last week of the school's first semester, Amanda and Summer were still scrubbing and inspecting during their free time. They'd made their way to the northernmost edge of the campus for the third time that day, intentionally avoiding the pile of upturned earth the teachers had used to fill in the hole above the temple.

Amanda tapped the long metal rod Petrov had given them for testing the wards against the air, which ignited a purple light where the teachers had renewed the protections, then she continued walking along the outskirts of the designated boundaries. "So what about you?"

Summer scoffed as she tapped the wards with her rod, dragging it against the invisible boundary and leaving a trail of purple light behind her. "What *about* me?"

"Everyone's talking about what's gonna happen here over winter break. You know, Christmas and New Year's and everything."

"Yeah, it'll be *so much* fun." The other girl didn't bother to hide any of her sarcasm.

"You're going home, then? I mean, I know the other kids here don't have anywhere else *to* go. You didn't come from LA, though."

"I'll go back home. Probably. I don't know. I haven't decided yet."

She doesn't sound too happy about it.

"Will it be only you and your parents?"

"Probably." Summer whacked her rod against another section of the wards. "It's gonna suck. They think I'm a waste of space. Or at least they act like it. You're going home too, right? I mean, to the bounty hunter, not New York."

"Yeah. I don't think he's expecting me to, honestly. Maybe I'll turn it into a surprise." *The look on Johnny's face when I show up at the cabin is gonna make all this detention pretty worth it.* "You know, if you don't wanna go home for break, I'd say you could stay with Johnny and me. Although he might kick us both out if I did that."

"What?" Summer barked out a laugh. "He have some rule about not bringing friends over?"

"More like a rule about not having friends in general." Amanda tried to hide her smirk. "He likes his privacy."

"And you."

"I mean, yeah. He taught me everything I know. Almost." The wards cracked and sparked as the girls whacked their rods against them in the same route they'd taken three times a day for the last three and a half weeks. "You'd like him, though."

"Probably not."

"He's big into explosions. Taught me how to throw grenades."

Summer stopped and turned to grin at her friend. "Maybe I *should* come home with you for break. If they let us out of this place."

Her rod came down in the air, but this time, there weren't any sparks or purple light flashing at the magical impact. Just nothing. "Whoa."

"Is that…"

"A hole?" Summer's eyes widened. "Looks like it."

"How did we miss this a million times?"

"Beats me, shifter girl." When Summer swung her rod at the open space again, the air shimmered around the tool. "Oh, shit. Not just a hole. That's an illusion."

"Then I guess we should go tell—hey!" Amanda darted after her friend as Summer stepped through the shimmering air and disappeared. "Summer?"

No answer.

Amanda spun and scanned the empty swamp around them at the edge of the school's boundary. Even the school buildings were hidden from view by the thick foliage and all the draping tree branches. *Crap. I should go after her, at least. Make sure she's okay before we tell Glasket what she found.*

That was how she could reason it, at least. Because now her

curiosity drove her to step through the illusion after Summer to see what was on the other side.

"Whoa."

Summer scoffed and thumped the end of her rod against the soggy ground. "Yeah, I thought it was gonna be cooler than this. It's only more swamp."

"Um... Hello? That's a dock." Amanda pointed at the long, sturdy wooden planks stretching out across the shallow waters before the swamp bed deepened and the murky water stretched out toward a wide river. "Look at this. What does that say?"

They stepped down the dock together and peered up at the wooden sign mounted on a pole and painted in green letters.

"'To the Everglades kemana,'" Summer read aloud. "No way. This is where all the other grades disappear and head off to the magical city in the middle of nowhere?"

"Looks like it. This is the one Ralthorn was talking about in class."

"Yeah, right before she dissed shifters in front of everyone. Including you." Summer smacked Amanda's arm with the back of a hand. "I'd say we should go check it out, but those weird boats over there don't look like they're ready."

Amanda gazed at the two flat-bottom airboats moored at the end of the dock, and a slow smile spread across her face. "Those are airboats."

"Whatever they are, we have to wait for next year to get into the kemana. We're freshmen."

Amanda tossed her hair out of her eyes and grinned at the other girl. "Hey, I'm a *twelve-year-old* freshman at a juvenile delinquent bounty hunter school. Exceptions for everything, right? Come on."

"Wait. Hold up." Summer took off down the dock after the shifter girl, laughing. "I mean, yeah, you're an exception to a lot of really shitty, outdated rules. I'm not arguing there."

"So what's the problem?" Amanda stopped in front of the first airboat and looked it over.

"The problem is there's no driver for these boats. Don't get me wrong, I'd love to hop on one of these things and go find the kemana, but I don't know how the hell these things work."

Amanda turned and scanned the long dock behind them and the shimmering light of the illusion that let all the other upperclassmen out to this part of the swamp for their kemana field trips. Then she met Summer's gaze and waggled her eyebrows. "Johnny let me take his airboat out all the time. Good thing *I* know how to work one."

The story is far from over. Classes continue for Amanda and Summer in *MAGIC IN THE MARSH*

Get sneak peeks, exclusive giveaways, behind the scenes content, and more. PLUS you'll be notified of special **one day only fan pricing** on new releases.

Sign up today to get free stories.

Visit: https://marthacarr.com/read-free-stories/

AUTHOR NOTES - MARTHA CARR

JANUARY 19, 2021

Yesterday was a weird day. It had a theme running through it of slow down, let others help and loving connection with others. The morning started with me trying to quickly flatten a few more boxes before the recycling truck arrived. Ever since Covid, there's a lot more boxes and that truck comes early. The good dog, Lois Lane was in the car waiting for me to drive her to daycare. Her boyfriend, Harry, the golden retriever was there and Lois was anxious to get going.

Normally, I'm on top of things like this so my brain was also busy chastising and looking for solutions to something that didn't need a solution. I mean, sometimes we don't get to everything.

The Offspring was there, and he suddenly looked alarmed and said, "Hey, did you cut your hand?"

I thought he had to be wrong but nope. I had given myself a pretty good paper cut and not even noticed. One band-aid later, I gave up on the rest of the boxes and drove dog number one to daycare.

I got home to walk the sweet pittie, Leela, who has too much anxiety for daycare. They very kindly asked me not to bring her back and showed me video proof. Leela does better at home with me.

I set out for the walk, glad to finally relax a little and was tromping around the brand new neighborhood nearby, walking briskly and feeling pretty good when my toe caught in a gopher hole hidden by new squares of grass.

I managed to hurl myself forward with such oomph I cleared the new front lawn and landed with surprising force on the cement driveway. Leela failed to notice and kept inspecting a nearby light post. I landed so hard I set off the Apple Watch, which asked if I needed emergency services. Boy, did I quickly click 'dismiss' on that one.

However, I was dismayed to see that no one came out of their door to see if I was okay, while simultaneously glad no one was making a fuss. Even in the middle of trying to figure out if I was okay, I let out a laugh. Leela was still busy.

I was surprised to find nothing wrong except for a weird tweak in my left arm. Since most of me was fine, I walked the mile back home but noticed the arm was not quite working right. It was obvious I would need to get it looked at…

However, there were a few deadlines to finish, first. I mean, what if they put on a cast? The Offspring checked in a few times to see if I'd done anything and it was fun pointing out to my grown son, that's what it looks like when I need something from him. That was mostly ignored.

Okay, so I finally went for that x-ray and yeah, I fractured my elbow. I jammed my hand so hard against the pavement, it cracked the bone at my elbow. Wow. Let's also remember, didn't break anything else. I still feel good about that.

I walked out of there with a large black sling, which I had to take off to drive myself home. Neighbors finally heard of my flying lesson and offers of help came pouring in, which I actually accepted. Food is coming, along with decorating this sling that will be my new best friend for a while. I was reminded that I'm part of a community, which can make a weird day like yesterday into a good memory.

By the way, if you're wondering, my hand is resting on the large keyboard so I can type, which they said was okay.

But wait, before you go… there was one more weird and funny twist to the day.

My friend, Beth called to check on me. A more polite and well-spoken person you will never meet. I missed the call and went to read the text of the message. It said, "Hey my fat ass happy Monday um…"

That's an interesting way to greet someone.

I listened to the message and discovered that when my iPhone hears my name, it interprets that as my fat ass. So judgie.

My friends have decided we should keep it as our new greeting. Maybe the phone will translate that as, hey Martha. More adventures to follow.

AUTHOR NOTES - MICHAEL ANDERLE

JANUARY 22, 2021

Thank you for reading to the back of this book and our author notes!

So, I'm not suggesting my collaborator-friend Martha Carr is trying to author-block me… But seriously? She takes a flying leap and smashes her arm against the pavement (when a perfectly good and kinda soft ground was available), so she can provide a sob story.

Well, maybe she didn't do it for THAT reason… maybe. What's the term for someone who fakes symptoms to get attention? Yeah… that's not her. I don't think. ;-)

BWAHAHAHAHA…. I can't wait to hear what she has to say when she reads these author notes. I suspect Grace (who works with Martha often through the day) will rat me out sooner rather than later.

When I found out about Martha's arm in the sling… You KNOW I had to ask the following (because this is how authors support authors) "Yes, that's nice Martha, you didn't break your head… But can you still *type*?"

Fortunately, Martha understands my dark humor.

FOOD

So, I'm on a mission of utmost importance for my bucket list... What is a bucket list? Glad you asked:

From Wikipedia:

Bucket list may refer to:

· A list of activities to do before dying ("kick the bucket") ß This one!

I want to learn how to smoke a brisket Texas-style. As a native Texan, I feel a call to my roots. My grandfather was a huge cook/pit boss and I always admired his ability to cook outside, with smoke.

The challenge is I have been BORED to tears tending any sort of fires in my life. So, it hasn't happened until I bought a wood-fired pellet grill. So, last night I did something I never, ever ever ever thought I would do.

I watched YouTube videos on how to cook a Texas-style brisket and one video on five things a guy screwed up cooking his brisket.

It got so bad, I was damn near dreaming about how to cut the fat off a full packer. I've also found out that the best brisket meat comes from Snake River Farms.

So I went there and looked to see what it would cost. I'll save you the effort, it was $179 for about a 15-pound brisket.

I don't think I'll be buying that brisket any time soon. I will consider it another bucket list item to attain AFTER succeeding with a Prime quality brisket.

To make a fantastic Wagyu Snake River Farms brisket and know that I'm not going to screw it up.

Goals.

For those that know, I'm considering low and slow, probably about 225 degrees or so for (maybe) up to 15 hours, paper-wrapped (not foil unless I do an injection), and I haven't decided whether fat up, or fat down. THAT right there probably just caused a few of you to throw your Kindle.

BBQ - it's a religion.

Talk to you soon, and sometime in the future I'll speak about my 2021 Brisket Challenge and my results!

Ad Aeternitatem,

Michael Anderle

WAKING MAGIC

Solve a murder, save her mother, and stop the apocalypse?

What would you do when elves ask you to investigate a prince's murder and you didn't even know elves, or magic, was real?

Meet Leira Berens, Austin homicide detective who's good at what she does – track down the bad guys and lock them away.

Which is why the elves want her to solve this murder – fast. It's not just about tracking down the killer and bringing them to justice. It's about saving the world!

If you're looking for a heroine who prefers fighting to flirting, check out The Leira Chronicles today!

OTHER SERIES IN THE ORICERAN UNIVERSE

SOUL STONE MAGE

THE KACY CHRONICLES

MIDWEST MAGIC CHRONICLES

THE FAIRHAVEN CHRONICLES

I FEAR NO EVIL

THE DANIEL CODEX SERIES

SCHOOL OF NECESSARY MAGIC

SCHOOL OF NECESSARY MAGIC: RAINE CAMPBELL

ALISON BROWNSTONE

FEDERAL AGENTS OF MAGIC

SCIONS OF MAGIC

THE UNBELIEVABLE MR. BROWNSTONE

MAGIC CITY CHRONICLES

DWARF BOUNTY HUNTER

OTHER BOOKS BY JUDITH BERENS

OTHER BOOKS BY MARTHA CARR

JOIN THE ORICERAN UNIVERSE FAN GROUP ON FACEBOOK!

BOOKS BY MICHAEL ANDERLE

Sign up for the LMBPN email list to be notified of new releases and special deals!

https://lmbpn.com/email/

For a complete list of books by Michael Anderle, please visit:

www.lmbpn.com/ma-books/

CONNECT WITH THE AUTHORS

Martha Carr Social

Website: http://www.marthacarr.com

Facebook: https://www.facebook.com/groups/MarthaCarrFans/

Michael Anderle Social

Website: http://lmbpn.com

Email List: http://lmbpn.com/email/

Social Media:

https://www.facebook.com/LMBPNPublishing

https://twitter.com/MichaelAnderle

https://www.instagram.com/lmbpn_publishing/

https://www.bookbub.com/authors/michael-anderle

Made in United States
North Haven, CT
28 December 2021